THE PACE

Shelena Shorts

Lands Atlantic
Publishing

The Pace
Published through Lands Atlantic Publishing
www.landsatlantic.com

This is a work of fiction. Names, characters, places, and incidents are the product of the author's imagination or are used fictitiously. Any resemblance to actual persons, living or dead, events, or locales is entirely coincidental.

Cover Photo by Suzanne Mazer and C. Paul

ISBN: 9780982500507

THE PACE

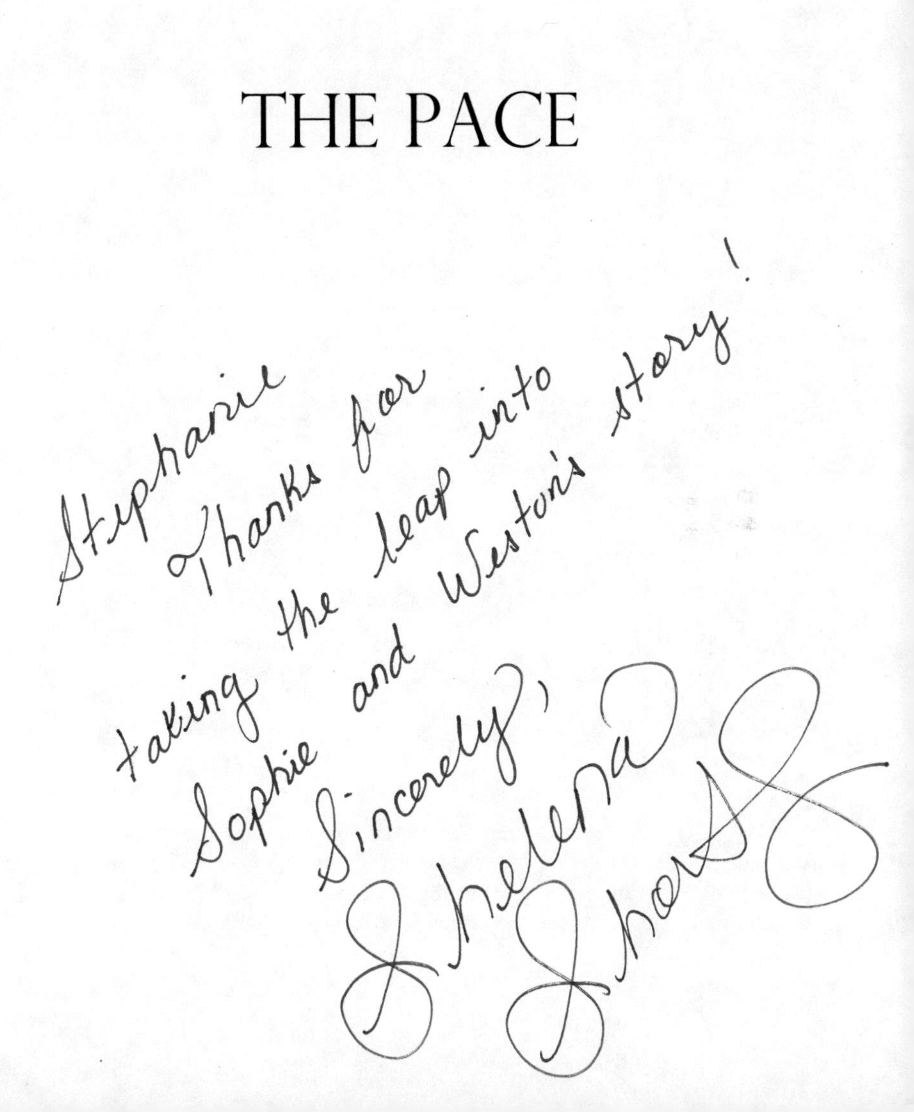
Stephanie
Thanks for
taking the leap into
Sophie and Weston's story!
Sincerely,
Shelena Shorts

Chapter 1

CRASH

Usually, the end of summer brought on a descending cloud of gloom. But not this year. For the first time, I approached September with the comforting knowledge that I could, once again, go to class in my pajamas.

Well, not really *go.* The truth is, when it came to school, I didn't have to go anywhere. I literally rolled out of bed, powered up my laptop, went to brush my teeth, and then logged into my classes. There were no more bad hair days, at least none that anyone else could see, and no more piles of rejected outfits on my bed. It was simple. Just thinking about it made my upcoming senior year seem a lot less dreadful. But I have to say, it didn't come easy.

The path to my virtual gold mine came at a price. It took enduring three moves to three different states before my mom realized I shouldn't have to start over as the new girl again. For her, moving wasn't a big deal. She'd always been outgoing and considered it as a way to, "see what's out there," but by the third move, I'd seen enough and she knew it. I can even remember the apprehension in her face when she approached me. "Sophie," she said, four months into my junior year, "I want to move back to California."

I could've flipped when she told me, but the weird thing was, I didn't. I actually liked the idea of moving back. That's where I was born and where my nana lived. My only apprehension was doing it in the middle of the year, and that's when she told me: Nana was ill. We couldn't very well leave her to take care of herself; so we moved, leaving behind my best friend Kerry, and the snowy winters of Virginia for the distant, familiar sun of California.

At first, I drowned myself in misery at the thought of starting over again, but then my mom discovered California had an *online* high school. That meant I didn't have to be the new girl after all. I wasted no time enrolling, and once that was taken care of, everything else just sort of fell into place.

My mom ended up finding a job at one of the medical centers at the UC Berkeley college campus, and then she bought us a yellow, two-bedroom house right outside of San Francisco. It was a small, old house, but she said it had "good bones." I just hoped the avocado-green appliances weren't part of the skeleton.

The nicest part about it was the layout. One of the bedrooms was upstairs and one was downstairs, and each had its own access to the two-story deck with its ridiculous hillside view. I would've settled for either room, but she insisted I have the one upstairs because it had more room to set up my workstation for school. It also gave me all the privacy I wanted, which turned out to be more than we'd both anticipated.

Within a few weeks, she decided I was spending too much time up there and missing out on being around other kids. Then, she began pressuring me to participate in my school's social events, saying I should get out and meet people. That was easy for her to say. She talks to people in elevators. The idea of roller skating, standing in line for ice cream, or going on a field trip didn't appeal to me. Plus, they all blatantly defeated the whole purpose of avoiding the awkward attempts at making new friends, so I cringed until she gave me another ultimatum.

My second choice was to have lunch with her on the Berkeley campus once a week. I mulled it over for about five minutes before deciding it wasn't a bad idea. She *was* letting me attend school from home, and the only visual interaction I did have with kids my age was seeing a green dot by their name if we were online at the same time. So, if all she wanted me to do was have lunch with her, and call walking the college campus interaction with kids, I certainly wasn't going to complain. In fact, I actually looked forward to it.

I found that being on campus was noticeably different from high school. I could show up in my sweatpants and a mismatched T-shirt if I wanted, and the only person from whom it would draw attention was my mom. It made it easy to keep up my end of the bargain, so I met her there every Thursday, and she agreed to let me keep going to school in my room.

It was a good deal, and it became such a tradition that we ended up keeping our meetings throughout most of the summer. The only exception was the last three weeks, when I was in Virginia visiting Kerry. It was the longest time I'd gone without seeing my mom, and she acted as if my absence had been an eternity.

When I returned, she wasted no time luring me back into our routine. "Oh, come on, Sophie," she pleaded.

"Come this Thursday. The food doesn't taste the same without you."

It really wasn't necessary for her to lay it on that thick. I didn't mind going. The food there was much better than the PB&J I usually ate at home, and letting her pick my brain for an hour was well worth not giving up my senior year online. So, on the last week of August, I headed to Berkeley, willingly, resuming our routine.

When I arrived, the campus was crowded. Classes had already started for the semester, and I expected it to be nearly impossible to find a parking space among the circling cars of students who were trying not to be late for class. For me, finding a space wasn't ever that serious, so I usually just drove up and down the rows until one became available. This time I got lucky. I found a space so quickly that I actually got to our favorite sandwich shop first.

I went in and saved us a table by one of the big glass windows overlooking the garden. It never quite felt like a school until I looked around and noticed that most of the patrons were under twenty-one and carrying backpacks. Some were sitting with their friends laughing. Others were just sitting alone eating and listening to iPods. I tried not to stare too much as I waited, but one girl in the corner caught my eye. I watched her pull out a stack of books from her messenger bag and start flipping through the crisp pages. It made me wonder what classes she was taking, and then I thought about my own schedule.

I was set to take a pretty standard course load, which included British literature, Algebra II, U.S. Government and Economics, Environmental Science, physics, and photography. My schedule wasn't too bad. I liked English and science, and I was excited about the photography. Government would be my least favorite.

I started to crinkle up my nose at the thought of government work when my mom bent down to give me a kiss on my cheek.

"Hey honey. What are you thinking about?"

"Just my schedule," I answered, dismissively.

She sat down across from me. "Oh. Are you nervous?"

"Nervous about what?"

"Your senior year. This is it, you know, before you're all grown up."

"Oh come on, Mom, don't start with the, *you'll miss me* stuff already." I dropped my shoulders in dread at an anticipated talk about my future. I wasn't sure what I wanted to do.

"I'm just saying. This is a big year for you."

"I know."

She paused for a few seconds and then leaned forward like she was about to tell me a secret. "I'm starving, and I'm not sharing today. I think I'll have that huge chicken salad."

I was glad she let the conversation about my cloudy future drop there. "Sounds good," I replied, wasting no time hopping up to place our order. Normally, my venture in line was uneventful, but this time I seemed to have acquired a shadow. I turned to see an older man in a tweed blazer. At first, he didn't say anything, but he was standing way too close for me not to notice his presence. I kept trying to scoot forward and he kept trying to stand beside me. He finally gently tapped his wrinkled hand on my shoulder.

"Excuse me," he said, politely. I turned around and raised my eyebrows in response. He was observing me as if

I were a painting. "You look so familiar." I gave him a quick look-over, and I was sure I'd never seen him before. He tilted his head downward, eyeing me over his spectacles. "I would recognize those jade-green eyes anywhere."

Now he was giving me the creeps. "Um, I'm sorry, I don't know you." I smiled as nicely as I could and turned around. I could still feel him staring.

"Did your mother go here?" he asked, not giving up.

I turned around slightly. "Uh, no she didn't." I tried to offer a final forced smile, hoping it would satisfy him.

"Are you sure? Not even one class?"

"Yes, I'm sure."

"You look *very* much like a young lady I taught years ago. She was in my photography class."

"Oh, that's nice." I wasn't sure what else he wanted. I smiled one more time and took two more steps closer to the register. Another minute or two passed.

"Maybe your aunt went here?"

OMG. I turned again. "No, I'm sorry. No one I know went here." Thankfully, the girl behind the counter called me up to order.

I'm not sure what that was about, but I wasn't used to people telling me I looked like anyone. People usually looked at my mother and then at me like I was adopted. She was fair-skinned and had a vibrant, strawberry-blond, naturally wavy bob. I had a year-round natural tan, and my dark hair was completely opposite from hers. Not only was it black but it was also straight, and slightly layered past my shoulders. The only features I have of hers are her slender build and green eyes.

I definitely take more after my Brazilian father, but he was never around growing up, so people didn't have anything to go by when figuring out where I got my looks. Instead, they always asked me where I was from. Any questions about me resembling someone else took me by surprise, and oddly, that man wasn't the first person on campus to approach me about it. The thought made me turn around to glance at the professor one more time, and he was still staring. I gave him a final nod and then took the food to our table.

As soon as I sat down, my mom started picking fries off my plate and then hammered away on planning for my approaching eighteenth birthday. It was only three days away, and she couldn't stop talking about it. For a minute, I thought she was turning eighteen again. She was always super excited about planning things, so I let her have her moment. My only request was that she keep it simple, and she said she would. I'd just have to wait and see if it held true.

The walk back to my car after lunch always seemed like it took forever, but I didn't mind. It gave me time to think, and the scenery was great. The campus had the most fascinating trees I'd ever seen. Saying they were not normal would be an understatement. They were downright bizarre. One of the paths had a massive sized oak tree, with a huge trunk that split into four or five huge branches. The branches shot upward and curved over so the tips were touching the ground, like an enormous claw.

The west end of the campus had a group of trees whose trunks looked normal, but then the big branches sprouted out in all directions, spiraling like a neat array of curly fries. They were the strangest, most serene things I'd ever seen. I definitely didn't mind the walk, and I hoped my photography class would have an assignment about nature.

Even if it didn't, I already decided I'd have to go back there and take a bunch of pictures of those anyway.

In the meantime, I needed something to do until school started, so I stopped at a used bookstore on my way home thinking I could find something to keep my mind occupied. It was a small store, and the woman behind the counter didn't have to raise her voice much to greet me. I smiled back at her and meandered my way to the hardcover section. I was a little rough on my books, so paperbacks didn't last that long with me. I needed something durable, and they had several shelves of them. I started at the top and searched my way through the titles looking for something old. Like a classic.

I had an odd interest in books that were worn, and it was even better if they had old inscriptions written in them—especially with dates attached. In those cases, I let my imagination run wild with what the previous owners looked liked. It gave the book more character.

About halfway through the romance section, my browsing eyes stopped on one that looked especially old. It was an Elizabeth Gaskell Victorian classic titled, *North and South,* and written on the inside of one of the browning pages was a faded message: *Happy 18th Birthday Sweetheart. Love Mom, October 8th 1962.*

Talk about weird. I shuddered a little at the reference and then tucked it under my arm. It seemed fitting, so I took it home, fixed myself a tall glass of lemonade, and started reading it while soaking up the view on my back deck.

It was a good read, but it seemed like a strange choice for a gift to a daughter. *Unless*, I thought, *the daughter was like the heroine in the story.* She must have been strong, bothered by social injustices, and had a tendency to follow her heart. I sighed at the visualization and the book felt heavy, as if weighted with a story of its own. Reading it certainly served its purpose in keeping me occupied until Sunday, which happened to be my birthday.

In the morning, I woke up like any other day and went to brush my teeth. Only this time, I was startled by a bathroom inundated with purple and pink balloons. *Mom.* It was so like her. Taped to the mirror was a white piece of paper covered in bold, plum-colored hearts and all-capped letters, which read, "Happy Birthday. I love you."

I smiled slightly before gently taking the paper off of the mirror and setting it aside. I looked at myself and stared. I didn't notice anything different. I still looked the same. I wondered if I felt different. *A little bit.* I was eighteen, and that was kind of cool.

Maybe I would've been more excited if I knew what I was going to do with my life, but I hadn't found my purpose yet, and it bothered me. I liked the medical field, but I wasn't sure I wanted to be a nurse. I wanted something more innovative. Something a little more out of reach, and every time I tried to think that far ahead, things went blank, so I didn't know. I blocked out the indecisive thoughts and started brushing my teeth, without looking back into the mirror.

"Sophie!" my mom shouted from below.

"Yes?" I yelled back, after I rinsed.

"Come on down. I have breakfast for you."

"All right. I'm coming." I was met halfway down the stairs by the smell of bacon. I reached the bottom step with a smile. It smelled good, and I was hungry.

I sat at the table while she insisted upon serving me all of my favorites. My plate was covered in scrambled eggs, fried potatoes, bacon, and an oven-baked grapefruit with cinnamon and brown sugar on top. My eyes widened. I zeroed in on the grapefruit first. By the time I was halfway done with the rest, she couldn't hold it in any longer.

"Do you want your present now or later?" she asked, practically bouncing out of her seat.

Not wanting to disappoint her, I answered, "Now is good."

She sprang from her chair and returned with a box that made me laugh. There I was turning eighteen, and she had wrapped my present in pastel pink paper with teddy bears on it. I rolled my eyes at the thought.

"Open it!" she said.

I untied the enormous bow and pulled back the wrapping paper. It was a box for a 10.0 megapixel digital camera. "Mother!"

"Do you like it?"

"Of course I like it. What were you thinking? You did *not* have to do this."

"Sure I did. You need a camera for your class, and you're always talking about taking pictures."

"Mom, I needed a camera. Just a regular digital camera. I didn't need all this."

"Would you stop it? You deserve it. It'll be something you can use for a long time."

I reached over to give her a hug, and she squeezed me, giving me a kiss on the cheek. "Thank you," I said.

"You're welcome." I stood up to put my plate in the sink when she added, "I'm not done you know?"

"Mom, I told you not to do anything for my birthday. You do enough for me already." I turned around and she was pouting. "Okay, fine. What is it?" I asked, holding back a smile.

Turns out, she had dinner plans, too. She was going to play up this milestone with all she had. There was no sense in trying to get around it, so I quietly returned to my room to wait until it was time to leave. I spent most of the afternoon talking to Kerry on the phone and taking pictures of the panoramic view. By 3:00, she alerted me that it was time to go. "By the way," she called up. "Wear some nice pants or something."

"How nice?" I yelled down.

"Just no jeans," she answered, tapering off.

All right. No jeans. I went over to my closet and scanned my wardrobe. I didn't have much in the way of dressy clothes, but I found a pair of black capris, and a black and white pinstriped tank top. I had a pair of black slip-on sandals that were dressy but comfortable, so I threw those on, too. My purse was an oversized burgundy bag. It was a little too casual for my outfit, but I liked the style, so I grabbed it anyway. I didn't wear earrings, only a necklace, which was a cross pendant covered in brown stones that I bought off consignment, and that was it for me when it came to accessorizing.

My mom was much more done up. She was wearing black capri pants, too, but she had on a teal satin shirt, with a gold chain around her waist, earrings, and a ton of bracelets. It was a far cry from her medical coat and scrubs.

It wasn't long before I figured out that we were headed to San Francisco.

She took me to a seafood restaurant with panoramic views of the bay. It was definitely not a place where we could've eaten in jeans, and the entrées were way more expensive than anywhere we usually ate. I really felt she was going overboard, so I told her again.

"Mom, this *really* isn't necessary."

"Sophie, you're my only daughter. I want you to have a nice birthday. My little girl is growing up. It's a big deal."

I felt a little uncomfortable. She went out of her way to make me happy, and I worried about what she would be like when I moved out. I couldn't picture her by herself, but I pushed it out of mind for the time being and shifted my attention to the menu.

It was a bit extravagant. I didn't understand half of what was on it. I ordered the only familiar sounding thing they had for my entrée, which was their Rock Cod Whole Fried Fish. The menu said it was their own fish and chips, and I liked fish and French fries, so I thought it was a safe choice. Then they brought it out to me, and it was staring at me, literally.

I didn't realize that whole fish actually meant *whole fish.* I was in shock looking at the little guy sitting on my plate all fried up. My mom started laughing, but I didn't find it funny. I was not about to eat something that was looking at me. She quickly offered to take the fish and gave me some of her lobster tail, which I ate with my fries. It was very good, and it made me full. But, not too full to start in on the triple-layer chocolate cake and vanilla ice cream that was waiting for us when we got home.

The next morning, it was official. My senior year had started. I turned on my computer and logged into my school homepage. All of my classes were listed on the main screen. I clicked on each, one by one, and printed the course syllabus and assignment checklist. Then, I worked my way through each class's typical Day 1 assignments, which usually consisted of posting something about me on the discussion board and responding to another classmate's posting. It was an attempt to get the students in the class to interact. In a traditional school, it would be like the teacher making a student stand in front of the class to introduce himself and reveal his hobbies, and then randomly forcing another student to verbally respond to the presentation.

It was completely ridiculous, but teachers were able to get away with it online, because there wasn't the complete embarrassment factor. Luckily for all of us, we didn't have to actually stand up in front of a class, but it was still awkward. "Hi, my name is Sophie, and I'm a senior. I like listening to music and reading on my deck."

Then, I could always count on a classmate's reply. "Cool. I'm a senior, too. I like music, too." I did that for all six classes. When I was done "introducing" myself, I opened up each course, found another classmate's posting that no one had replied to yet, and said what everyone else says: "Cool. Nice to meet you. I'm a senior, too." Then, I moved on.

I went right to my assignment checklists for the whole semester. I could see every assignment, when it was due, and I could start them as soon as I wanted. Surprisingly, I had a lot due that week. The 12th grade was looking like it was going to be a bear. I grabbed my Zune and lay on my bed listening to my favorite playlist until I felt motivated to start it all. It took about an hour for the motivation to kick in, but eventually, it did.

By the following week, I had a regular routine down, and I even got ahead on my assignments. I was reaping the benefits of online learning and was stoked about an upcoming photography project. For the assignment, I was able to use a subject from nature. The bizarre claw tree on campus immediately came to mind, so on Thursday, I headed to lunch with my camera tucked in my bag.

This time, I couldn't wait for our lunch to be over. I was eager to get my pictures, and my mother was being extremely inquisitive. She asked what seemed like a zillion questions about my classmates. She wanted to know if I had anything in common with any of them, because she was dying for me to find a local friend. I tried to give her a little hope.

"Yeah sure, Mom, I met a few seniors who like music."

"Really?" she said, perking up. "That's so nice. You're a senior and you like music, too."

"I know. Can you believe it? What a coincidence," I replied, eyes wide.

"Very funny, Sophie. You *need* to open up and meet people. Go to the social gatherings. You may find out that you actually have a lot in common with them…besides music."

"All right, I will," I said, hoping that would satisfy her.

When we finished our lunch, I took more time on campus than usual. I captured a bunch of pictures of the oak tree, and then I headed back to my car. When I reached the parking lot, I received a text message from Kerry. It read: CHEM TEACHER SO HOT. I laughed to myself as I neared my car. I didn't have time to text her back right then, because it was really rude to take a long time getting out of the space while the vultures were hovering. Instead, I got in my car, set the phone down, and decided I would text her back at the first red light I came to.

I turned to back out of the space, and my phone went off again. *What now?* I thought to myself, as I glanced in my lap. I picked up the phone and opened the message. Kerry again: YUM YUM, it read. I smiled, set the phone in the console, and resumed my previous task.

Just then, a tremendous jolt and crunch sound happened simultaneously. I slammed on the brakes and said a word my mother wouldn't have approved of, and then I snapped my head around to see what had happened. That's when I realized I'd backed right into a car passing by. A quick rundown of questions flashed through my brain, such as: *What just happened? How bad is it? What do I do? Do I call Mom? Do I call the cops? Do I get out? Is this person going to kill me? Am I an idiot?* The only answers I could come up with were, yes, I was a complete idiot, and yes, I should get out and apologize quickly.

I opened my door and walked toward the back of my car. I didn't even look at the damage to my car. I was too busy quickly coming up with an apology in my head. My thoughts were interrupted by the image of a huge dent in the side of the shiny black car, made by yours truly. Horrified, and not knowing what to do, I searched for the owner who was making his way around his own car, sizing up the damage as well.

"I'm so sorry," I said, looking like a deer in headlights. "I don't know what happened. I didn't see..." About halfway through my attempt at an apology, the boy looked up from his car to me. His eyes got wide. *Oh great,* I thought. *I've really done it. I've ticked this guy off. And how embarrassing, does he have to be so cute?* I swallowed and stared at his face, which was incredibly proportioned. There wasn't one feature that overpowered the other, and the perfect combination was topped off with strikingly dark brown hair that curled slightly at the tips. I didn't know which feature I preferred to focus on, so I settled for his equally dark eyes, which were, by that time, piercing through my guilt. He looked so intimidating and strong, but boyish at the same time. I didn't feel afraid. I felt terribly guilty and completely and utterly embarrassed.

That was until he took two long strides and was standing less than two feet from me, and then I held my breath. "It can't be," he said, looking at me intensely. He was a good five inches taller than me, and I wasn't short, so I started to get intimidated after all.

"I'm sorry," I said instinctively. "I didn't see you. I must not have been paying attention…"

"What are you doing here?" he interrupted, saying the words slowly and clearly, as if to make sure I heard the question. Well, what I was doing was ruining a perfectly good afternoon for the both of us while also ruining any self-esteem I had. There I was standing two feet in front of the most beautiful face I had ever seen, watching the muscles in his jaws flex as he bit down on his teeth, and I was feeling like I should be in time-out.

"I don't know," I answered. "I thought I checked. I didn't see you." *Didn't I say that already? I'm rambling again.*

"I meant, do you go here?"

"No, I'm just having lunch with my mom."

"On campus?" His eyes narrowed.

"Um yes, my mom works here." At that point, I really felt like a toddler. I had to stop talking about my mom and get myself out of this nightmare. "Yes, I come here all the time," I said assertively, shaking the hair out of my eyes and straightening my posture to look more mature. "This is the first time I've had this happen, and I'm sorry. I think I need to get you my insurance information. It was my fault."

"Are you all right? You're not hurt are you?" he asked.

I looked down at myself, and I appeared to be perfectly fine on the outside. My brain was working a little slow, and my stomach was acting funny, but I wasn't about to tell him that so I said, "I'm fine. Let me get you my information."

I turned toward my car to get it when I thought I heard him say, "It's all right. Don't worry about it."

"Don't you want my—"

"I said don't worry about it."

He slid back into his car, and I stood there looking confused as he drove off with his words still lingering. By that time, a few people had gathered. A guy, gripping a backpack with one hand, zeroed in on my personal space like a reporter.

"Did he hit you? Are you okay?" he asked.

"Yes. I mean, no. He didn't hit me. I hit him, and yes, I'm okay."

"Do you know that guy?"

"No."

"And he just drove off?"

"Um. Yes," I replied, still trying to figure it out for myself.

"Do you have any idea how much that car is worth?"

"No." Of course I didn't, and as a matter of fact, I didn't even know what kind of car it was.

"Well, you're lucky. That's a Maserati," he informed. "It costs more than a college education."

"Great."

"Not for him it isn't."

At that point, he was starting to get on my nerves, so I shook my head and did a 180 on Anderson 360 to assess the damage to my own car. A busted brake light and some paint scratched off in the back left corner. My car definitely got the lesser damage of the two. I let out a big sigh and got back into my Jeep. What was I thinking? *I'm going to kill Kerry. Yes. That was it.* It may not have been what I was thinking when I rammed into that car, but it was definitely what I was thinking afterward. I was going to have to make those arrangements *after* I called my mom to tell her the grand news.

Chapter 2
CHECKMATE

I didn't want to call my mom while I was still on campus, because I was pretty sure she would insist upon seeing me in person to make sure I was all right. Instead, I waited until I got home. That way I could make it seem like it wasn't a big deal. As soon as I told her, she immediately began the rundown.

"Are you okay?"

"Yes Mom, I'm fine."

"How did it happen?"

"I don't know. I'm not sure. I guess I just didn't see him." I hoped that would be enough information. I was not about to fill her in on the text message thing.

"All right, I'll call the insurance company and let them know. How much damage did you do to the other car?"

"Well, I put a pretty good size dent in the car, but it's hard to tell."

"Well, it's okay. Don't worry about it. The insurance should take care of it."

"Well Mom, that's the strange thing," I said. "He sort of drove away."

"He did what?"

"He just said don't worry about it and drove off."

"Odd."

"Yeah, I know."

I could tell in her voice that she wasn't completely buying the recap, but after insisting that I was serious, she settled on just having my car looked at to see what the damage was and assured me we would take care of it. Next, it was on to Kerry. I text messaged her back and just said: CALL ME.

Once she did, I filled her in on what her little message caused me to do. She was laughing and asked me what I was thinking.

"I was thinking about your chemistry teacher being hot. Remember?"

"Well I can't help it if you don't pay attention, but I *am* sorry," she said, giggling. "So what are you going to do? How much damage did you do to the other car?"

I explained to her how he drove off and how I was still confused by the whole thing. She, of course, picked up on the "he" of my explanation right away and wasted no time asking me if he was cute. I couldn't lie, so I found myself having to explain every little detail of his looks until she was convinced he must have thought I was cute, too.

"Yeah whatever," I replied. "I'm sure he just thought I was great. 'Moron puts a big dent in my car and babbles like an idiot. Oh yeah, and she hangs out with her mom on campus.' Right, I'm sure he was real impressed."

She thought about that for a second and then said, "Good point, but why did he let you off the hook then? Who does that?"

"I don't know. Maybe he didn't want to get the police involved."

"He likes you," she said back quickly.

"Yeah sure," I countered, in complete sarcasm.

I didn't consider myself a genius, but I was sure whoever it was I rammed into, and then babbled to about my mom, was not interested in me. Besides, he was in college, and according to the parking lot reporter, he had a really expensive car, so I couldn't imagine any reason he'd be interested in a high school girl. I tried to push the whole afternoon out of my head, but it stayed on my mind all evening. I kept picturing his face and trying to think of what things I could have said to him instead of the lame apologies, but there was no way to make up for ramming into someone's car. All I could do was say I was sorry. Although, I suppose I could've left out the part about meeting my mom there. That was embarrassing. *Whatever*, I thought. It didn't matter. I wasn't banking on running into him again, literally or figuratively, so I had to fill my thoughts with something else, which turned out to be very difficult to do.

Early the following week, my mom had an insurance adjuster come out to our house to look at my car. The damage was going to cost about $550.00 to fix. That wasn't bad at all, except for the fact that our insurance deductible was $500.00, and I didn't have that much saved up. I decided right away that I would need to get a job. My mom made me promise to keep my grades up and to keep our Thursdays together.

I ended up going back to the used bookstore, because I remembered seeing a small hiring sign that had been in the window for a while. It probably meant they didn't pay much, but I didn't care. I just needed a job, and I wanted to do something that interested me, so I went.

When I walked in, the same people were at the counter, and I got a little nervous, so I proceeded to the aisles as if I were looking for a book. While rehearsing what to say in my head, I saw a girl stacking books. She looked about my age, with auburn brown hair that was cropped at her neck and pulled back behind her ears. She was naturally pretty even though she was a little heavy on the eyeliner. I walked up to her and initiated a conversation.

She was relieved to have a girl her age interested in working there, and it worked out really well, because her dad was the owner. She told me her name was Dawn, and then she took me to the front and introduced me to her dad as someone she knew. I barely had to say two words, before he asked me to come around the counter to go over days I'd be able to help out.

After the easiest interview I could've imagined, we settled on Thursday, Friday, and Saturday afternoons. It was a good schedule. It gave me the beginning of the week to get a jump on my schoolwork, I could still fulfill my lunch with Mom, and it would still let me sleep in on Saturday. It sounded like it was a great opportunity, so I took it without hesitation.

I was set to start on Saturday for training, so I wanted to be sure to get my assignments done before then. By Thursday morning, I was a little behind on my work, and I wanted to cancel lunch with my mom, but I kept it anyway. I tried to tell myself that I didn't want to disappoint her by canceling, but the truth was, I was hoping to see that little black car again. I wondered if he would still park in the same lot or if he would be sure to park at the opposite end of the campus.

While I was looking for a parking space, I scoped out the lot to no avail. I began to think I was stupid for even looking. What was I going to do if I did see it? I couldn't very well go up to him and strike up a conversation. "Hey remember me? I hit your car." That would be ridiculous. I was silly for even looking for him. Then, I got to thinking about why he'd driven away to begin with. That was kind of rude. The more I thought about it, the more stumped I became. I wasn't sure if he was just so angry that he needed to cool off or what. None of it made sense, and it was starting to irritate me that I couldn't figure it out.

I found a space at the far end of the lot and headed to meet my mom, still a little annoyed that I was looking for someone who had me so flustered. I didn't like not being able to understand things. That's why I liked science so much. There was always something to figure out, and there was always an answer for everything. Things just needed to be analyzed, evaluated, and solved. I was good at that. So it bothered me that I had caused a problem and the solution was left dangling in midair, hovering like a constant whisper in my ear. Most people would count their lucky stars that they got off that easy, but not me.

My mom was in focus for about half of our lunch. I found myself searching around the café looking for any sign of him only to come up short with every attempt. She could sense I was a little off, and she pressed me on it. I finally had to give in and tell her I was wondering if the guy I hit was anywhere on campus. She asked me if I was afraid, and I laughed out loud.

"No, Mom, I'm not afraid. What's he going to do? Make me fix his car? That would be horrible."

"Well, he might decide that he should've gotten your information after all, once he thinks about it," she added in.

"Yeah, I suppose you're right, but so what if he does. I did hit his car."

"You did, but he should've gotten your information then, not after the fact. He shouldn't be looking for you now. That would be odd."

I was feeling very full at that moment. I had barely eaten anything, but I was ready to end the conversation about the whole thing. It seemed all so pointless anyway. There were 35,000 students there, and the odds of me seeing him again were slim to none. We finished our lunch, and I headed back to my car still wondering how far I would take this. If I knew his name, would I go look it up in the directory? Would I become a stalker? I shook my head at the thought and quickly tried to get a grip.

As I approached the parking lot, I told myself it was just some guy. So what if he was cute and had eyes that could melt butter? And so what if he just happened to be leaning up against my Jeep at that very moment?

Reflexes kicked in, with my eyes blinking a few times to confirm what I was seeing. He was definitely standing there. My hands got sweaty and my heart skipped about four beats. Thinking about running into him again and really doing it were two different things.

A million things went through my mind, so I slowed up my pace to give myself more time to reach my car. I had no choice but to walk right up to him since he was standing at my door. Leaning casually, with his arms crossed, he was wearing dark denim jeans, and a heavy charcoal-colored V-neck sweater. I thought that was strange, since it was about 65 degrees outside. It made the whole encounter seem very surreal, and I wondered whether I was imagining it all, but then he spoke.

"You again."

"So, did you come back to collect?" I asked, biting my lip and coming to a stop in front of him.

"No," he said, half smiling.

"So, what…" I raised my eyebrows, hoping he would give me something to go on.

"I just wanted to ask you a few things. Shall we?" He motioned toward a nearby path. I looked around and saw a few cars circling and waiting for my space, so I figured it would be a good idea to move away. I nodded my head to indicate yes and waited for him to lead the way.

"You first," he said, with a small smile.

I walked in front of him, toward the wooded path, glad he couldn't see my face. I was beaming. When I reached the edge of the path, I gathered my composure and turned around.

"So?"

"So," he said, giving me nothing more. He was just looking at me with very engaging eyes, which was making it hard for me to concentrate. I had to do something to break the awkwardness of the whole situation.

"So, if you didn't come to collect then—"

"What is your name?" he asked, fully composed.

I ignored his question. "Do you do that a lot?"

"Do what?"

"Cut people off."

He laughed. "That's fair, I suppose. I'm sorry. No, I didn't come to collect," he answered, leaning in. "Now, can you tell me your name?"

"Sophie," I said, with my eyes narrowing, trying to figure him out.

"Sophie," he repeated, as if he was trying to hear the ring in it. "That's a nice name. How old are you…may I ask?"

He could've asked me whatever he wanted, anytime he wanted, for all I cared, and for the first time, I was so glad to be eighteen. I couldn't wait to say it out loud.

"Eighteen," I said confidently.

"When did you turn eighteen?" he asked, curious.

"A couple of weeks ago."

"What day exactly?"

I looked at him, trying to figure out what the big deal was, and I could tell from the seriousness of his expression that I had no choice but to admit I was a newbie. He wanted specifics. "September 2nd," I answered. "How old are you?" I shot back, just as curious.

"Nineteen." He was staring at me strangely, but a little more at ease.

"And do you have a name?" I asked.

"Yes."

"Are you going to tell me what it is?"

"Wes." He was holding back a smile.

"What? What's so funny?" I asked, starting to feel self-conscious again.

"Nothing, I'm just amazed to have run into you."

"Actually, I ran into you, remember? Speaking of, how is your car? I feel terrible."

"You shouldn't. It's fine. I told you not to worry. It's already fixed, but I did notice that yours isn't."

"Oh, I'm saving up for it."

"How much will it cost you?"

"Just like $500.00, but I didn't want my mom to pay for it, so I got a job, and I'll take care of it. It's no big deal."

"You talk about your mom a lot," he said, with that half smile of his. "You said she works here, right? What's her name?"

Oh great. I was talking about my mom again. I wanted to find a rock and crawl under it, but he was leaning in, waiting attentively.

"Her name is Gayle."

"And she works where?"

"The medical center. She's a radiologist."

He acted like that was interesting to him for some unknown reason, and he was about to say something but was interrupted by a beeping noise coming from his watch. He looked at the time and told me he needed to head to his class. I snapped out of my gazing state as we started walking back toward my car. There was no exchange of phone numbers, and I was too much of a coward to ask for his, so I told him I was sorry about the car again and he assured me, for the third time, that I shouldn't worry about it.

I was so ecstatic on my way home that I didn't know what to do with myself. Although, I was now worse off than I was before. It was better than I remembered. There was no doubt in my mind that he was the most perfect being on my planet. Wes, who is nineteen, only a year older than me, was all I kept repeating in my head. It was very much doable, if only I knew what I was doing. I had been cooped up in my room studying for the past year, and now was the one time I wished I had prior experience interacting with people—more specifically, guys.

My stomach started getting that feeling again. It was a weird, fluttering feeling. I needed to get a grip if I was going to function at any sort of schoolwork when I got home. But for the car ride there, I let myself enjoy the elation.

The only way I managed to get any work done was to blast my music in my ears. I tried to drown out the extra thoughts in my head with constant noise in order to focus on my lousy government work. Give me something to analyze and figure out, and I was fine, but I didn't like having to remember facts, and I especially didn't like it when my mind was wandering off.

I was able to get through some questions, but I needed to start remembering the order of events. I tried to sit there with the rhythm of the song in my head while creating little rhymes for the facts. It wasn't working, so I shut the book and lay on my bed, just listening to my music instead.

When my mom got home from work that evening, she called me from the entryway. It was very rare for her to call me as soon as she got home, so I knew something was up. I went to the top of the stairs, and she motioned for me to come down. She was holding an envelope in her hand that was addressed to Gayle Slone. She handed it to me and said, "I suppose you don't have to go looking after all." I opened the envelope, and there was a check for $500.00 written out to my mom from Weston C. Wilson III. Along with it was a note in perfect cursive:

Dear Ms. Slone,

I hope this letter finds you well. My intention is to relieve a bit of a burden I may have caused for you and your daughter. She and I had an incident in the parking lot a week ago involving our cars, and I have since felt terrible about the damage it has caused. I hope this amount covers the cost to repair her vehicle. Please accept it as my apology.

With Kind Regards,

Weston,

I couldn't believe it. He had gone behind my back, to my mother, to pay for something that was my fault. I didn't need anyone to pay for my mistakes. It was so frustrating, and what was even more frustrating was having to explain the entire ordeal to my mother. I hadn't planned on mentioning seeing him again at all, and there I was explaining away a letter that he'd apparently dropped off at her office, which just happened to have a check in it for the amount of my deductible.

It took me about thirty minutes to get my mother to believe that I actually had hit *him* and that he must have figured out how to reach her, because I told him, in passing, her name. I don't think she believed me fully, but her suspicion was sidetracked when I ripped up the check right in front of her.

"What are you doing?" she asked, looking at me like I was insane.

"I'm ripping this up."

"Yes. I see that. Why? What are you thinking? That will fix your car."

"Mom, I know. I just don't want this guy to pay for this. I clearly hit him, and he is already letting me off the hook by not having me pay for his car. I'm not about to let him pay for mine, too." *Was he crazy?* I thought.

"Look. Sophie, I'm not sure what's going on here, but this all sounds way too abnormal."

Before she could continue in her rambling fit, which was loaded with the insinuation that I was hiding something, I cut her off.

"Mom, I know. I'll fix it. I'll nicely tell him thanks, but no thanks. *If* I see him again."

"You are so strange, Sophie. I won't pretend to understand you."

"You don't have to," I said, walking back up the stairs. I added, "Love you," over my shoulder. She just shook her head and walked toward her room. I went upstairs and closed my door. I wanted to feel completely alone while I tried to figure this out. I held out the letter again and reread: Weston C. Wilson III. So that was his whole name. I sat with a small grin on my face as I thought about how sneaky he was to have pulled that off, and then I felt stumped again, because I didn't know why he was being so nice. I didn't deserve it. I wanted to call Kerry and ask her what she thought, but I knew she would flip and go down the, "I told you so," road. I wasn't in the mood, and I wasn't entirely convinced that was the case anyway.

For the next twenty minutes, I sat trying to figure out what to do next. The more I thought about it, the more I started to feel a little bit more confident. It was much easier feeling that way when I wasn't standing in front of him. Plus, I knew that he had gone out of his way to see me and send my mom a fancy donation. It was my turn to make the next move.

I sat on my bed looking around my room, brainstorming. I was thinking of things I knew about him, hoping it would help me figure out what to do. What I knew was that he went to Berkeley, he drove a black car, he was nineteen, and his name was Weston Wilson. I jumped up with an idea and slid into my desk chair to begin my search. Surely there was an online student directory.

Right on the school's main homepage was a link titled, "Student Emails." Once I clicked on it, it wanted me to enter a user name and password, which I didn't have. I let out a big sigh and leaned back in my chair. There had to be a way to access a student directory, so I pressed on.

I decided to type, "Student Directory," in the main search box, and that's when a query page opened up. It allowed me to search by student, or faculty name. After narrowing down the search to students, I typed his first initial and last name. There were several W Wilsons enrolled, but the Weston C. Wilson III stood out like a sore thumb.

Just looking at the name on my computer screen made me smile, and then I found myself feeling a little stalkish, but I quickly dismissed it. *He* was the one waiting by my car and sending my mom letters. No, I felt no shame.

Under student number, it said, "Unlisted," but his campus email address was there. I clicked on it to send an email. There was a lot I wanted to say, but I didn't want to sound too wordy or desperate, so I settled on a few sentences:

```
Dear Weston,

Thank you for your offer. It was really
nice of you. Unfortunately, I'm unable
to accept.

Thanks anyway,
Sophie
```

I hit send and decided to finish my government work. For some reason I felt much better. I had taken a stance on something I could feel good about, and that put me at ease for the time being, but the next day was a different story.

I woke up and went straight to my computer. I wanted to check my email to see if there was a reply. I logged into my account, and I had one new message. It was from Kerry. Normally, I would've been happy to hear from her, but that day I had to admit, I was a little bummed that I didn't get a reply from Weston C. Wilson III. I told myself it had only been a day, not even, and that he probably didn't even check his campus email that often. I had to tell myself that about ten times, because that's how many times I checked it. I was fidgety all day, pacing and hovering around my computer.

Saturday came around and there was still no email. I had to show up for my first day at work that afternoon, so I had no choice but to try to put it out of mind. I was actually happier to start than I thought. It did take my mind off of things.

I found out more about Dawn. It turned out that she attended the same virtual academy as me. Apparently, thousands of kids attend my school. She was a junior and had been attending the school since middle school. My mom was going to be ecstatic when she found out I had met someone who went to the same school as me. I rolled my eyes at the thought.

I spent a lot of the afternoon learning how the books were received and checked in as well as how to work the register. It wasn't that hard. There was nothing to scan. All I had to do was enter the price that was written on the book and add them all up until it was time to press the Total button. It didn't take that much talent. I felt pretty lucky that I'd found this job. It was easy, and the place was low-key and quiet.

The only people who worked there were my boss, Mr. Healey; Dawn; her older brother, Danny; and Ms. Mary. Danny and Mr. Healey were there most of the time; Dawn was there five days a week in the afternoons; and Ms. Mary and I alternated afternoons to help out. It was a pretty easy job, and it kept me from being bored. I had an entire store of books to flip through whenever we weren't busy. It was a decent escape.

The following week began with me burying myself in my assignments and by Thursday, there was still no email. I had gone to campus for my normal lunch, and I physically felt my shoulders sink as I approached my car and saw that he wasn't there. I was ready to call Kerry for advice. There would be no, "I told you so," at this point.

I called her later that evening. She was just as stumped as I was about what was going on, but she told me she thought I should let it go. According to her, it was all too weird. I agreed, but it still didn't stop me from checking my email one more time that day. Much to my disappointment, there was still no reply.

I spent a lot of time thinking that evening. I took a long shower to clear my head, and then I sat in my reading chair, in the dark, with my eyes closed, listening to complete silence. My mind tried to figure out how I had ended up in this situation. I had never been the type of person to be bothered by anyone. I could always easily dismiss people who bothered me or hurt my feelings. I was perfectly happy being by myself all of the time, and I never really had any interest in guys. Most of the guys, with whom I ever got close enough to have a conversation, were so predictable, so I had no interest in a boyfriend before. But all of a sudden my mind was constantly fixated on this one nineteen-year-old guy, who I had probably spoken to for a total of fifteen minutes. It was not normal.

I cursed those brown eyes. I had never encountered anyone that made me feel like they were looking into my soul. I felt oddly exposed and vulnerable, but good at the same time. One afternoon, running my car into someone in a parking lot, had changed my thinking forever. It was a mental battle I was going to have to fight, and I knew it would only have two outcomes. The first one was that I would get over this in about a week, and the second was that I would dislike boys forever. I was leaning toward the second one until things took a drastic turn.

About a week and a half later, I was working on my science homework one evening and took a break to check my email. I was shocked to see a new email from Weston. I paused for a good two minutes because I wasn't sure what to expect. My stomach started to feel fluttery again, as I slowly clicked the mouse to open the email. It read:

Dear Sophie,

I am sorry you feel that way, but I'm not surprised. Please know that I tried to go about things legitimately, but you made it very difficult. As a result, I have taken the matter of fixing your car into my own hands. I cannot, in good conscience, have you drive around in a damaged vehicle. You deserve more.

Sincerely,
Wes

I read it three times and still couldn't figure it out. Fixing your car, matter into my own hands, good conscience, you deserve more. What in the world did that mean? The guessing game was getting old. I was so worked up; I needed to get out of the house. I slipped on some flip-flops and headed to my car in my T-shirt and shorts. It was about 7:00 p.m., so I called into my mom's room to tell her I was going to the store. I just needed to get some air. I wanted to take the top off of my Jeep to increase the effect, but I was in too much of a hurry to deal with that.

When I walked outside, I noticed my Jeep backed into my driveway. I didn't remember leaving it like that. In fact, I was positive I hadn't parked it that way. My eyes narrowed as I walked around the back end, and then I shook my head. My car was completely fixed. I ran my hand over where the busted light and dent had been as if it was going to bite me. I was not imagining it. My car was fixed, completely. No sign of damage whatsoever. This had gone too far.

Dumbfounded, I walked back into the house and went straight upstairs. The email was still on my screen. I hit reply:

```
I want to talk. Meet me somewhere.
Please.

Sophie
```

I hit send and waited. I really didn't expect a reply that night, but I waited anyway. I put on my favorite songs and lounged around my room periodically checking my inbox. By about 9:00, I had new mail. It was from Wes:

```
If you insist. Tomorrow, at the
overlook. Noon?
```

That wasn't good enough. I needed some answers before then, so I replied back:

```
No, now is good. Overlook, ten minutes.
I'm leaving now...
```

I had no idea if he was going to go or not, but I was itching to get out of the house anyway. I needed a drive, and the overlook would be a good place to go anyway. It was a natural soother, located off of a windy road overlooking a river, hills, and city. In the daytime, you could stand there in awe of the beauty of the water and the mounds of green hillsides. At night, the hills were lit up by the town lights. It was a perfect place for me to go to clear my head whether he came or not.

About halfway there, I realized that I had left the house in the same checkered shorts, T-shirt and flip-flops, and I was horrified thinking that he might actually show. That was just great. It was only going downhill for me, but I was in investigation mode. I was more concerned with wanting to know why he was going out of his way to fix my car, and moreover I wanted to know how the heck he had actually pulled it off without my knowing. I hadn't gone anywhere that day, and I was sure it took longer than a day to have a car fixed.

I pulled off into the overlook. The space was just off the road, like a widened gravel shoulder. It was very dark out there, so I decided to stay in my car with my doors locked. I wasn't about to go out there by myself, and the view was almost as good from the car anyway. Besides, I was afraid of heights, and standing near the edge in the dark didn't sound appealing.

I cut the ignition but left on the music and sat waiting and thinking. Within about five minutes, a car pulled in from the opposite direction, with headlights glaring. As it pulled farther in, the lights were diverted toward the cliff, and by then, I could tell it was the same black car I had hit. This time, I paid closer attention to it, since I was curious. It was fixed on the side I had hit, and it was a very nice car—not too flashy. It just looked like a little black modern sports car to me.

I watched as he rolled his car to a stop, got out, and leaned casually up against his door. I took it as my cue. If I wanted to talk to him, I was going to have to get out and walk over there. I supposed it wasn't too much of a demand. I had just dragged him away from whatever it was he was doing to come meet me at 9:30 at night, so it was a minor compromise.

As I approached him, I saw he was wearing jeans and a heavy navy blue zip-up jacket. I was instantly embarrassed by my shorts and flip-flops, and I was actually starting to feel a little chilly out there on the overhang. Even still, he was a bit overdressed.

I walked over to his car and leaned next to him. Neither one of us said anything for a few minutes. I was the one to break the silence.

"Are you going to tell me why you fixed my car?" I said, looking at him.

"I told you, it bothered me to know you were driving around in a crashed vehicle." He didn't look my way, but I could tell he had a small half-smile on his face.

"I would hardly call it a crashed vehicle. It's very durable. The damage was barely noticeable," I corrected.

"It's all in how you look at it I suppose."

"Okay well, that didn't give you the right to steal it."

"I didn't steal it; you have it back."

"Yes you did. I didn't give you permission to take it."

"I told you," he said, turning toward me. "I had to take matters into my own hands."

I rolled my eyes and shuddered at a cool breeze, and he noticed.

"You're cold."

"No I'm not," I lied.

"Yes you are. Anyone would be, coming out here in that," he said, as his eyes examined me from head to toe.

"You're trying to distract me," I shot back. "And it won't work. I want to know how you took my car and fixed it in a day without my knowledge or permission. And I don't like being lied to."

"I didn't lie to you."

All right, that was it. I was done with the going around in circles, and as cute as he was, I was getting a bit fed up.

"All right then, I'm leaving," I informed him, walking back toward my car. I really didn't want to leave, but I was flustered. I reached my car and turned back to see what he was doing. He hadn't moved an inch. He was still looking out over the cliff. Threatening to leave always worked in the movies. Right? One person got mad and acted as if they were leaving, and the other person folded in submission. But, it was clear to me that he wasn't folding.

I let out a little grumble, swallowed a little bit of pride, took a deep breath, and headed back over to his car. This time, I stood right in front of him.

"Are you going to, at least, let me pay you back?" I asked, crossing my arms firmly.

"No."

"You have to let me pay you back. Please."

"I don't want your money."

"You're impossible."

"Only to you," he said, with a little laugh.

"Then what can I do? I can't just do nothing," I said, uncrossing my arms and putting my hands on my hips.

"For one, you could go home and stop coming to dark places at night by yourself." He raised his dark eyebrows, waiting for my reply.

We both stood there staring at each other without moving or saying anything for a few minutes. I'm sure we were both trying to figure the other out. That's what I was doing anyway, and it wasn't working. I'm not sure what he was thinking about, but my thoughts ranged from frustration to wondering what it would feel like to have him grab me and give me a big kiss. It was so cliché, and the thought made me blush. I had no idea what this thing was between us, but I liked it. I didn't want my time with him to end, and I knew I didn't want to have to check my emails anymore to communicate or wait to see if he would show up in the parking lot on campus.

"So what now?" I asked, hoping for a solution.

"Whatever you want."

"You won't let me pay you back for fixing my car, so is this it, or will I see you again?"

"What do you want?" he asked, shrugging his shoulders a little, putting the decision back on me. I hadn't felt more shy or desperate in my whole life. I just wanted to walk away, but I knew that I would spend the next several days in my room wondering when and if I would see him again if I didn't truthfully answer the question.

I looked down at the ground between us. "I want to see you again."

"All right." He was much more at ease than I was, and he casually stood up straight, as if to leave.

"How will I reach you?" I asked, a little too quickly.

"Do you have a number?"

"Yes."

"Are you going to give it to me?"

I looked at his empty hands. "Do you have a pen?"

"I'll remember it," he said confidently, not making any movement toward getting a pen. I couldn't tell if I was being blown off or if he was playing it cool, but I didn't want to press it any further. If he wasn't planning on calling, it didn't matter if I wrote it or not, so I just told it to him.

"I'll call you." He nodded, seeming satisfied, although he wasn't concentrating too hard. "We should go home," he added, tucking his hands in his coat.

"Aren't you warm in that jacket?" I asked, curious.

"Not at all; I don't like being cold. I'll see you later."

He got into his car first, but he waited for me to get in mine and pull off before driving away in the opposite direction. As I drove home, I had a permanent smile on my face. There was so much I still didn't know, but I at least felt there would be time to figure it out. One of the things still bothering me was how I was going to pay him back for fixing my car. It would be quite difficult since he would have to accept it, and I was pretty sure he wouldn't. It wasn't going to be easy, but I would have to try. In the meantime, I just accepted the fact that he had one up on me. I smiled at the thought and then reached to turn on the heat. It *was* a bit chilly.

Chapter 3
THE PRIZE

I really didn't like lying to people, especially my mom, but Wes' most recent stunt left me no choice. I had to come up with something to explain away the fact that my car had been fixed without either of us knowing. I wasn't able to come up with anything remotely believable at first, so I backed in the driveway so she wouldn't see that side of my Jeep unless she went out of her way to look at it.

The next day, I called her while she was at work to tell her Wes got in touch with me again and offered to have a guy fix it, and that I agreed. She was fine with that, but she started asking more questions about him. I had to tell her he was only nineteen and that he was really nice. The only thing she thought was weird was how he was paying for it to begin with. I told her it was a good question, but I didn't know.

She asked fewer questions than I expected, and I thought we were finished with the whole ordeal, until she came home and saw that it was actually fixed. Even she knew it took more than a few hours to do a little body work and a paint job, but I acted like I had no idea how fixing cars worked. Then, I told her I would ask him if he called. That's when her eyes got big.

"He has your phone number?"

"Yes."

"How did he get that?"

"I gave it to him."

"Why?" she pressed.

"Because he's really nice." I wasn't sure if that was true or not, but I had to play up that card. Then, I added, "And he fixed my car. I may want to talk to him."

"Sophie, I don't know about that. He's in college."

"He's only nineteen, Mom, and I'm eighteen," I reminded her.

"But he's in college, Sophie. That's a big difference from things you have experienced."

"Mom. Wasn't that the whole reason you wanted me to meet you every week? So I could interact with kids my age?"

She hung up her coat and started off toward her bedroom. I followed her, seeking out an explanation. "Well, yes, but I thought that it would inspire you to meet people from your own school, or even maybe give you the urge to go back and experience regular school. I didn't mean for you to meet a boy there."

"Well, I have met someone at my school. Dawn goes to my school, and Wes is only a year older than I am. So, I don't see what the problem is."

"The problem is that you have literally skipped over the normal progression of a teenager, and I'm not sure you're ready to skip right over to college dating."

I sort of understood what she was saying. She did have a point. I had no experience even talking to a guy on the phone. I didn't have a clue what I was getting myself into, but deep down I knew what I wanted, and I knew I hadn't missed out on any prerequisite teenage experience. I was fine with my life. I had to make her at least see that, so I tried to reassure her.

"Mom, I don't feel like I've skipped over anything. High school life has never interested me, and I don't believe I need to go to some dance or school function just to be friends with a nineteen-year-old. You don't give me much credit."

She took a deep breath and said she wasn't sure if she liked the whole thing, but she eventually relaxed and kissed me on the cheek before closing her bedroom door. I supposed I was out of the woods with explaining away the car thing, and I would have to wait and see if she would leave the other issue alone.

I went back up to my room after a pit stop to the kitchen for a bowl of ice cream. I decided to sit out on my back deck and eat it. The view was the main thing that sold me on this house. It just felt like home, and I could've stared out at it all day long. It was completely peaceful until about 7:00, when my cell phone rang. I practically threw my bowl trying to free my hands to answer it.

"Hello?" I said, trying to sound calm.

"Sophie?"

"Yes. Wes?"

"Are you expecting someone else?" he inquired.

"No."

"Did I interrupt you?"

"Well, I did just finish having to explain away your little car fixing stunt to my mother."

He started laughing. "I'm sure you came up with something good."

"No thanks to you," I added.

"Well, I tried to go about it so she wouldn't question anything. You're the one who wanted to be difficult."

"So, is that why you're calling? To call *me* difficult?"

"No, actually, I was hoping I could come pick you up Saturday night."

I could *not* believe I was actually talking to this beautiful guy, who was asking me out. Or at least I thought he was. I had to check to be sure.

"Are you asking me out?"

"You could call it that." I could visualize his little grin through the telephone.

"Well, okay, I suppose." I wondered where we were going. I wanted to prepare myself. If it was a movie, that would be easy. I hoped it wasn't something like bowling or somewhere I could embarrass myself. Then I wondered if it would be a party. That's what college kids did, and that would be horrible. I would feel completely out of place and self-conscious, especially arriving with him. I had to know.

"Where are we going?" I asked, curiously.

"Well, you were a little grumpy the other night, so I was thinking maybe a carnival. Is 7:00 okay?"

"Oh, I work until 7:00 on Saturday," I said, disappointed.

"Where do you work?"

"At a bookstore."

"Which one?"

"Healey's Used Books," I answered half-heartedly, not sure how uncool it sounded.

"I know that one. I've been there before. It's a nice place."

"Oh, well you should stop by sometime," I suggested.

"Maybe I will."

I still wanted to salvage his invitation, so I countered, "I can do 8:00."

"Okay, I'll pick you up then. And you may want to wear something a little more than shorts and a T-shirt."

I felt like jumping up and down on my bed after I got off the phone with him. I couldn't believe that I had the opportunity to go out with him. I wasn't fully convinced it was happening, but I was certainly glad it was. I called Kerry and filled her in on the news. Of course she blurted out, "I told you so," but she was also a little skeptical. Neither of us had really dated before. She had just started seeing someone at her school, so she sympathized with the fluttery stomach, but she was useless when it came to what I should do. I would have to figure the whole dating thing out on my own.

I went to work on Saturday, and I was fidgety all day. We were very slow, and I was working the register, so time just crept by all afternoon. I finally resorted to going over different outfits in my head to figure out what I wanted to wear. I liked being casual, but he was always dressed so nicely. I didn't want to feel underdressed or overdressed. It was going to be hard to pick out something.

The bell sounded at the front door, and I lifted my head to greet the customer.

"Hello," I said, shifting my hair to the side. I was both pleasantly surprised and taken aback to see Wes walking through the door. He greeted me back and walked by, casually, like he was a normal shopper. My heart started to pound as I watched him disappear through the aisle. He went down the non-fiction section and was gone for about twenty minutes. I was itching to go back to see if he needed help, and I was sure Mr. Healey wouldn't mind, but I figured I would play it cool. Besides, if he wanted to talk to me, he would've stopped when he came in.

I was pretending to read through a magazine when he came to check out. He had two books with him, and I tried to act surprised, as if I hadn't seen him coming a mile away.

"Hey," I said, looking up.

"Hey." He smiled, setting the books down on the counter.

"You found some books," I observed, relieved that his trip hadn't been a complete waste.

I picked up the books to enter the prices. I was very interested to know what he was into. One was a science fiction book titled, *Isolation,* and the other was a book titled, *An Old Soul*. Both selections surprised me, but I held up the second.

"What's this one about?"

He thought for a few seconds and replied, "Something about people remembering lives they've lived before."

"Interesting," I said, ringing it up. "That'll be $5.25." He handed me a ten-dollar bill.

"You think so?"

"Yeah sure." I thought it was kind of cool that he was such a deep thinker.

As he tucked the books under his arm, I realized I hadn't bagged them yet, and I had a handful of change to give back. All of a sudden, my no-brainer job turned into an extremely difficult task as I tried to force my brain to concentrate. *What was I doing? Staring at him while I was ringing them up? How hard is it? Enter the price and put it in a bag, not hard,* I thought. He was getting a kick out of my sudden lack of multitasking skills. He had a little smile on his face as I handed him his change. "I'll see you later," he said, and I could've sworn I heard him laugh.

I got home from work around 7:15. The first thing I did was hurry up to my room to take a shower. The inside of the bookstore smelled like old books. And the last thing I wanted to smell like was musty vanilla; so to be sure I didn't, I washed my hair, too.

For my outfit, I decided on a pair of jeans and a white peasant top. It was a tad see-through, so I put a tank under it. Then, I looked in the mirror and realized I needed some color. After a few scans of my handbag collection, I decided on one with the most vibrant colors. It was my vintage, '60s, multi-colored crochet shoulder bag. It was perfect against the plain backdrop of my shirt.

At a few minutes to eight, I went down to the living room and waited. My mother was just sitting on the couch looking at me. Her legs were crossed, and one was rapidly swaying back and forth. She was more nervous than I was. Just when I was about to tell her to relax, the doorbell rang.

I walked to the foyer as casually as I could, but when I opened the door, my heart did a cartwheel. The second I saw him, I instantly smiled and he returned the gesture. I noticed his eyes give me a quick look-over.

"You look nice," he said shyly. If I hadn't been mistaken, I would have thought him to be a little nervous, too.

"Thanks. Come in. I'd like you to meet my mom."

He nodded and stepped in. I noticed he was wearing dark jeans and a very nice black, zip-up jacket, with a high-collared baby blue sweater peeking out at the neck. It looked very good on him, to say the least. There was no doubt that he was model material, without even trying to be. The definition in Wes' face was natural, and it didn't deserve to be disrupted—unless it was by his captivating smile, which was now directed at me.

I instinctively grabbed his hand and led him into the living room. The coolness of his palm sent a chill up my spine, and I wondered how cold it was outside. By the time we reached the living room, my mom was already standing.

"Mom, this is Wes. Wes, this is my mom, Gayle." I suppose that's what I should've said. I didn't know.

"Hello, Wes, it is very nice to finally meet you," she said, motioning him to come in and sit down. I only hoped this wasn't going to last too long. "So, Sophie, tells me you guys met when she crashed into you." It wasn't a question, but Wes took the cue.

"Yes, ma'am, she did. She didn't do that much damage to my car though, so it was fine."

"Well, I thought it was awfully nice of you to pay for all the damage to both vehicles yourself. What do your parents do?" I shot a look over at her that could have frozen boiling water. I couldn't believe she'd asked him that. I wanted to reach over there and shake her. She must have sensed my horror because she quickly corrected herself—her next question didn't sound *as* rude, but still rude, nevertheless.

"Well, I mean that, it's not every day a college student can pay for someone else's vehicle when they were not at fault. I was just wondering if your parents helped you, or if you had to pay for this yourself." My anger turned to complete embarrassment when he answered her.

"Well, Ms. Slone, my parents died when I was younger." I turned my head to look at my mother and by the look on her face, I saw that she was just as embarrassed as she should've been. Wes continued. "My uncle raised me for a while, and then he died when I was eighteen."

"I'm very sorry to hear that," my mother interrupted, and for the first time, I saw my mother in complete mental discomfort. He all too nicely tried to make her feel better.

"It's okay, Ms. Slone," he assured her. "If you were wondering how or why I took care of Sophie's car, it's because I wanted to do something that would help her. My parents were very wealthy, and my uncle was a renowned scientist, so I have quite a bit of savings. She seems like a very nice girl, and I didn't want her to have to worry about it."

Wes looked completely comfortable with the whole conversation, but I felt terrible. I stood up and told my mother we were going to be late. I wanted to leave immediately.

As soon as we got in the car, I apologized for my mother's prying.

"I'm so sorry."

"Don't be. She was asking normal questions," he said, trying to reassure me.

"Still, it was very personal, and she shouldn't have pried."

"Sophie, those are very normal questions. I get them all the time. It's fine."

I let out a big sigh and stared out the window. I was trying very hard to block out the whole incident, but I couldn't. He'd lost both of his parents and an uncle. I couldn't imagine going through that. All of a sudden, I felt like my life had been so easy. My one complaint was having to move around too often. I tried to sympathize.

"I'm sorry," I said again.

"I already told you. No worries."

"I meant, I'm sorry about your loss."

He looked directly in my eyes and gave me a slight nod, as if to tell me he was all right. We drove for a while without saying anything. I wanted to change the subject to a happier note, at least from my perspective.

"I love carnivals," I said. "I haven't been to one since I lived in Virginia."

He smiled slightly. "I'm glad."

"Of course, I never win anything," I admitted.

"You might tonight," he added. I smiled in response to his optimism.

The seats in his car were on the tiny side compared to my Jeep, but there was enough room for me to turn my body, so I perked up a bit and twisted so I was facing him. Occasionally I could see his eyes turn toward my direction to check if I was still watching him. But for the most part, he kept his eyes on the road and smoothly shifted gears.

It seemed like we drove for a half-hour. I lost track of where we were going, because I wasn't even watching the road. He had put on a CD that I had never heard before, but I liked it. After a while, I just closed my eyes and started listening. I almost fell asleep in an odd state of tranquility, which was interrupted when he lightly nudged my knee to let me know we were there. I immediately perked up and saw two gigantic Ferris wheels lighting up the sky. It was a big carnival. I felt so excited; it was almost like I was a kid again.

He parked the car, and as I gathered my purse from the floor, he walked around the front of the car and opened the door for me. I could immediately hear the sounds of the bells and horns and people laughing. I couldn't wait to play some games. He put his hand on the small of my back as he guided me toward the ticket booth. After he'd purchased some tickets, he asked me if I was hungry or thirsty. I told him I wanted to play a few games first, and then we could get something to eat.

We started walking down the midway and were immediately bombarded with luring tempters. Lined up on both sides of the aisle were game hosts calling to us from their booths. "Step right up. Take a shot. Let's see what you got. Win your prize." It was hard to walk right past some of them, but I knew what I wanted.

I immediately zeroed in on the roll-down game. It was one of my favorites, because it really didn't require that much talent, and I like games where you took your chances. We both sat down on the stool and the guy behind the counter said it was $2.00 per person to play. Wes put down two dollars.

"Aren't you going to play?" I asked.

"No, I want to watch you." I was glad there was really no way for me to embarrass myself. All I had to do was drop the little wooden ball on the decline and watch it roll into the little numbered slots. If I got a total number over 28 or under 14, then I would win a prize. I'm sure there was a strategy to playing, but I just dropped my ball and let it roll. The first time I played, I got 25. I stuck my bottom lip out a little, and I heard Wes chuckle as he put down another $2.00. I looked at him, unconvinced. "You really want to watch me play this again?"

He leaned in closer, being sure to maintain eye contact. "I could watch you play this all night." I felt my cheeks blush a little as I turned forward and let the next ball drop.

I started concentrating really hard as I rolled the next balls, and my score that time was a 22. Still no win.

It may not have taken any real talent, but it was starting to get embarrassing. He kept putting down two dollars every time I lost, encouraging me to keep trying. I did want a little stuffed animal, and Wes seemed to get a kick out of it, so I kept playing. I lost track of how many dollars Wes gave the guy before I won my first stuffed animal. It was a little koala bear about the size of my hand. The guy gave it to me and I started laughing. Wes said, "What? You don't like your bear? You worked so hard for it." He was holding back a smile.

"Yes, I do like my bear, but I was just hoping for that great big one up there. It's cute." I was pointing at a huge white bear with a red ribbon around the neck.

Wes turned to the guy and asked, "What does she have to do to earn that bear?"

The guy looked at me and then back to Wes. "You're going to need a lot more dollar bills if *she* wants to win that."

I saw Wes' eyes narrow as he looked up at the guy. "Well, maybe I'll have better luck," he said. He sat back down, and I started to feel guilty for having said something. I didn't want Wes to waste any more money. Plus, I could tell Wes was a little irritated, and the guy looked all too willing to take his money.

I quickly sat down next to him. "Wes, you don't have to do this. I really don't need that bear."

"I want you to have it," he said, squaring his shoulders toward the game, putting two more dollars on the counter. On his very first try, he got 29 points, and then he looked at me and said, "I guess it's my lucky day." Every time he rolled, he got the exact amount he needed to win. I watched in amazement as he carefully selected which side of the lane to release his ball. Sometimes he put it on the left, sometimes toward the middle, and sometimes on the right. He knew exactly where to drop it.

I would've been embarrassed about having frivolously squandered away my rolls before, but I was too busy getting a kick out of watching that guy's face as Wes kept winning. At the height of Wes' victory, the guy went to hand him the bear, but he declined. Instead, Wes pointed to me, indicating that the prize was mine. I took it and gave it a big squeeze.

"Thank you," I said, beaming.

"You are very welcome."

We started walking, and he told me he was hungry, so he wanted to grab something to eat. I was a little hungry myself, so I was glad he offered. As we were walking, I thought it would be a good time to feed my curiosity.

"So, do you come here often?" I asked, trying not to sound too interested.

"No, not at all. Why?"

"Well, I was just curious. You seemed like you play that game a lot. I was just wondering."

"Oh no. I haven't been to one of these in a very long time."

I wasn't sure I believed him, but I was having a great time, so I dropped it. We reached the little eatery stand, and he ordered a hot dog with French fries. I had a slice of pizza and a Coke. When we were done eating, he asked me if I wanted a funnel cake. I was stuffed, but I was not about to pass on one of those.

He hopped up and offered to go get me one, but I went with him and ate it as we walked. He didn't want any, so I was stuck eating it all by myself, and that was boring. I wanted to share.

"Are you sure you don't want a bite?"

He smiled that perfect smile of his. "Yes, I'm sure."

I held it up and waved it in front of him, hoping he'd change his mind. He started smiling and motioned to gently move my arm down when a large rush of cool air came between us, sweeping up the powdered sugar from the funnel cake. I grabbed the plate, but not in time to stop a white gust of powder from finding a new home all over Weston's face and designer jacket.

Oh my God! My mouth dropped opened. "I'm so sorry!"

He started laughing. "It's okay."

"No, it isn't." I started dusting it off of him frantically. I managed to get most of it off of his jacket, and I stopped before reaching his face. It was splattered with white powder, and he was still smiling. I was sure he wouldn't be so happy if he could see himself. Then again, he was still ridiculously cute. Powdered sugar and all.

He was making no motion whatsoever to clean himself off, but I couldn't let him walk around like that, so I reached up with my hand and started brushing his face gently. His cheeks were cool to my touch, and incredibly soft and smooth. I got all of it off except for the remnants, which resided on his lips. I fought thoughts of tasting it, but then I got a grip. "You have some on your lips," I informed him. In slow motion, I watched, no stared, as he licked his lips clean of every last speck of dissolving sugar.

"Um," he said.

I cleared my throat and blinked. "Uh…maybe I should throw this away."

He was holding back a smile now. "Maybe you should."

I threw the rest away, all the while fighting the fluttery sensation that was going wild inside. He snapped me out of my trance by asking me if I wanted to get on some rides or if I wanted to play some more games.

"Well, if you hadn't let me stuff myself with the funnel cake, then maybe I would say rides, but since you did, let's play some games."

"All right, you pick. What do you want to play?"

We walked for a while and passed the dart throw game, the shoot out game, the game where you have to knock the cans down with the ball, and a basketball game. All of them required some sort of skill, and I had already wasted a bunch of his money, so I picked the horse racing game. I loved that game, too. It was an exciting game, but it still only required a bit of luck. Once again, Wes only put down enough for me to play. I was starting to suspect he didn't want to whip my butt in any of them.

On my first game, there were four other people playing, and I thought to myself, *I can beat them.* All I had to do was roll the ball in the high number holes to make my horse go faster than all the others. When the bell went off, I started rolling my ball and my horse got a quick jump ahead of the rest of the field. My chances looked promising at first, but shortly after that, it seemed like my balls were always going in the lowest number. My horse finished dead last. I frowned, and Wes instantly put down two more dollars with a grin. I quickly slid the money back over to him.

"Oh, no you don't. I'm not doing this again. You keep your money. You play. I want to watch you."

"But I was having so much fun watching you."

"Well, I'd rather watch *you* win. Besides, my bear needs a friend." I poked out my lip in a little pout.

He reached over and moved my hair behind my ear, smiling softly. "Well, then, in that case, let's get your bear a friend." He casually squared off with the game and effortlessly won another enormous bear just for me. Once again, he had no problem rolling his ball in a professional fashion, where each one dropped where he wanted it to. Not only did his horse win the races, it won by a landslide. I was just as tickled to get that bear as I had been to get the first, but I was no longer convinced that he was winning with luck.

"Are you going to tell me that you really haven't played these games in a while?"

"I never said that," he said innocently.

"Well, then how do you expect me to believe that you're that good if you don't play a lot?"

"I do play a lot. I have these games at home."

"You have them at home? Like on a computer?" I needed clarification.

"No, I have the actual games." I looked at him skeptically. "It's true," he said. "I have them in my basement."

"I don't believe you," I said, half-joking. We were walking then, and he had taken one of the bears to lighten my load.

"Well, I'll show you sometime."

That was a good sign. I took that as an extended invitation for another date. That thought made me feel really good and curious at the same time. It was starting to get late, and he asked me if I was tired and ready to go. "Just a little," I admitted. "But I'm not ready to go." He chuckled and said some part that I tuned out about returning me safely to my mom, and another part about it being a long drive home.

"Can we just do the Ferris wheel before we go? We still have the tickets." I was trying to make the evening last longer.

He looked confused. "Are you sure you want to do the Ferris wheel?" he asked. I was afraid of heights, but I was not about to let him in on that little secret. I just wanted to spend a little more time with him. And if that meant being a little dizzy for a few minutes, then it was well worth it. I wasn't ready to go home.

"Yes, I'm sure," I answered confidently.

"Okay, but we can do something else, if you want."

I had already said it, and I didn't want to sound like I was desperately trying to hang on to the moment so I reassured him, "Yes, I like Ferris wheels." He looked a little bit perplexed but motioned with his hand for me to go ahead of him. I was starting to feel stupid for suggesting the whole thing. I hoped he couldn't see my desperate attempt to keep the date going.

There was a very short line, so I didn't have much time to think about it. When we climbed into the car, he offered to take my teddy bear and set it across from us. I clutched the bear instantly and told him I preferred to hold it. I thought having something on my lap to squeeze would help with the dizziness and nausea I might feel.

The first few times around weren't so bad. He asked me a lot of questions about where I'd lived before, how we moved to California, how long we lived in California, where I went to school, and things like that. It had taken my mind off the ride, but by the fourth or fifth time around, I looked out over the edge and felt instantly queasy.

"It helps if you don't look down," he said, putting his arm around me. How embarrassing, and was it that obvious?

"I'm fine," I lied. Regardless, I took his advice and stared at my bear for the rest of the ride. As we got off, he put his arms on my elbows to steady me. It was completely embarrassing.

"I'm proud of you."

"Proud of what?"

"Proud you overcame your fear of heights."

I guess it *had been* that obvious. On our way out, he still had his arm around me as if I was going to fall over, and I have to admit I wasn't complaining about that part. Once we got in the car, I wanted to take the focus off me and my nausea, so I started asking him questions.

"Why do you have carnival games in your basement anyway?"

"I get bored easily. I like to do fun things to pass the time." He looked at me, and I noticed for the first time in the dark car that his eyes had a glassy look to them. I could almost see my reflection. It was like a subtle shine to a lake in the evening. It was mesmerizing. He looked away quickly. "Since I live alone, I need a lot of things to keep me busy."

"How many games do you have?" I asked, still slightly distracted by the beauty of his eyes.

"I have a lot of games down there, but those are the only two carnival games I have." He kept his eyes on the road.

That was interesting. "So, you just happen to have the two games I played tonight in your basement?" He was quiet. "That sounds like a coincidence," I added.

"It's funny how the world works. Isn't it?" he asked, rhetorically.

"I guess so." We drove for a few minutes listening to the soft music play, and then I added hopefully, "You're going to let me see them, right?" He glanced back over to me and smiled slightly.

"You can see them whenever you want."

I wanted to ask him so many more things, but I didn't want to babble. Talking too much had already gotten me in the Ferris wheel predicament. I thought it would be a good idea to enjoy the ride home and only speak if he did first. I was amazed—fifteen minutes went by and not a word. But, it wasn't the kind of silence that was awkward. It was a natural silence. It was comfortable. The kind filled with pleasant thoughts.

As we pulled up to my house, I thanked him and opened my door. He opened his at the same time. "You don't have to get out."

"Someone has to help you carry your bears." He came around to help me pull them from the back seat. He took one of the big ones, and I grabbed the little bear in one hand and wrapped my arm around the other big one.

We stepped up to my front door, and I thanked him again.

"I really appreciate it," I said. He smiled with a slow blink and stared into my eyes.

I was completely smitten. And as if his presence, alone, wasn't enough to give me butterflies, he leaned down and touched his lips to my cheek in a way that lingered long enough for me to notice that it was not like a kiss from a friend or relative. As he gently pulled back, he took the tiny bear from my hand and said, "I want to keep this one." I smiled, thinking it was a reasonable request. After all, he had paid a small fortune for it.

Chapter 4
DRIVEN

My mother was waiting up, and she cornered me as soon I was walked through the door, which was fine with me because I had a few words for her. She didn't let me get two words out before she told me how terrible she felt for making Wes feel so uncomfortable. She said she had no idea that he would have lost both parents, and she hoped she'd have the chance to make it up to him.

"Good luck with that," I told her.

"Come on, Sophie. How was I supposed to know?"

"You aren't supposed to know that, but you don't ask people where they get their money from. That's rude."

"You're right. I was just trying to make sense of the whole thing. I didn't mean...." She tapered off as she examined my two large bears. "It looks like you had a good time." It sounded like a question, so I said, "Yes. I did."

"Good. I'm glad. I really am."

"Why are you so glad now?" I asked, suspiciously, as I freed my hands to take off my jacket.

"Well, he seems really nice, and I feel sorry for him a little, and I think he means well. Not to mention he is some serious eye candy."

"Mother!" I spat, unable to contain a smile. I scooped up my animals and headed upstairs.

"Well, he is," she added. "And I've never seen such perfect teeth!"

"I'm ignoring you," I sang.

I wasn't ready to have a boy talk with my mother. In fact, I was going to avoid it at all costs, but I was happy that she seemed open to the idea of me hanging out with him some more. I certainly wanted to.

That night, my face hurt from smiling so much. It was ridiculous how giddy I was. I felt so beside myself. I think I even sat on my bed once and turned to see if I was sitting next to myself. I couldn't believe the emotions running through me. I wanted to see him again, and he'd only been gone five minutes. I tried very hard to bring myself back down to earth.

Trying to go about my days like nothing was unusual after meeting Wes was very difficult. I tried hard not to be glued by the phone waiting for his call. I went out for a lot of drives to relax myself. The weather was still decent enough for me to take the top off my Jeep, and I loved the fresh air. Some days I'd go to the mall to look around and some days I'd go sit out at the overlook for a little while, just anything to make the time go by faster before I talked to him again.

He called me more frequently than I expected, but I found myself wanting more. One day he called, and I must have sounded down because he came right out and asked, "Is everything okay? You don't sound like yourself."

I didn't want him to think I was clingy, so I tried to play it cool. "Yes, everything's good."

"It doesn't sound that way to me. What's up?"

Okay fine, I had nothing to lose. "I was hoping to see you again," I admitted.

"I'll see you Thursday, and then I'm bringing you to my house this weekend." On Thursday, we would cross paths, after my lunch on campus, but that was hardly what I had in mind.

"I know, but still. I'm just being silly." I felt my lip poke out, and I was glad he couldn't see me. Saturday was only a few days away, but somehow I was miserable with the thought of not seeing him until then. I felt an ache in the pit of my stomach. I missed him more than I wanted to admit to myself, or to him.

When we hung up, I decided to get some homework done. I was already a few days ahead, but I wanted to stay busy. I had to do a paper on how water pollution affects the environment, so I did some research for that. A few hours and ten websites later, my brain was full of information on pathogens, sewage, viruses, protozoa, and eutrophication. By the afternoon, I was ready for a break. I didn't have to go to work, so I decided to take a drive to the overlook to keep my head focused.

On my way out of the house, I instantly perked up at the warm breeze that was still in the air. I started to smile at the thought of the afternoon drive when my heart skipped a beat at the sight of a little black car sitting right in front of my house. After taking a quick breath to calm my nerves, I let out an involuntary grin and walked over to the passenger side door. His window slid down.

"What are you doing?" I asked, surprised.

"You said you wanted to see me."

"But you have class today."

"I know British literature quite well. I think I'll be okay if I miss a class." He was leaning over with a smile. "Get in."

I couldn't get in the car fast enough. "Where are we going?"

"Where were *you* going?" he countered.

"The overlook."

"What for?" he asked.

"Just for a drive."

"Okay, we'll drive then," he said, putting the car in gear.

"How do you do that?" I asked, looking at his shifter. He followed my eyes.

"This?"

"Yeah, you drive this car so smoothly. I tried once, and I almost broke my mom's neck."

He laughed. "You just haven't had the right teacher."

"That's a nice way of putting it." I happened to notice I was in sweatpants and a T-shirt while he was, once again, dressed nicely. I would have to start paying attention to what I was wearing before I left the house. I wasn't used to worrying about seeing anyone in particular out in public before. "Where are we going?" I asked, diverting the attention from my attire.

"Just for a little drive, not too far from here."

I was fine with the drive part, but I was hoping I would have a little time to spend with him. I had some questions that I'd been saving to ask him in person, and now seemed like a good enough time.

"Do you mind if I ask some questions?"

"No, not at all," he said, with his eyes still on the road. "Go ahead."

I shifted in my seat a little. "Well, I was wondering about your parents."

"Yes?"

"How did you lose them?" I hoped I hadn't worded it too poorly.

"That's a good way of putting it," he said. "Well, my father died flying a small plane many years ago, and my mother died from the flu when I was seventeen."

"How old was she?" I asked, thinking it was strange.

"She was only forty-two." He looked over and must have seen signs of thinking going on in my head because he clarified. "She was in another country when she got sick. They didn't have the treatment we have here."

"And your uncle?"

"Cancer."

"My grandmother died from cancer, too," I added. He looked over at me with sympathetic eyes and said he was sorry. For the first time, I knew how he felt when he said it was okay every time I apologized to him for his loss. It wasn't his fault that my grandmother died, and there really wasn't anything for him to apologize for. It was just a part of life. I guess people feel the need to say they're sorry when they hear about it. It was just a natural compassion, I supposed.

"Do you have any more family in the area?" I asked.

"No."

"No one?"

"No."

I wasn't sure how to respond to that, so I just sat quietly. We drove for a few more minutes until he broke the silence.

"So, you live with your mother. Where is your father?"

I've never liked answering that question before, but I didn't seem to mind then.

"He went back to Brazil when I was young."

"Do you still talk to him?"

"No. Not really. My mom says he tried to keep in touch, but as I got older, he just stopped communicating."

"What brought you to California then?" he asked.

"My grandmother got sick. She died earlier this year."

At least I was lucky enough to have a family member still living, but he had no one. I stared out the window, wondering how I would feel to be all alone, and it made me sad. I was sure I wouldn't be as composed as he was. I was glad when he interrupted my thoughts.

"Here we are," he said, pulling into the parking lot of what looked like a field house.

"What is this?"

"It's a race car track," he said, pulling up to a side gate. He got out and manually pulled the gate open on each side. Then, he casually got back in the car and smoothly pulled in.

"What are we doing here?" I asked, looking around. It didn't look closed, but I didn't see any people either.

"You said you wanted to drive."

"You're going to drive on here?" I pointed to the track.

"No, you are," he informed me, getting out of the car and walking around to my side. "Well?" he said, holding my door open, waiting for me to get out.

"What?"

"*You're* going to drive, on the track."

"Drive what?"

"Drive this," he clarified, motioning to his car. He *was* crazy. I shook my head.

"No. I don't think so. I can't drive your car. I don't even know how."

He leaned in the car and grabbed me by my arms. "Come on, up you go," he said, pulling me out.

"Would you stop it!" I said, swatting him away. "I'm not going to drive this thing. You just got it fixed. Are you nuts?"

He laughed, shutting the door behind me. "No, I want you to drive it. I want to show you how. Besides, everyone should know how to drive a manual shift."

"But I'll mess it up. I can't."

He put his hands on both of my shoulders and leaned in. His eyes were that deep brown I loved, but I couldn't see my reflection this time. "No, you won't," he said, pausing. "Please, I'm missing class for this. The least you can do is make this worth my while." He tilted his head downward and looked at me through his long, dark eyelashes. I let out a big sigh and stared at him for a few minutes. He didn't look like he was going to change his mind.

"Fine."

He smiled immediately.

I dragged myself around the car and slid into the driver's side. I sat there, afraid to touch anything, and he was smiling the whole time.

"Are you sure we can drive on this?" I asked, hoping for an out to my predicament.

"I'm positive."

"How do you know?"

He leaned back into his seat, completely relaxed. "Because it's mine, courtesy of Weston C. Wilson II."

"I thought you said your dad was a pilot?"

"He was," he assured me. "My family had a lot of hobbies."

So that was great. He had a race car track in his family. It was sure to be an absolute embarrassment. I would've rather been doing my government homework. Well, maybe I was exaggerating a little, but I was horrified.

"You're going to need a neck brace you know?" I added.

"I'll be fine, you'll see." He was getting a kick out of this.

"How much is this car worth anyway? Wait, don't tell me. I don't want to know."

"Stop worrying," he said. "The car will be fine, and so will you. I promise."

He instructed me to push the clutch all the way in and hold it while I started the car. My leg felt like Jell-O. It was shaking. "Now, push in the clutch with your left foot and keep your other foot on the brake." That was easy. I could do that. "Now keep your feet exactly where they are and move this up like that." I watched him put the gearshift in first gear and then put it back in neutral. "Now you try it."

"You want me to move?"

"Yes, but not yet," he smiled. "Just put it in gear and wait." I followed his instructions reluctantly.

"Now just stay like that and close your eyes."

"What?" I said, looking at him.

"Just do it," he said, encouraging me. I did.

"Now listen very carefully." His voice was soothing. "I want you to feel the car. You are going to *slowly* let out the clutch a little, and *as soon as* you feel the car start to move, push the clutch all the way back in. Now, try that." I just sat there. "Go on. Try it." I gripped the wheel and started to ease off the clutch, and as soon as I felt the car start to move, I shoved it back in. It was hard on the poor clutch but easy on our necks.

"Good," he said. "Now do it again." He had me do it a few times. "Do you feel where the clutch is catching?"

I nodded.

"That's where the gears will catch. Now, I want you to think about that spot where the clutch catches *and* the gas pedal. They are like a seesaw. The car will move when the seesaw is in balance. What you need to do is slowly ease off the clutch, so it is where you felt it catch before. This time you want to hold the clutch still, right before it makes the car move. Then, you need to give it some gas slowly. Once the seesaw is balanced, the car will start to move and you can slowly give it more gas and let the clutch all the way out. We will drive for a few feet and when I tell you to brake, I want you to take your foot off the gas and push the clutch all the way back in and stop the car. The clutch has to be all the way in every time the car stops. Got it?"

"I can't do this," I said, opening my eyes.

"Yes, you can. We are just going to go a few feet. I want you to practice the seesaw. That's all. Just try it."

I ran down everything he said in my mind again and started to release the clutch. I gave it some gas and let out the clutch. Both of our heads flew back into the headrests and bounced violently off. The car stalled.

"Oh my God. I'm sorry," I said. "I told you." He was laughing.

"No, it's okay. I should've warned you. You don't need to give it as much gas as you do your Jeep. This car is very sensitive to speed. Just a tiny bit of gas will go a long way. Just give it a tiny bit." He held up his thumb and index finger pinched together.

I started the car and tried it again. I let out the clutch a little, felt the car start to move, and gave it just a tiny bit of gas. "Now let off the clutch the rest of the way." We went about ten feet. "Okay, now stop the car." I braked a little too fast, but our heads only moved forward a few inches. "Good," he said. "Not too bad. Now try it again, get us going a little, and then stop, again. Get used to the see-saw."

He had me practice starting and stopping a bunch of times, but I eventually got it down pretty smoothly. I only stalled once, not counting the first time. I did much better than I expected. I turned to him and said, "Okay, your turn."

"Oh, no. You're not done," he said, shaking his head. "You need to try moving through the gears."

"Why are you insistent upon me ruining this car?"

"You are not going to ruin it. Trust me. Now, instead of stopping the car this time, all you are going to do is let off the gas and instead of braking, you're just going to push in the clutch and change gears. Then, you slowly let out the clutch and give it some more gas." He took my hand and motioned through the gears with me to show me where to move them, and then he set me free. I replayed everything he said in my head and then gave it a try.

"Good. Now try second gear . . . Good, now try third." Third gear was a little shaky, but I managed. We were driving. "Now just keep her steady," he instructed. We drove around the track, one whole time, at thirty miles per hour. I didn't want to go any faster. I had to admit, driving the car was sort of fun. I felt powerful in a way. And, had I not been worried about wrecking it, I might have enjoyed myself, but I figured I should quit while I was still ahead.

"Can I stop now?" I practically pleaded.

"You can stop whenever you want."

I was glad to hear that and wasted no time pulling over, being sure to remember to put the clutch in as I braked.

"You did it," he said, putting the gearshift in neutral and pulling up the emergency brake. "Always remember to pull this up when you stop the car."

I nodded again and swiftly opened the door and got out. Our necks seemed to be in good shape. I wouldn't call it a smooth ride, but it wasn't half-bad either. He was a very good teacher, but I was glad to be out of that seat.

Of course when he got in, we smoothly picked up speed until we were back around the track. I was a little envious. It was effortless to him. "I want you to meet some people," he said. He pulled up to a building that looked like an aviation hangar. We got out and walked into the office. There were a few guys working there. Wes led us over to the counter area. "Kenny, Curtis, Jimmy, this is Sophie." They each came up to me and shook my hand one by one. Curtis looked like the oldest, and Kenny was wearing a mechanic suit, so I took him for a mechanic, and Jimmy was wearing a racing suit. He looked about our age.

"So Wes, it's good to see you," Kenny said. "What brings you by?"

"Just showing Sophie how to drive." They all laughed and looked at me. I didn't get the joke.

"Sophie, you might want to steer clear of this one on the track," Curtis interjected.

"Why is that?" I asked, curious. Wes grabbed my hand and was trying to pull me toward a side door.

"Leave her alone, guys," Wes said, still pulling me. I wanted to know, so I stopped and separated my hand and waited.

"Because he is a crazy man on the track. He has no fear." They all laughed.

"I'll keep that in mind," I said, pondering this new information.

"Bye guys," he said, holding onto my hand again. I waved over my shoulder, to be polite, as he gently pulled me away.

"That was interesting."

"They don't know what they're talking about," he said, and then, leaning in closer to my ear, he added, "I want to show you something." I kept following him as a tingling sensation lingered on my ear from his cool breath.

He opened up a door that led to a large garage, which housed several race cars. I was in awe. I'd never been into car racing, but those cars were very cool.

"How many are there?" I asked, touching the window nets and running my hands over the painted numbers and sponsor signs.

"We have seven here. We use four for the driving school and we race three."

"You race?"

"No, not anymore. I thought I would try college for a while." He winked. "Jimmy is our driver."

"So what, you like *own* all this?"

"Yes. I inherited it, I suppose. It sort of runs itself now. Curtis manages it, and I just sort of enjoy it."

We walked around the cars. He let go of my hand, and I was reluctantly free to explore the hangar. "These are *real* cars?" I asked stupidly.

"Yes, they are. One day, I'll get you to drive one," he said.

I laughed out loud. I was absolutely positive that would never happen, although, I did want to sit in one.

"Can I get in one?" I asked.

"Of course." He motioned his hand, obligingly, toward the closest car. He had a devious smile on his face, but I ignored it. I tried to grab for a door handle, but there wasn't one. "How do I…" I started to ask, but then it registered. "Wait, I'm not supposed to *climb* in, am I?"

"Yes," he said, chuckling, and that explained his insidious invitation.

"Never mind," I said, turning away from the car, as the embarrassing vision flashed through my brain.

"Oh, come on. Get in," he pleaded, stepping into my path.

"No way," I countered, crossing my arms. I was not going to fumble my way through a car window in front of Wes. "Not a chance."

He sighed and then raised his eyebrows in preparation for a negotiation. "I'll help you." He went to hold onto me and gave me that long stare with those mesmerizing eyes. What was it with this guy? I couldn't help but notice his obvious joy in the idea of me foolishly climbing in the window, and although I could see myself clumsily doing it, I couldn't help but want to give him what he wanted—even if it meant I would possibly regret it later.

"Fine," I said, uncrossing my arms. He scooped me up like a child, and I could feel the hardness of his arms under my ribs and thighs. I wrapped my arms around his neck instinctively. He smelled so good. Fresh, like rain with a hint of something sweet. My stomach started feeling all fluttery again.

He turned my feet toward the driver's door and led me through the window. From there, I was easily able to slide in. An early episode of the *Dukes of Hazzard* came to mind, and it wasn't that bad.

Sitting in that car was no comparison to Wes'. There was no luxury at all. It had the feel of a bumper car at a carnival. There were gauges I didn't understand, and I was very certain I wouldn't ever drive one of them. He would look good in one though. I was sure of that. I started to climb out and was stumped.

"You come out the same way you went in," he said, with a little grin. I knew I shouldn't have fallen for that look. I awkwardly climbed my way out, and I was glad to have been in sweat pants. Halfway out of the window, he grabbed me by the waist and pulled me to him until my feet settled on the ground.

"Thanks," I said, still standing within inches of him.

"It's no trouble." He slowly raised his hand to move my hair out of my face. I remained perfectly still as his fingertips glided across my forehead in an effort to slide bangs behind my ear. He looked at me with intense but peaceful eyes, and my heart started pounding. I dropped my gaze and zeroed in on his plenteous lips. My eyes were also intensely drawn to the gentle creases on the sides of his mouth, which seemed to be the remnants of previous smiles. Instinctively, I reached up, quickly, and put my lips to his. I think it was a knee-jerk reaction to divert his attention from my nervousness, but whatever it was, I kissed him. He softly placed both hands on the sides of my face and a warm chill went through my spine. He kissed me back, gently, and my thumping heart turned to a racing heart.

Very slowly, he pulled back a few inches, and when I opened my eyes, he was studying my face. Self consciously, I wondered if I had done it right. It felt right to me, but I couldn't read his expression. I searched his eyes for some sort of sign, and it made me feel a burning in my chest. There was a yearning for me to be closer to him, so I pulled him back to me without thinking it through and started kissing him again.

I don't know what came over me, but I needed the warmth that the closeness of his lips brought me. Everything felt so right. Our lips moved with one another in the same rhythm, as if we had kissed a thousand times. I felt my muscles turn to mush, but instead of sinking toward the ground, I felt like I was floating. He embraced me tighter as we kissed for an immeasurable moment, and then he pulled back slightly, pausing with his forehead to mine. I could feel his breath on my cheek, and we stood still while silent thoughts lingered in both of our minds. Then, as if to offer some sort of reassurance before responsibly suggesting that we should go, he tilted his lips back to mine to complete one more brief but soft encounter between our lips.

I ran through our whole kiss in my mind as we walked back to the car. It was my first *real* kiss, and I wished I could read his mind to gauge his reaction. It was so very frustrating. I was used to being in such control of myself, and for the first time, I felt like I was unraveling into someone else. Someone who wanted this guy more than anything else in the world. The feeling I had when I was with him was indescribable. My brain knew so little about him, but my heart felt like it knew everything, and that made me sure I wanted him. I knew that day, that I would never be the same again. I didn't just *want* him in my life, I felt like I was *supposed* to be with him, even if it didn't make sense.

Chapter 5
SILENT STORIES

The drive to his house on Saturday felt like we were constantly headed upward. We were driving on a windy little two-lane road off the highway. The turnoff was not too far from the overlook, but it was a turn that no one would have taken had they not been looking for it.

"So you live out here by yourself?"

"Yes." There was a pause, and then he added, "Is that strange to you?"

"No. Well, I was just wondering why you choose not to live on campus."

"Well, I don't like being around a lot of people. I like my privacy."

"Don't you feel lonely out here?" We passed some driveways here and there, but I couldn't really see any houses. I liked my privacy, too, but I also liked the idea of neighbors I could at least see. Somehow it made me feel safer to know that people were around, even if I didn't actually talk to them.

"No, not at all. I bought this place so I could be alone."

"You bought it?" It was peculiar to hear him talk about buying a house. The only thing I had bought was my car, and I needed my mom and Kerry to help me decide on that. Buying a house was the last thing on my mind. It made me feel so young.

"Yes, my uncle had a house about twenty miles away. I lived there for a while after he died, but I decided I needed a change, something for myself. So I sold that house and bought this one."

"How long have you lived here?"

"Since I was eighteen."

I decided to put the rest of my questions on hold. It was an absolutely beautiful drive. I could see the sky and far away hills peeking through the trees on the hillside, and I wondered what the view would be like once we got to a spot where I could actually see it. When he invited me to come up early, I was initially bummed, because I had to work in the afternoon, but I was starting to be glad he had. It meant the view would be much better.

He slowed and made the turn into a paved, narrow driveway, which was bordered by tall trees on each side. We meandered through a wooded trail sloping back downward and then up again on the hillside.

My eyes widened. "Shut up."

"I didn't say anything," he said, confused.

"No, shut up," I said again. That was all I could seem to say staring at his house. It was a contemporary-style home made out of cedar, and it sat situated on an upslope. There were so many complex angles and levels that I couldn't tell how many floors the house had. On the left side of the house was a four-car side load garage situated under one of the levels. There were several windows on all sides of the house. I have never seen a house like it.

"What?" he said.

"Are you kidding me?" I asked, as he rolled to a stop in front of the house.

"You can't be serious." I got out of the car and looked at the house. It was amazing. It looked so big, but cozy all at the same time. It reminded me of a ski resort I had been to once in Virginia, only on a slightly smaller scale. I imagined a fireplace in every room. "You live here all by yourself?"

"Yes."

"It's beautiful."

"Come on. Let's go in." He grabbed my hand, and I was surprised at how natural the gesture was to him. His hand was cool and relaxed, and I was the opposite. My hand burned at his touch. I had to concentrate hard to keep my heart in check so my hands wouldn't get clammy. He seemed to have no problem with that.

He guided me up the front steps, which ran parallel to the house. When we reached the glass front door, I could see through it to a wide hallway that opened up to a massive view from the back of the house. The entryway, inside, made my mouth drop open. There was one huge skylight that ran the entire length of the hall, with horizontal beams going across it. It had to be three stories high. On each side, the beams stretched out over open balcony areas that were upstairs. We walked in, and I couldn't decide which was more spectacular—the view from the windows at the back of the house or the view from the skylight.

We continued past the kitchen on the left, and then we went down a couple of steps into the living area where the exposed beams continued to support the ceiling. "This is absolutely amazing," I said. "Look at the view. You can see everything." He stood there in satisfaction at my reactions.

"Can I get you something to drink?"

"Sure," I answered, walking over to the window. There had to have been a twenty-mile view from anywhere in the back of his house. You could see the whole town. I turned around to examine the decor. There seemed to be only the necessities. There was one contemporary black sofa and two chairs with throw pillows that looked like they had never been moved.

Just beyond the living area, and a few more steps down, was a dining room. I decided to explore it during his absence. It was surrounded by glass windows on three sides. It had a simple rectangular table with seating for eight. It, too, looked like the room had never been touched. There was a huge canvas painting on the wall behind me. It was very abstract, but I could see what looked like two arms reaching for each other. I was intrigued at first by the size of the painting and then by the use of color. It was breathtaking and vibrant, and yet somehow it made me feel sad at the same time.

I walked back into the living room when I heard the clanking of ice in a glass. "Is Coke okay?" he asked.

"Yes, thank you." I took a sip. "You don't need me to tell you that this place is great. I'm sure everyone says that." I took another sip.

"Would you believe me if I told you, you're my first visitor?"

I coughed a little. "No."

"Well then," he said. "I won't tell you."

"Can you show me the rest of the house?" I asked the question but then it felt a little awkward to ask for a full house tour, so I added, "I want to see the basement. You know, your games."

"Ah," he said. "That's right. You want to practice." He turned and headed toward the other half of the house. We crossed under the main hall, and I glanced at the exquisite skylight again. He led me down a few steps and into a doorway, which opened up into one large room with square columns situated throughout. There was a bar, TV area, pool table, foosball table, air hockey, a race car game, dart game, several arcade games, and the two carnival games. I smiled right away.

"So this is where you play?" He nodded. "How fun," I said, narrowing in on the product of my first big bear win. They looked like they were taken right out of a carnival. Just the two of them took up an entire area of the basement. "You weren't kidding. You *do* have the games. How old are they?" I asked, noticing the authentic antique details.

"About forty years, I think. I'm not exactly sure when they were built, but they have been in my family that long."

"Amazing," I said, feeling like a kid in a candy store. "Can I try it?"

"Sure." He took my drink.

I sat down on the little round stool and let the first ball drop. Of course, my score didn't end up a winner. I pouted. "Show me how you do it," I demanded.

Slowly, he leaned over me and reached for a ball. I felt warmth permeate all over me when he bent down, placing his chest just inches away from my back.

"You see," he said, "you can't just let go of the ball and expect it to drop where you want. I figured out that these places beat people because the ground is not level.

Of course it looks that way, but it isn't." By this time, his cheek was just inches from mine, and he wrapped his arms around me, placing his hand over mine. I was barely concentrating on anything he said until he molded my hand around one of the wooden balls.

"See, once you figure out which way the lane is leaning, you can choose your paths." He moved the ball over slightly, and we let go of it at the same time. I watched as that ball and two subsequent balls earned a score of 29. *Perfect,* I thought. *Just like he was appearing to be by the second.* I turned myself around. He was still kneeling on one knee, so we were looking eye to eye. I wanted to kiss him again, but I waited. I had kissed him the first time and the awkwardness of timing a second kiss was hovering. I didn't want to make the first move again. If he wanted to kiss me, I decided, he would have to kiss me first, which much to my disappointment, he chose not to do.

Instead, he broke the silence between our gaze by standing and pulling me up by my hand. "Is there anything else you want to play?" he asked. Trying not to appear too rejected, I scoped out the rest of the basement. If he was going to be difficult, then that was his choice, but it put me in the mood for a challenge. I chose the air hockey. He chuckled, and I silently grumbled.

We played several games, but it only took two minutes into the first before my game-face was annihilated. I was there, playing my hardest, with tightened lips, determined to beat him, and he was playing with his eyes practically closed. I couldn't help but laugh at myself, and before I knew it, he was laughing, too. I couldn't tell if he was laughing at me or with me, but it didn't matter. It was the most fun I'd had in a long time.

After a while, we walked back toward the steps to the main level. We passed a door that had a little square window at the top. "What's this to?" I asked.

"Oh, that goes to the pool."

"Pool?" I looked at him for clarification.

"Yes…pool." He said it slowly, as if I didn't know what a pool was.

"I heard you," I assured him, wanting to give him a whack right upside his perfect head. "I'm just surprised you have one *inside*." He locked his melting eyes on me, and I blushed. "Can I see it?" I asked, trying to divert his attention.

"Of course." He propped the door open with his back and waited for me to enter first.

My eyes were greeted by a full-size lap pool. "Are you kidding? What do you have this for?"

Innocently, he responded, "I like to swim. It relaxes me."

"Yeah, I get that. But we're in California. Most people have outdoor pools."

"This lets me swim year-round."

"I see." That made sense. I slid off my flip-flops and dipped my foot into the water. "Wow, it's warm. *Really* warm," I observed. As a matter of fact, the entire room was feeling hot. Or maybe it was just me visualizing him in his trunks. "Okay, I'm ready to go up."

We never went to the top levels, but I did see enough of the house to notice that there were no pictures anywhere. We had pictures everywhere in my house, and my room was covered in pictures of places I'd lived, pictures of me and Kerry, and pictures I had taken with my new camera. Pictures told stories and brought life to a room.

"You don't have any pictures," I said out loud.

He looked around as if to check on my observation. "No, I guess I don't."

I found it very odd that he didn't have any memories of his family or loved ones around. It made the room feel lonely. "You don't have pictures of your family or friends?" I asked. "Or places you've been?"

"No, pictures for me don't really bring happy memories."

I looked around, thinking about what he'd said, and I also noticed that everything was new other than the two antique games he had downstairs. It didn't seem like a place where you call home. It felt like a vacation property. Somewhere you go to spend time to get away. "Everything here is new. Are you *sure* you live here?" I was half joking and half serious.

He laughed again, "Yes, I'm sure."

"Well show me what makes this *your* house then."

He looked perplexed. "What do you mean?"

"Well, I don't know all that much about you, and I was hoping to get an idea from your house, but everything is so new, and it doesn't even look like it has been touched, except for your games. But, you can't play games all day, so what else do you do here all alone?"

He looked at me, studying my face again. I hoped I wasn't making an odd request, but I wanted to understand him and so far, he was becoming more of a mystery to me. No pictures of anyone anywhere, living in a bright, huge house all alone. I didn't see much personality in any of it. "All right," he said. "I can show you what I like."

"That works."

He led me to the living area to sit on the couch. "Well, you already know I like to race cars, but when I'm home, I just read or watch TV." He pressed a button on a remote. A flat screen rose up from behind the fireplace. "I watch sports," he said, flipping through his sport channels. "And I watch the Discovery channel a lot." We were making progress, but I sat there waiting for more in silence. He took the cue that I wasn't satisfied. "And I like music." He opened large doors to built-in bookcases where he had hundreds of records. Actual records, that would need to be played on a record player.

"Have you ever heard of an iPod?" I asked, sarcastically.

"Yes, I have one of those, too." He was smiling.

"What else?" I asked. He pondered for a second, and then he headed toward the kitchen.

"Come on," he said. "I'll show you what I eat." I started laughing. It all seemed so ridiculous, but I was actually curious. I wanted to know everything about him.

He opened up his cupboards and refrigerator to show me his favorite foods. He had tons of bottled water, lots of cereal, his freezer was packed with chicken and steaks, and his refrigerator had a variety of fresh fruits and vegetables. He picked up a raw broccoli spear and took a bite.

"Eww," I said. "That's gross."

"You asked me what I like. I like vegetables. They're good for you. You ought to try them. You of all people should know that," he said, still chewing.

"What's that supposed to mean?"

"You know, your mom being in the medical field and all. You should eat healthy."

"Okay whatever. What else?" I was having fun. I had learned more about him in the last five minutes than I had in weeks.

"What else do you want to know?"

"Why do you live in such a big house?"

"Well, I just wanted the view, the privacy, and a place big enough to hold my cars."

That *sounded* reasonable, but the last word lingered. He was such a boy.

"Your cars?" I asked. "Let me guess, more race cars?"

"No, not those kind."

I really didn't care for seeing any more new fancy sports cars or race cars. I wasn't going to be suckered into driving any more of them, and I wasn't planning on climbing in any more car windows, so unless he had maybe a monster truck in there, I wasn't really interested.

"Trucks?" I guessed.

"Nope."

"Oh," I said, disappointed. Now it was getting mysterious again, and I definitely didn't like that. "Bikes?"

"No, just cars that have been in my family for a long time."

"And you like them enough to buy a big house for them?"

"Those are the only things that keep memories alive for me. You talk about photos as reminders for places you've been and people you love. For me, the cars out there," he nodded his head back toward the garage side of the house, "tell the best stories of the past. They truly tell where people have been. That's how I keep the memories I want alive."

Now we are getting somewhere. He was becoming more real to me by the moment. I wanted him to keep talking. "Can I see them?" I was curious as to how the cars he talked about could tell stories.

He led me around the kitchen, opposite from the dining and living room entry and down a few steps into a wash room. Through the washroom was the garage. He opened the door to the cleanest garage I've ever seen. The walls and floor were painted a light gray color. The only things inside the garage were three cars hidden under white cloth car covers. We stood there looking for a few minutes. He realized I wasn't satisfied with the viewing.

"Do you want me to take the covers off?"

"That would be good."

"Where should I start?" he asked. I didn't understand. "I can start at the most recent or the oldest," he clarified reluctantly.

"The oldest," I answered, still without fully understanding. He walked around the car farthest from us, and I followed. When he pulled the car cover off, I took a double take. I thought it was some sort of joke, and then I took a closer look and saw the perfection and authenticity of it.

"What is it?" I asked, leaning over the shiny black vintage car.

"It's a 1921 Ford Model T Speedster. This one has been in my family the longest." He was looking at it with pride and joy, and I could completely understand why. It was a beauty. There wasn't a scratch on it anywhere. I walked around and touched what seemed like every inch of the outside.

"Is everything original?"

"Yes, everything," he confirmed.

"Amazing." I turned around, now curious to see what was under the others. He took my cue and walked over to the second car. He smoothly pulled back the cloth. It was a newer model car, but nonetheless breathtaking.

"And this one?" I asked.

"A Rolls Royce. 1958, Silver Wraith."

It was another beauty. Silver and royal blue with white tires. I wished instantly that I had my camera with me. It was definitely not something someone gets to see every-day.

"This one meant a lot to my uncle. I keep this one for him."

"Wow. That's really nice." I thought for a minute. "What was it you said your uncle did?" I was starting to sound like my mother, but I couldn't help but be overly curious. It was never-ending with Wes. There was something amazing around every corner. I wondered how much more there could possibly be.

"He was a doctor," he said. "More so a scientist, you could say."

I remembered him mentioning something like that before, but it still didn't give me the answers I needed. I wanted to know what kind. Did he inherit money, too? There were so many questions, but I didn't want to be rude, so I settled on a simpler question.

"What was his name?" I was looking at the details of the car, so I didn't appear to be prying too much. Wes seemed to ponder his answer, which I noted.

"His name was Oliver Thomas."

"Oh," I said, satisfied for the moment. "And what about this one?" I pointed, diverting his attention to the last covered car. He looked at it and then back to me. He walked over to the car and took a long pause before pulling the cover back. As the cover slid away from the hood, I knew right away. It was a black Mustang.

"Now, *this* is cool," I said. "What year is it?"

"1963." I stared at it and a vision of him driving it crossed my mind.

I opened the door to sit in it without asking, and he quickly grabbed my elbow. I looked at him, taken aback.

"Sorry," he said, letting go. "This one has special meaning. Please don't." He looked nervous and concerned.

"Oh, sure. No problem," I said, hoping I didn't offend him. He started re-covering the car and then he worked his way back over to the others, covering each one without saying much. I followed him over to the last car.

"These cars are great. You have a nice collection. I'm sorry if I—"

"Thanks," he said, interrupting. "And don't apologize. I didn't mean to snap at you back there." He was covering the car in hard concentration, and his expression was unreadable. I was pretty certain that he regretted showing them to me, and yet he still managed to find a way to apologize. I felt so meager. Who knew how much those vintage cars were worth, and I tried to jump right into one with dirty shoes and all. I rolled my eyes at my stupidity. I was about to apologize again when he finished up, but he spoke first.

"Sophie," he said, moving in front of me. "You don't have anything to apologize for, really." He stopped and looked away, searching for the words to explain. "I just haven't shown anyone else these cars before. They are very special to me, and I'm not sure I'm ready to open up those stories yet." Once his eyes met mine, I studied their warmth and nodded in comprehension.

"Fair enough," I said.

He smiled and reached his hand out to me as a peace offering. I took it, without hesitating, as he led me back into the house. It was a strange feeling leaving that garage. There was a sense of history hovering in the air. It was similar to what I felt when I was at work, only this was a thousand times stronger. At work, those were just minor little pieces of the past, but these were monumental heirlooms, and the aura they gave off was inexplicable. I glanced back, over my shoulder, one more time as we exited, wondering what interesting stories they had to tell.

We ended up leaving and going to a little sandwich eatery that was on the way to my house. It was right off the highway, and I had seen it many times, but I'd never actually eaten there before. We chose a window seat so we could soak up the great view it had, and he offered to order for us, which provided me with a few moments alone. I tried to clear my mind of my own personal insults at my prior mishap. By the time he returned with our food, I was much more at ease. I was, however, a little hesitant to ask him any more questions, since I had already overstepped my boundaries with his valuables. Thankfully, he took control of our conversation once we got situated.

"So why did you get a job at Healey's?" he asked, taking a bite of his sub. I smiled a little.

"Because I needed money to fix a couple of cars I dented. Remember?"

He chuckled. "No, I mean why Healey's?"

That was a good question, I suppose. Most teenagers would probably not choose to work at a used bookstore. It was not really deemed cool. Dawn seemed to have a decent enough social life, but she hadn't chosen the bookstore. She sort of got stuck with working there.

"I don't know." I shrugged. "I used to go there to buy books, and I just saw a hiring sign right about the time I rammed into you." I searched his face for some sort of reaction at the memory. There was nothing out of the ordinary.

"And you like working there?"

"Yeah, sure, I guess." It gave me something to do, plus I liked having my own money coming in. I was curious as to what he thought, so I figured I would use his own question on him. "Why? Is that strange to you?" I asked.

He smiled again and looked down. "No, not at all."

"Books can be very cool, you know." I was trying to sell my apparently odd choice of employment. "Especially at a used book store. Talk about telling stories. You can't help but wonder how many places those books have been. It's very neat."

"Oh, I believe you," he said, swallowing a French fry. "I have quite a collection myself."

"Why does that not surprise me?" I was staring at my own food, now, realizing I'd been playing around with it. He noticed as well.

"It helps if you actually eat it." He smiled.

I was too busy absorbing every word he spoke to think about eating, but I bit off a French fry and showed him the remainder.

"I like books, too," he continued. "It's nice to see someone appreciate old things as well as new things. Most young people nowadays seem so wrapped up in technology, they don't have time for hobbies that involve thinking."

Now that we had my boring life summed up, I was feeling like a nerd—plus, he had called me young. I didn't like it. I needed to divert the attention away from myself.

"What are you studying at Berkeley?" I asked, between bites of my own sandwich.

"Chemistry," he said, matter of factly. Instantly, I didn't feel like the nerd anymore, but I did feel a little inadequate. Not only was he good looking, wealthy, and incredibly charming, he was smart, too.

"Wow. I would've never thought," I replied, and I knew instantly that was a mistake, because he wasted no time with the obvious follow-up.

"What *would* you have thought?" he asked, leaning back, taking a break from his sandwich. I had to think for a minute.

"Well..." I looked him over, contemplating deeply. "Maybe finance?"

He laughed. "That's a good one, but no."

We were finishing up our food by then, and he started gathering our trash to throw it away. I would've wanted to prolong the afternoon but I, unfortunately, had to go to work. It was the first time I wished I didn't have to go in. I had more questions.

"Why chemistry?" I asked, as we threw our trash away. He didn't seem like the chemist type, although it did run in the family, so I don't know why I found that so surprising. It could've been because I kept envisioning him on a magazine cover and not in a lab coat.

"My uncle piqued my interest. He was working on some medical breakthroughs that could have cured many people when he died, so I thought I would continue on for him. We'll see." He shrugged, opening the door for me.

It was hard to keep my eyes on him because we were walking by then, but I could tell he was trying not to boast too much about it, but there was no way he could hide it.

I added compassion to my list of good qualities about him.

I daydreamed all afternoon at the register, and my curiosity grew by the second. There were things that didn't make sense to me, and I wanted to resolve them. I had met a guy, who I liked more than I should, and yet there was so much left unknown. He had more money than even a middle-aged person would responsibly know how to manage, and yet he had no family to help him. He was incredibly kind and open, but complex at the same time. I couldn't decipher whether I was overthinking things, as usual, or if there were missing pieces that I should try to locate. If I hadn't liked him so much, I probably wouldn't have wasted my time, but I *did* like him.

In fact, if I believed in love at first sight, I would have said I loved him already, but I refused to go there. So many things were too mysterious for me to allow myself to fall hopelessly for someone who may not reciprocate my feelings. I wanted to know everything about him and more so, I wanted to know why he was interested in me. He could have had anyone he wanted. It didn't make sense.

I went into an insecure abyss that afternoon and made it my mission to fill in the missing pieces before getting deeper into a situation that could be potentially painful.

Chapter 6
RESEARCH

There were a couple of things I already knew, and I ran through them in my mind. He said his dad died many years ago; his mom died a few years ago; and his uncle died last year. He also told my mother that his uncle was a renowned scientist. I knew their names, although I had neglected to ask his mother's name, I did have two names to go on, so I figured I would start there.

I felt like I was sneaking around behind his back, and it really wasn't a good feeling. He had never been anything but kind to me, and here I was checking up on him—but I had to find out more about him if I was ever going to understand him, guilt or no guilt.

I typed Weston Wilson II in the search box on my computer screen. Four links popped up right away. I clicked on the first one. It was an article from the *California Chronicle*:

Millionaire Heir Presumed Dead
From a Plane Crash Over Australia
July 19th 2008

> Authorities discovered the crash site of millionaire Weston C. Wilson II, Monday afternoon. His son is reported to have been the last person to see him take off in his KR-2, personally-crafted, single-engine airplane from a secluded airstrip at his Australian home. Officials say that no one would have been able to survive the crash. Although no body has been discovered, personal objects were found in the charred wreckage confirming the aircraft was the one manned by Wilson. Authorities also searched the area and found no sign of survivors.
>
> Wilson was well known for his work in aircraft design and for helping fund the California Blood Research Center throughout the 1980s. He is survived by one son.

I looked back over the article, because something didn't make sense. The first detail I noticed was the one indicating that he was survived by one son. I knew that had to be Weston, but Weston told me his father died *many* years ago, and this article was dated just last year. Wes also made it seem like his father had died before his mother, but there was no mention of her in this article. I tried to do other searches to see what else came up, but there was nothing contradictory. All of the articles were similar.

I spun around in my desk chair and stared at the wall. It just didn't make sense. There was no reason for him to lie to me about his father's death, but for some reason I was sure he had. I went over the article several times looking for some other explanation. I got nothing. This man was a mystery to me, just like his son. Frustrated, I decided to go downstairs and grab a snack and a drink while I pondered the information.

I knew I didn't want to keep asking him about his family, and I knew I didn't like the idea of him not telling me the truth. I started to feel very foolish, both for liking him so much without knowing him and also for looking up something I probably shouldn't have. I mean, I was prying and going behind his back investigating his family without him knowing. It wasn't like he deserved my mistrust, but at the same time, I had to protect myself. I wasn't stupid.

When I got downstairs, my mom was in the kitchen, too. She turned away from the pantry.

"Great minds think alike," she said, dangling a package of cookies.

I smiled. "You have the munchies, too?"

"Yeah, I do," she said, pulling one out for herself.

I grabbed one from the package as she held it out to me and headed over to the fridge. I liked milk with my cookies, so I grabbed a glass from the cupboard and began pouring my milk and chewing.

"How are things with Wes?" she asked.

I almost spilled my milk. Her question was simple and not really out of the ordinary, but it still took me by surprise. That meant I was definitely feeling guilty for my insecurity. "Fine," I replied, still chewing. I wasn't in the mood to go into details, or admit to my mother that I had already suspected him of lying. She was just barely okay with me seeing him, so I figured my best bet would be to tell her I had work to do and get out of there as fast as I could. I wasted no time grabbing a few cookies and giving her a kiss on the cheek before disappearing.

Back in my room, I pondered the conclusion that there was no reason for me to be uptight. It was just dates mixed up. So what? Maybe he didn't want to tell me his loss was so new. Some people just don't like sympathy. I resolved myself to being content with that explanation, so when I finished my snack, I brushed my teeth and got in the bed.

The getting in was the easy part, but actually falling asleep was a whole other matter. I lay there tossing and turning from one side to another for about an hour. The question of why kept bouncing around in my brain, and I couldn't shake it no matter which way I lay.

He was nineteen years old, and if his father died last year, he would've been eighteen. There would be no need for him to live with his uncle for a while, unless he just wanted to stay with family, but he said his uncle *cared* for him. Why would an adult need to be cared for? Why even mention the uncle? *The uncle*, I thought. I threw back my covers and slid into my desk chair again, hoping for some sort of resolution.

He said his uncle was a renowned scientist. Surely there would have to be something else I could find. It was the only other name I had to go on, so I searched his name, too. My first couple of searches for Thomas Oliver brought back too many results, and none of them sounded anything remotely doctor related, so I narrowed it down to "Dr. Oliver Thomas." An article from the University of Berkeley popped up. I straightened my posture in interest, because I knew that had to be him. I quickly double clicked on the link.

It was a university article dedicating an academic hall to Dr. Thomas for his research in blood and cell structure for the university. The article described Dr. Thomas as one of the first scientists to discover blood typing, ways to store blood, as well as innovative cell research in his later life. According to the article, the hall was named after him shortly following his death on December 1, 1959.

My eyes narrowed as I reread 1959. I dropped my head down on my arms in frustration. I was only making the situation worse. I was reading about people for no reason. It wasn't even the right person. I closed out of the web page and tried another search.

I typed in "Dr. Oliver Thomas Renowned Scientist." This time, I was referred to a medical journal discussing experimental cures for cancer. I almost closed it out, but I saw a line again about blood research, which was a phrase I'd come across far too often for it to be a coincidence. I paused, let out a tired sigh, and kept on reading. This article had been written by another doctor who was working on finding cures for cancer and HIV with the use of alligator blood. The article said Dr. Oliver Thomas was first known to have tried such blood transfusions on patients in 1916, only to abruptly cease his research due to the poor outcome of the patients—who all died within 24 hours of receiving the blood.

With the help of new methods of obtaining antibodies from alligator blood, scientists were now able to conduct new studies in hopes of finding a cure for many diseases. I scrolled down to find anything relevant to what I was looking for, and I saw the same date of death listed for the doctor: 1959.

I tightened my lips together and closed out of that web page as well. I searched Dr. Oliver Thomas' name every other way I could imagine and each time, the only doctor going by that name had died in 1959 at his home outside of San Francisco, which would be at right about the location Wes said he had lived. I built up more air than needed in my chest, and I let out a huge sigh, which sent my bangs flying away from my eyes. I turned off my computer screen. *Ridiculous,* I thought.

I went back over to my bed; it was midnight by then. One thing I didn't like was being misled, and for some reason, that is exactly what Wes had done. I didn't understand why. He had been so nice, so perfect. I didn't know what I was going to do about the new information. Telling my mom wasn't an option, because she was just starting to like him, and I couldn't tell Kerry because I didn't want to listen to her talk bad about him, which is what she would do. Even though I knew she'd be trying to make me feel better, it would only make me feel worse. I didn't want people to mistrust him. The thought of that made me roll my eyes in the darkness. It was like I was protecting him undeservingly. Why would I care if people thought he was a phony? It made me angry to care so much.

Somewhere in the back of my mind, I was telling myself to leave well enough alone. There had to be a reason he told me that story, and whatever the reason, I was pretty sure I wasn't going to find out. I certainly wasn't about to call him and tell him I had played the part of private investigator behind his back—and by the way, tell him he'd lied about his dad and an uncle who died before he was even born. No, I wasn't going to tell him that. My only other two options were to ignore it and keep things as they were or to stop seeing him. Neither choice appealed to me. So, for the time being, I decided I would avoid the situation altogether.

I played up having projects and homework for over a week. I only saw Wes on my way from having lunch with my mom. I could tell he sensed that I was trying to keep my distance a bit, but he didn't question me on it. He seemed content to give me as much attention as I wanted. I wasn't sure if that was a good thing or not. I was glad he didn't ask me what was wrong every five minutes, but I was worried about why my distance and lame homework excuses weren't bothering him either.

Aside from seeing him once for almost two weeks, we talked just about every day on the phone, but other than that, I buried myself in my school work and used it as an excuse to stay home. At first, I was proud of myself for whatever internal mind game I was playing, but after a while, I realized I was fooling myself. I couldn't keep up the schoolwork façade much longer. I had to decide to see him or just break it off altogether.

I told myself that I didn't want to be bamboozled by him, but it wasn't working. I needed to see him—bamboozled or not. I justified my submission by vowing to demand the truth from him. If he wasn't going to be honest, then I was fairly sure I would be able to walk away. I was content with my decision except, I had spent so much time racking my brain about Wes and what I was going to say to him, that I was blindsided by other issues in my own house.

I was having breakfast with my mother when I noticed she was acting a little nervous. I sat at my normal spot at the table, eating a bowl of cereal, and she sat down with a cup of coffee and nothing else. That meant she wanted to talk.

"Sophie?" she said, as if she wasn't sure I was sitting right in front of her.

"Yes," I answered, bracing myself for whatever talk she was about to have with me. I hoped to goodness it wasn't going to be the boy talk.

"Sophie, I met someone," she said hesitantly. "A man. He's really nice," she clarified. It was worse. It was a man talk. I kept looking at my bowl and chewing so I wouldn't have to look her in the eye. I should've known something was weird with her when I saw her digging in my cookies the other night. That was out of the ordinary for her, but I was so wrapped up in my own problem, I didn't even notice.

"And," I said, between bites.

"And, I would like for you to meet him."

Oh no, I thought, fighting hard to refrain from rolling my eyes. It was all too much. I had my own problems to deal with. I wasn't about to play the mother with her. I tried to get my point across without sounding too selfish.

"Mom, you don't need me to meet him. I'm sure anyone you choose to hang out with will be fine." The word "please" kept repeating in my mind over and over as I waited for her reply.

"Well, I would like your opinion. He's really persistent, and I'm not sure about him. I could use your input," she added.

"I'm sure he's fine."

"I want your approval," she countered.

Her eyes were desperate and conflicted, and I wished I had more time to decipher them, but the truth was, I was just dying to get out of there.

"You have my approval, Mom," I said, standing up to put my bowl in the sink.

"Really. Just like that? You don't even want to meet him?"

"Uh, yeah, I do. Just not yet…I'd rather wait."

"Okay. Fair enough," she said, nodding and assessing my expression. I threw in a little forced smile and when she was satisfied with her assessment, she went back to drinking her coffee. Relieved, I smoothly made my exit.

I wasn't sure why my mother would need my approval. I didn't care if she'd met someone. I suppose I might have been weirded out by the idea of her bringing someone else into our lives before, but I was eighteen now, and I had my own future to worry about. In a way, I was happy for her to have someone else. I had always worried about her being alone after I moved out, so the idea of her meeting someone didn't bother me at all. But, that didn't mean I had to play, "Meet the Daughter." No, I was glad she'd let me off the hook, for now.

I went to work on Saturday, still hesitant at the idea of confronting Wes about the discrepancies I'd discovered, but after an hour of complete boredom, I text messaged him: NO MORE WORK. WANT TO MEET? I set the phone down on the counter and after only a minute, I stared at it, wondering why he hadn't replied. I didn't even notice Dawn sneak up behind me.

"Are you waiting for it to jump up and dance?" she asked. I looked up to notice her eyeing my phone. I let out a chuckle.

"Yeah, I suppose so."

"Hmm…I'm betting a guy…no, not just a guy. A really cute guy," she said, hypothesizing.

"What makes you say that?" I asked, trying to sound innocent.

"Because you wouldn't be watching it that hard if it wasn't."

She had a point.

"I'm just a little nervous," I admitted.

She pulled up a stool and sat beside me, closing in so Mr. Healey couldn't hear us. He was busy doing whatever he always seemed to do, but she acted like he was eavesdropping. I shrugged my shoulders casually. "It's nothing really. Just a guy. I think we are going to have a 'talk' today." I put up quotation symbols with my fingers when I said the word talk.

"Ah hah. You mean like doing it?"

"No!" I snapped, loud enough for her father to turn his head our way. "*Just* a talk," I clarified.

She looked at me like I was hiding something, but then she eased off. "Sorry."

I wasn't sure how to reply to that. Wes and I weren't even close to going there, but she didn't know that, so I just said, "It's okay." Just then, the phone started vibrating on the counter. Both of our eyes turned to watch as it shifted in a circular motion.

"It won't bite," she said.

"Oh, shush," I said, grabbing the phone and elbowing her simultaneously. I don't know why I was being so weird. I think I was just nervous because of what I had to say. If he accepted, there was no turning back, and if he declined, I feared I was too late to salvage anything, if there was anything at all worth salvaging.

I looked down at the message from him: YOU DON'T NEED TO ASK. JUST CALL ME AND TELL ME WHEN. An involuntary smile went across my face, and I felt a huge sigh of relief, which I was trying to control. I couldn't help but feel all warm inside, but there were still major details left to hash out, so I wasn't going to let myself feel all fluttery until they were resolved.

"You *are* aren't you?" Dawn accused again.

"Oh please, get your head out of the toilet. I barely know him."

"If you say so," she said, going back to her own business of passing the time.

I was telling her the truth. I had more immediate things to think about, such as calling him and working out the details. I already knew that I didn't want him picking me up at my house. I had to figure out somewhere to meet, because I wanted to drive. I would feel more in control that way.

I chose to meet at the marina after work. I thought the pier would be a good place to talk. It wasn't anywhere out of the ordinary. People went there all the time, but it also allowed for privacy. It was perfect.

Chapter 7

TRUST

When I pulled into the parking lot, his car was already there. I parked a few cars down, and then I got out and looked around for him. It was hard to see if he was in his car because his windows were tinted.

As I approached his vehicle, he stepped out. He looked beyond good, as usual, but I was taken aback by the winter hat he was wearing. It did seem like an unusually cold evening for early November, but I didn't need to be bundled up the way he was. I started thinking he was just trying to look good with the accessory, and if he was, he pulled it off very well.

"I guess it gets a little cold out here this late in the year," I said, as he approached me.

"Maybe a little, but I think we'll be okay," he assured.

I liked the sound of "we" a little too much, and walking beside him was making it all too easy to forget my apprehensions, but I needed to stay focused. Lucky for me, he was being very accommodating. He was patiently giving me as much room as I needed.

"I'm sorry I haven't been out much lately," I said. I paused, but he remained attentive without commenting. "I had two tests and two projects due, plus my mom met someone new. It's been really crazy around my house." It wasn't a total lie. I did have tests and projects, and my mom *was* seeing someone new, even if I'd only found that out in the last day or so.

"You don't have to explain anything." He was sincere as always, which was making him that much more alluring.

"Well, I think I do. The truth is, it's very hard to focus when I'm around you. I needed to clear my head." We found a stopping point on the pier, and he turned to look at me. The dark backdrop of the night was making it impossible to concentrate on anything other than the attraction I felt for him.

"Clear your head about what?" he asked.

I needed to choose my words very carefully. I thought I could accomplish what I wanted by being a little more honest than I'd intended. "Well," I said. "I feel like I don't know who you are. You know everything about me. You've even met my mom. I feel like you're too perfect to be true, honestly."

He shook his head and looked at his feet. "I'm far from perfect."

"I don't think so. I mean, you're so mature, and you have all your goals lined up, and you're so responsible, and you own your own house." I turned toward the water and leaned on the rail. "Your parents must have really been good people."

"They were," he said, leaning his elbows on the rail next to me.

"I'm just amazed at the way you're able to handle everything." I paused, hoping not to give away my suspicion. "How old were you when you lost your dad?"

"I was three," he answered, without a stutter. I looked out over the water, trying not to appear too rehearsed. After a moment, I asked him something I hadn't thought about before.

"So your mom raised you alone, or did you have a stepfather?"

He shook his head immediately. "No, my mom was alone. She spent her life taking care of me after my father died." He was staring off into the water reflecting. "I owe her more than you can imagine."

"She must have been a great woman," I offered, feeling pity again. Listening to him sound so open and genuine with me made me almost forget what I'd discovered.

"I'm not so sure I could be as strong as you," I continued.

"Don't underestimate yourself."

"I'm not. It's true. If something happened to my mother, I would be lost. I wouldn't have anyone. At least you had your uncle." It wasn't a question, but I hoped it would spark a reply from him.

"Yes, I did. I was very lucky."

My pity was turning into rage, but I remained composed. "Did he teach you everything you know, or did your mother?"

He reflected a moment. "Both, I suppose."

"What do you mean?"

A small group of girls and guys our age walked by, a little too rambunctious to carry on an uninterrupted conversation, so he waited until they passed.

"My mother taught me how to be caring and kind, and my uncle taught me how to take care of myself."

It all sounded so wonderful—if only it was the truth. I couldn't stand it anymore. I knew it didn't add up to anything I'd found out about him, and yet he was so convincing. Frustrated, I asked, "Why are you telling me this?"

He looked at me, confused. "Because you asked."

"No, I mean, why are you telling me things that aren't true?"

He leaned off the rail at my accusation and faced me. "I don't know what you mean." His voice was calm, but his eyes were studying me intensely.

"You said your father died when you were three. I found an article that said he died last year."

His eyes narrowed as the information registered. "That article was not about my father."

"So are you telling me there is more than one Weston Wilson II who died in a plane crash?"

"No—"

"Look Weston, I don't want to bring up things that are painful for you, but I don't like being lied to either."

"I'm not lying to you." His attention was diverted as he looked over his shoulder. I peeked around to see the distraction for myself. He was looking down the pier. I could barely make out the group that walked by us before. I couldn't hear them anymore, but it looked like one of them was climbing the rail. I quickly focused back to my own conversation.

"Then why did you tell me you lived with an uncle who died fifty years ago?" Upon hearing my question, he whipped his head around.

"How did you know that?"

"I found an article about him, too."

He dropped his head and closed his eyes. It was enough of an indication to me that what I'd found was correct. I felt a tightening in my chest as I realized that he hadn't been truthful. Then, I began to feel panicked. I wasn't even sure who he was. I started to step backward, away from him, but he stepped toward me, holding me by my shoulders. Instinctively, I tried to wriggle free, but he tightened his grip.

"Please, Sophie, listen to me. I didn't lie to you."

"Then what do you call it?" I countered.

He looked over his shoulder again in irritation at the group, and his distraction made me even more angry. "What do you call it then?" I repeated, bringing his attention back to me.

"I don't know, but I didn't lie. I can't explain it."

"Is your name even Wes?"

"Of course it is."

I pulled his arms down to free myself. "Listen, I don't know what's going on with you or why you're lying, but I can't be friends with someone I don't trust. Unless you're going to tell me the truth, then I can't keep seeing you." I waited for his answer, not even sure that hearing the truth now would suffice.

"I am telling you the truth," he said. "I wouldn't tell you lies." It was as if he wanted to say something more, but he chose not to. He was giving me no reasonable explanation to stay, and although something in me wanted to, I knew I couldn't be with someone who was dishonest. After a moment of staring at his perfect face, I took a few steps backward. "Fine, I'm leaving."

He lowered his shoulders at the realization that it was over, but this time he made no attempt to stop me. I turned toward the parking lot and began my walk back from the pier, having reluctantly made up my mind to forget about this seemingly perfect but mysterious boy. Within a few moments, I felt that dreaded lump build in my throat. I couldn't tell if it was because I was mad or if it was because I was making a mistake, but I kept walking, determined to hold my ground. Somewhere inside, I was hoping to hear him call my name, but he didn't. Instead, the silence was broken by the sounds of ear-piercing screams. I stiffened and turned back quickly to see where the sound had come from. It was down the pier.

Wes and I simultaneously began to head toward the source. He picked up his pace to a light jog, and I was running heavily to keep up.

By the time we reached the end of the pier, we saw one of the guys climb to the top of the railing and jump over. "Oh my God!" I yelled in shock. There were four other people leaning over the rail. "He just jumped. Oh my God. Why?" I asked, completely frantic.

Another girl was screaming. "I can't see her. I can't see."

Wes was looking over the pier.

"What happened?" I yelled.

"Lisa! She fell over! She was playing around!" a girl yelled, looking at me in desperation.

"No, I saw a guy," I corrected.

"That's her boyfriend. He's going after her." She turned back to the water, and I looked over as well. It was a long drop, and Wes put his arm around me to hold me steady. We could hardly see anything. A faint glow from the nearby park made it light enough to see a break in the black water. We were all leaning over.

"Clay!" a boy shouted down.

"I can't find her. I can't find her!"

He went back under, and I started taking off my coat.

"What are you doing?" Wes asked.

"I'm going in," I answered, sliding out of my coat.

He slid it back on. "Are you crazy?"

"We can't just let her drown," I snapped, looking around, wondering why everyone else was just standing there. Wes studied my face.

"Damn it," he said, looking over the edge. "No, *you* stay."

"I can't just—"

"*I'll* go," he said, taking off his coat. He climbed the rail faster than I could have told him to stay, and then he was gone. We barely heard a splash at the bottom, but we could see the little ripples from where he went in.

"Somebody call 911!" I was frantically looking around the water for any sign and suddenly feeling guilty for causing him to go in.

"Look right there!" someone shouted. Clay broke the surface again.

"I can't find her!" he yelled up, even more frantic.

"Clay, wait," a girl yelled. "Someone is in there helping you."

He went back under. I searched the water, getting more worried by the second. Another moment or two went by and Clay appeared at the surface again. Where was Wes? I covered my mouth with both hands and tears welled up in my eyes. It was awful. Too much time had passed. I started crying, and my hands shook uncontrollably. The water was so dark, and there were no signs of anyone in it except for Clay going under and coming up.

"Damn it, Wes," I yelled. "Come on!"

"He'll be okay," a girl said, touching my back. I shoved her off. None of us would have been in this predicament had they not been acting so foolishly. The railings reached seven feet high for a reason—so idiots like them wouldn't go over. I was uncontrollable. I took off my jacket and started climbing.

"You can't," said an unknown voice. I ignored the warning. I knew there was probably nothing I could do, but I couldn't understand how anyone could sit back and watch while other people were in trouble. They needed help, for goodness sake, and what kind of people could just stand up here and watch! It was mind-boggling. I had to do something. I was on the second rail when someone shouted, "Look! Over there! Look!"

I followed the pointed finger.

"Look," shouted a girl. "He's got her. He found her!"

My eyes focused hard on the spot where a person broke the surface. I could see her and then I could make out Wes' cream sweater. By then, Clay was swimming over to them, but Wes was swimming faster to the dock. We ran along side on the pier. It took us about a minute to run around to where he pulled her to land. He rolled her over and started administering CPR, and I dropped down on my knees to help. He was breathing for her, and I took over with the chest compressions. Moans and cries were audible from all directions as people started gathering. Clay pulled himself from the water in exhaustion and dropped to his knees beside us.

"Come on, Lisa," he was saying. "Come on. Please, come on."

Wes appeared to be working on her more rigorously, the more Clay pleaded. He was working so quickly, I could barely keep up the compressions. I looked at Wes for instruction, and I noticed he was losing color. He looked awful. "Wes."

"I'm not stopping. She'll be fine," he said, trying to reassure me.

That's not what I meant. I was worried about him. I kept compressing until my arms got tired. I was about to give up when I felt a jolt under my hands. Her chest jerked upward, and Wes quickly rolled her on her side. Water started coming up from her throat and she began vomiting massive amounts of it. Her vomiting turned to gagging and then to coughing. Clay moved me out of the way to get to her face.

"Lisa, Lisa! Oh Lisa, you're okay. You're fine. Lisa, you're going to be just fine."

He was relieved. "Thank you," he said, and I couldn't tell if he was thanking her, God, or Wes, but I imagined it was all three. I was overwhelmingly relieved for him. Wes and I leaned back on the ground, and then I noticed Wes fall all the way back.

"Wes!" I said, springing over to him.

"Are you okay, man?" someone asked, noticing that something was wrong as well. All Wes did was nod and close his eyes. I felt him, and he was freezing.

"He's cold," I shouted. "Someone get his coat! It's on the pier." About six people stood there looking at me. "Please!" I shouted. "He's freezing!" One of the girls turned around and started running to get it. Wes lay back on the ground. His color was fading rapidly.

"Sophie."

"I'm right here, Wes. I'm right here. You're cold. Someone's getting your coat."

I knew he needed more than a coat, but my mind was too cluttered with worry to think straight. A bystander pushed his way through the growing crowd. "Take off his shirt," he shouted. I tensed at his rapid approach and hovered over Wes in a protective fashion. "He needs to warm up. You have to take off the wet clothes."

I didn't want anyone touching him, but I knew we needed to do something.

I leaned away, and the man quickly started pulling off Wes' wet sweater. His chest was ice cold and turning blue. I could see the shocked reaction in the faces of the hovering crowd. I wrapped my arms around him in an effort to keep him warm until help arrived. I was shivering profusely, but his weakened body was completely still. Panic started taking over.

"Here! Here's his coat!" the girl shouted as she returned, nervously throwing both his coat, and mine, on the ground. Someone helped me put his on him, and by that time, we could hear the sirens coming. Wes started to stir.

"Sophie?"

"Yes? I'm here."

"I need you to take me home." Looking at me, his eyes were glassier than I had ever seen them before. He put his arms around me and pulled me so close to him that my ear was touching his cold lips. "Please. Sophie, you have to get me out of here. I can't go to the hospital. I can't."

I pulled back so he could see my lips. "Wes, you'll be okay. The ambulance is coming. They'll help you."

He roughly grabbed my face. "No! You don't understand. I *can't* go. Please! Trust me. I'll be fine, but you have to get me home. *Promise me*."

"Wes..."

"Please!" He said it with such urgency that I didn't know what to do. It seemed my only choice was to get him out of there. I made an effort to stand him up.

"What are you doing?" a man asked.

"He wants to go home."

"You can't take him home. He needs medical attention."

"He'll be fine. He's just cold," I lied.

"Look at him," someone said.

"He wants to go home, so I'm taking him home. He says he'll be fine," I growled.

Wes was able to stand up, and I was glad about that because I felt very certain no one was going to help me get him away from there.

"Are you sure?" asked the group simultaneously.

"Yes, he's sure. Just get *her* help," I ordered, pointing to the girl on the ground.

I walked him to my car with his arm around me and what felt like most of his weight on me. I helped him sit in my Jeep, just as the ambulance was passing. I could feel that his pants were still soaking wet as I lifted his legs in the car. "Are you sure?" I asked him. His eyes were rolling slowly toward the back of his head. I was losing my calm. "Wes? I can't do this! I don't know what's wrong. Please!" I pleaded.

He looked at me again and was able to faintly say, "Just help me get warm. I'll be fine. Trust me."

Damn it. Why is this happening to me? I don't trust anything. What am I doing? I cringed as I shut the door and ran around to my driver's side door. Once I got in, he drifted in and out of consciousness. "Wes! What do you expect me to do? You need help. I can't help you. I don't know what I'm doing." I could barely put the key in the ignition.

He looked over at me with desperate eyes. "Sophie, I'll explain everything to you later. I promise. Just please, listen to me. My heart rate is dropping and is about to be so slow you won't be able to feel it. Trust me when I say, I'll be fine. I just need to get warm. Just *please,* don't let them take me." That was the last thing he said before passing out.

He looked like death. He was pale and cold. I wanted to drive him straight to the emergency room, and I was angry with myself for hesitating. All I wanted that evening was the truth. Instead, I'd ended up with more lies, a drowning girl, and Wes dying beside me. And now, I was fleeing the scene. *What the heck am I thinking?*

I angrily glanced over at him, waiting for him to give me further instructions, but there was nothing. I started going over the last things he'd said, and the words "be fine" and "trust me" kept repeating in my head, only I wasn't convinced on either count. I drove down the road, going below the speed limit, as if jarring him in any way would hurt him. It was silly.

Most people in a state of emergency would be driving crazy and rushing to get somewhere. I, on the other hand, was creeping along. Half of me wanted to head to the hospital and the other half didn't have a clue where to go.

All of the reasons someone would want to avoid medical attention popped up in my mind. Maybe he didn't want people to find out who he was. That was it. I decided it was a common theme with him, and then I remembered the lies and discrepancies between who he said he was and who he could actually be. All of a sudden, I felt angry again and glanced over at him with pressed lips. *Maybe I should let him die,* I thought. *No,* I couldn't do that. *Crap, crap crap!* I wasn't going to purposely let him die, nor accidentally for that matter. I would have to get him home and at least make sure he was okay.

I pressed on the accelerator once I knew for sure which way I was headed. Then, I cranked up the heat, remembering his assurance that he would be okay if I got him warm. It appeared to be working. As the heat kicked in, he started stirring a bit, but his movements were labored. He covered his eyes with his hands and mumbled something about, "Time, make it stop. No, the time, no, stop it." He wasn't making any sense, but he was at least coming back to consciousness a bit, so I turned the heat on higher. After a few minutes, I was scorching hot and had to roll my window down to get some cool air. His brief moment of mumbling ceased as he slipped back into unconsciousness. Consequently, I rolled my window back up and suffered from the heat to make him more comfortable. It didn't work. He was out cold, and he remained that way the rest of the way home.

When I pulled into his driveway, I cringed at the visual of the long flight of stairs leading up to his front door. There was no way I was getting him up those steps. He was going to have to walk. I turned off the car and went around to his side. I opened the door and leaned in.

"Wes," I whispered. There was no response. "Wes!" I said louder, and there was still nothing. I shook his arm trying to wake him, but there was still no movement. Instinctively, I put my hands on his face. His skin was cool, but not nearly as icy as it had been at the pier. He was improving. I turned his face toward me. "Wes? Wes! Please. You have to get up." He started scrunching up his forehead in disgruntlement, and I knew there was no way he was going up that flight of stairs.

I looked around for other options. My eyes scanned the outside of his house for another entryway, and I zeroed in on the garage. If I could get in there, then it would only be a few steps up into the kitchen, and I was hopeful he could manage that.

I began quickly searching for his keys. The first place I looked was in his coat pockets, and they weren't there. I then searched the pockets of his pants, which were still completely soaked. The keys were there. I ran up the steps and fumbled my way through the front door, opening the garage from the inside. I went ahead and pulled my Jeep into the garage to shorten the walking distance. My car was the runt of the litter amongst the perfect classics sleeping soundly beneath their cloths, but I didn't care. Any other day, I wouldn't have dared pull my dirty Jeep in there, but on that night, I pulled right in.

By the time I made it around to his door, I was out of breath from running the stairs and worrying. It made my patience wear thin quickly. I spoke his name only two more times before grabbing him by his jacket collar and shaking him profusely. "Weston!" I shouted. There was still nothing. I shouted it again, and he flinched away. "Wes! Listen to me. You're home." I was shouting and shaking him at the same time, trying to get his attention. "Please! Wes, I need to get you inside. You have to get up!"

He covered his eyes again, as if to block the light, only there was no light to block. I pulled his hands down and shouted, "Get up! Walk with me." He made a small effort to move his legs, and I capitalized on it by pulling him out of the car. He kept his eyes closed in agony.

I guided him toward the kitchen doorway. He was extremely limp and heavy, but he was walking the best he could. It was taking all of my strength to hold him up. Once in the entryway, he moaned and mumbled again about time, and slowing, and not being able to see me. He was pleading with me not to let him sleep past tomorrow. He was delusional. Ideally, I would have liked to get him to his room, but more stairs were out of the question, so I settled on the living room.

When we reached the couch, I set him down and he immediately fell over. I tugged on him enough for him to make the effort to lay the length of the couch so his feet were comfortably propped up. I was relieved the hard part seemed to be over.

All I needed to do next was keep him warm and wait, at least, I hoped. I looked around and was happy to find the fireplace switch, but I wasn't happy with the distance between the fireplace and the couch, so I moved the coffee table out of the way, and then I grunted and pushed the couch right in front of the fire. My next obstacle was deciding on what to do with his clothes. He was wearing his coat still, and it looked very uncomfortable, and even more of a problem, he was still wearing cold, wet pants. They both needed to come off.

I rolled my eyes at the thought of having to do it myself. I wanted to leave him right then and there. I had done what he'd asked me to do. I'd brought him home, I'd gotten him warm. My job was done. I figured if I just left him there, he would be fine, but as I walked over to check him, I noticed that he didn't look well. His coloring was relatively good, but it didn't look like he was breathing.

I stood over him, watching him very closely, and he seemed too motionless. Nervously, I unwrapped his coat and placed my hand over his bare chest. I put my ear to his mouth. It was hard to tell, but it felt like a very faint breath was slowly escaping him. I couldn't be sure, so I searched for a pulse. There was nothing on his neck or wrists. Concerned, I lay my ear over his heart. There was also nothing. I listened harder, and when I still didn't hear anything, I started to panic. I stood up and began pacing back and forth the distance of his living room. *What have I done?* I hadn't helped him at all.

I had agreed to bring him home, because he said he would be fine, but that didn't include him dying on me with his heartbeat fading. I was about to call for an ambulance when I remembered something he'd said, in the car, about his heart going so slow I wouldn't be able to feel it. I quickly turned back and knelt over him, placed my ear over his heart, and listened. At first, there was nothing, and then I pressed closer and I thought, I wasn't sure, but I thought that I heard a faint rhythmic flutter. I breathed out a sigh of relief and leaned back on the floor.

I studied his sleeping face, searching for something to tell me what to do. An image of him shivering on a hospital table and being wrapped in blankets flashed before me, and I blinked rapidly, trying to clear my head. The image was quick, but vivid enough for me to realize what he needed. I hopped up and began searching for blankets.

Reluctantly, I headed upstairs. I felt like I was trespassing since he hadn't taken me up there before, but I shook off my worry with the idea that I was just getting him something he needed. I didn't see any sort of linen closet. I started peeking in rooms, looking for a bathroom.

I found a study with a sofa lounge, a couple of rooms, and a hall bath, but no blankets. I went up another flight of steps and came to a loft area that led to the master bedroom. The back wall of the room was full of windows that overlooked the blackened sky. I felt awkward being in his room, so I went straight over to the bathroom without delay. Inside, there was a gorgeous walk-in shower and beautiful marble floor. Upon entering, I was overtaken by the smell of him.

I inhaled the sweet scent, and my eyes followed it to a red bar of soap resting by the sink. I shook away the thought of the luscious smell and refocused. I made my way over to the linen closet, where I noticed little dials on the wall. A closer look confirmed they were controls to turn on the heated floors and overhead heat lights. His bathroom had all the bells and whistles, and I'm not sure why I expected anything less.

I found some blankets and headed back downstairs. He was in the exact position he'd been in when I left him. Awkwardly, I began unzipping his jeans. I was surprised at how quickly I became controlled. It was a necessity, I told myself, and so I very professionally pulled down his still-soaked jeans and put them on the floor. His wet boxers were clinging to his physique, but I left them alone. I wasn't even about to go there.

I covered him with the blanket and curled up in a chair next to him. After about an hour, I realized how exhausted I was. I needed to get some sleep, but I was at his house.

I glanced at my watch and saw that it was almost 9:30. I had to make a decision quickly about what I was going to do. I didn't feel comfortable spending the night in his house, but I felt even more uncomfortable at the thought of leaving him alone all night without knowing if he would be all right.

That night was the first time I'd outright lied to my mother. I called her and told her I was having a good time hanging out with Dawn after work, and that I wanted to stay over at her house. I was surprised at how easily she believed me. She was either so happy I had a new friend in town, or she was wrapped up in her new personal life. Whatever the reason, I was glad she believed me easily.

I left him alone long enough for me to run home and get a change of clothes. I almost laughed at myself as I walked through his house with an overnight bag. It was surreal. I was on autopilot, because I didn't feel like I was making any of the decisions. At least not any rational ones. It was completely senseless. I had lied to my mother, and I was about to spend the night with a guy I barely knew.

I checked on him one more time that evening to see how he was doing, and he felt warm. I figured the fire was working, so I decided to leave it on all night. Upstairs, I peeked into the bedrooms, and I felt too uncomfortable making myself at home in one of them, so I went to the study. The couch in there seemed much more appropriate. I settled in there and made sure to leave the door open, in case he woke up in the night.

Of course I couldn't sleep. I don't even know why I bothered trying. After about an hour, I got back up to check on him. He was still sleeping, but he looked extremely flushed. I felt him, and he was burning up. I jerked my hand back and hit the fireplace switch to turn it off. He was way too hot now, but oddly, he wasn't sweating.

I looked around the kitchen for a thermometer, and there was nothing. Back upstairs, I searched the bathroom. I opened a few drawers, and there was a digital ear thermometer. I rushed back downstairs and placed it in his ear. After a quick beep, I pulled it back. It read ERROR. Trying it again, I watched as it flashed 104 degrees and then read ERROR again.

I threw the thermometer on the floor in frustration. After about twenty minutes of silence, I grabbed it and tried it on myself. My temperature reading was 98.4. The thermometer was working fine.

I was two seconds away from being certifiable. I roughly placed it back in his ear, promising to call for an ambulance if the reading wasn't normal. Lucky for him, his temperature read 103 that time. It was still high, but it was manageable. I pulled back the blanket and monitored him for a little longer. Once his temperature was at 100 degrees, I relaxed. Then, I started to feel bad for almost leaving an unconscious person sitting three feet in front of a burning fire all night. Not very smart. The night was taking its toll on me.

Chapter 8
First Reveal

The morning brought much greater peace of mind. The first thing I did, after brushing my teeth, was go downstairs and take his temperature again. It was 97 degrees. It seemed a little low, but not enough to trigger an alarm. He looked like he was sleeping peacefully, so I looked for something to do. There weren't too many places where I felt free to go in his house, but having slept in the study all night, I felt comfortable passing time in there.

With the full light of morning, I was able to see an amazing collection of books. There were hundreds stacked on two full walls, from floor to ceiling. Most of them were nonfiction books on medicine and animals, but some were fiction titles. One section of volumes didn't have titles on the bindings, so I found those most intriguing. I pulled a few out and flipped through them. Some looked like accounting books and others appeared to be journals.

I ran my hands over some more until I came across one that stood out the most. It looked extremely old. I carefully pulled it down and set it on the desk. It was a leather-bound, relatively thin book, but it was taller than a normal book, so it was easy to see amongst the others. I gently opened the first page, and I saw handwriting that was extremely slanted and hard to read. The fading ink and browning pages didn't help, but I could make out the words, "Medical Journal January 1, 1916–December 31, 1916, Dr. Oliver Thomas, London, England." This was the doctor I had read about. I was sure of it. I sat up on the edge of my chair and leaned over in hard concentration.

January 2, 1916

I have been continuing the work of Dr. Oscar Haase, with limited success. The malaria concern is still growing as more soldiers are transporting the disease from places outside of England. In an attempt to save their sons and loved ones from the horrific disease, many mothers are bringing them to me in hopes that my experimental cold-blood transfusion will save them.

January 31, 1916

I have been able to keep a few patients alive long enough to see the cold-blood serum reverse the effects of the malaria momentarily, but within a day, the patients become violently ill from a reaction to the blood. It is an awful sight to watch. Much of the difficulty comes from the problem of coagulation during the transfusion.

February 20, 1916

After more research, I have decided to add additional blood types to my sample. I am still researching one of the types, and do not feel comfortable documenting the nature until I have further information. The other type, about which I do feel confident, is the alligator blood. The proteins in this particular sample have been proven to kill a wide range of bacteria and viruses. Whether or not it will be successful in the human body remains to be seen.

April 3, 1916

Given the complexity of my research and expanding needs, I have acquired the help of a nursing student, Amelia. She is reporting patient conditions to me, as well as caring for them while I continue searching for a breakthrough healing agent.

May 1, 1916

Today I leave for a journey to acquire the necessary samples I will need to mix my new serum. I am hopeful that I will return in time to save the waiting patients.

I turned the page to see what looked like several pages of the journal missing from the binding. Someone had ripped them completely out. I glanced back and forth to see how much time was missing. From the May 1 entry, it skipped to November 15, 1916. Six and a half months of missing journal entries. Why would so much be missing? What had happened to the doctor? Did he return in time? What was the serum he brought back? These were all questions I had, and so, I eagerly kept reading.

November 15, 1916

Our last patient died today. We tried our best to care for him. Unfortunately, my sample was of no help to the young man. Like the other patients, the cold-blood seemed to reverse the effects of the disease momentarily, but the patient deteriorated more rapidly than the others. Apparently, the new serum is even more incompatible with human blood. It appears the human blood clots against the cold- blood intrusion causing rapid swelling of the vessels and eventually bursting the vessels to the heart. This will be my last attempt at transfusing cold-blood into humans. I will return to my studies of normal transfusions.

December 22, 1916

Amelia brought in a patient today who was suffering from massive internal bleeding. I immediately diagnosed him as a hemophiliac. He was in need of an emergency transfusion to help thicken his own blood. I was not prepared for any new patients so soon, so Amelia volunteered some of her own blood, making it possible for me to complete the transfusion. It seems to be helping him some, but I fear he is too far gone. He will need something else to save him—possibly a miracle.

December 23, 1916

Amelia has been talking to the patient. During brief moments of consciousness, she was able to obtain a name, Weston. We will search for his family tomorrow. I am afraid the news will not be good.

December 24, 1916

Amelia brought in Mrs. Wilson. She is grateful for what we have been able to do so far, but she worries the outcome will not be good. I have examined the patient, and he appears to be hemorrhaging in his brain. It is only a matter of hours.

December 25, 1916

Amelia has offered more of her blood to help with clotting, but it will not help. Mrs. Wilson is pleading with me to try anything I have, but I cannot bring myself to try the cold-blood serum. We will just have to wait to see if the patient pulls through on his own.

I heard a thump downstairs and jumped to my feet. I peeked over the balcony and saw Weston lying on the floor. I sprinted down the stairs and knelt by his side. He was covering his face with the blanket.

"Sophie," he mumbled.

"Yes," I replied, even though he hadn't said it like a question.

"I can't see you."

I tried to pull the cover back. "That's because you need to uncover—"

"No, I can't concentrate. I can't see you."

I yanked the covers back and put his face in my palms. I lowered my eyes to his. "Look at me," I said. "I'm here. You can concentrate, if you look at me." He opened his eyes. They were mesmerizing. "See," I said. "You can see me. Look at me." His face was tormented. His eyes were like glass. I was so stunned to see my own reflection that I involuntarily moved my cheek to his. His skin was soft and cool. He didn't flinch away.

"I'm right here. I'm right here," I repeated. He hesitated a moment and then put his arms around me with much more gentleness than the previous evening. I helped him onto the couch, and his closeness filled my soul with a comfort I didn't know I needed. We lay there for a few moments with my cheek to his. I couldn't see his face, but I could tell by his hold on me that I was giving him as much comfort as I was receiving.

I tried to pull back to look him over, and he tightened his arms. "It's okay," I said. "I need to check you over."

"No, please. Stay just how you are. It's almost better now, please." He sounded almost afraid. I rescinded my retreat and lay with him for several more moments.

Eventually, he jerked up onto his elbow and began frantically feeling around for something. "Where's my watch?" he asked, urgently.

"I put it with your clothes."

He started trying to sit up. "Where is it? I need it."

At a time like this? "Wes, lie back down. It's okay—"

He cut me off again. "What day is it?"

"Sunday."

"No, what is the date?" He was searching my eyes intensely.

"November 15."

"What year?" he countered quickly.

Confused at his continued delirium, I replied, "2009."

He closed his eyes and relaxed. "I'm sorry."

"It's okay. You don't need to apologize, but you do need to let me check you out."

He let his blanket fall to his waist. The sharpness to his lean physique was distracting. I wanted to close my eyes to focus, but instead, I searched around for the thermometer, which gave me something else to concentrate on.

"What are you looking for?" he asked. His eyes completely fixed on me.

"The thermometer." I was feeling around with my hands.

"What for?"

"So I can take your temperature." I wondered if I was really meant to answer that. It seemed a bit rhetorical.

"That won't be necessary." His voice was soft and assured.

"Why not?"

"Because, I can tell you it will be roughly 80 degrees."

"What?" I looked at him, confused. "You think your body temperature is 80 degrees. Right now?"

He nodded.

I quickly went back to looking for the thermometer. Once I found it, I hesitantly reached toward his ear. He didn't pull away, so I continued. His temperature was 80.2 degrees. I looked at him, and he had never taken his eyes off of me.

"I don't understand."

He looked at me with abashed eyes. "You said you wanted to know the truth."

"Yes, I do," I said, assertively.

He paused. After a few moments, he replied, "Do you mind if I get dressed first?"

I sort of did mind. I wanted to make sense of it all, but at the same time, it was very hard for me to concentrate with him sitting there bare-chested and pantless. I cleared my throat.

"No, I don't mind," I conceded, but I didn't release him from my stare. I wanted him to know that I wasn't going to forget the truth he owed me.

A corner of his mouth turned up softly.

"Okay," he said, standing up. "I'll be right back."

While he was gone, I pondered what he'd said and was trying to maintain a clear head. It was very difficult. I was on the brink of exhaustion from trying to figure him out. My nerves had been through the wringer, and my brain was stressed beyond comfort. I leaned my head on the arm of the sofa and closed my eyes. I took slow breaths, and I told myself to relax. He seemed better now, and for some unknown reason, I trusted him to tell me the truth. After all, I had just saved his life. It was the least he could do.

He came back downstairs wearing a black hooded sweatshirt and jeans. He must have taken a quick shower because his hair was dark and freshly wet. I started to prop myself up when he reached out his hand for me. I placed mine in his, and he effortlessly pulled me upward so that I was standing within a few inches of him. He was staring so deeply into my eyes that I felt a blush permeate both sides of my face.

"You're in your pajamas," he noted, with a smile.

I looked down at myself and realized that I was, indeed, still in my pajamas. It was awkward.

"Um…yes. I guess I am," I said, embarrassed.

"You stayed the night?"

I nodded my head nonchalantly and replied, "Well, I couldn't very well let you die alone, could I? Someone had to watch you."

He let a soft smile reach across one cheek. I couldn't figure out if he was purposely making me lose focus or if he was stalling, so I took the opportunity to nip it in the bud.

"You owe me the truth," I reminded him.

"Let me make you breakfast. You have to be hungry."

"I don't want food. I want to know what is going on."

"Please?"

I rolled my eyes, and he wasted no time taking hold of my hand and pulling me toward the dining room. He sat me at the head of the table.

"Please, just sit here, and I'll be right back. We can talk and eat."

I sat there motionless and tired, but it was hard to keep a rigid disposition because the view was overwhelming. It was impossible to sit there and not feel a sense of peace. I scanned the entire landscape and wondered what people were doing in those areas stretched out for miles. I imagined everyone going about their mornings as usual, and I was sitting there experiencing the most abnormal morning I could imagine. I turned away, trying to shake the frustration that was coming over me again.

My attention was brought to the large painting. I remembered being wowed by it on my first tour of the room. It was just as stunning the second time around. I watched the two figures and examined how their arms greeted each other, and then I corrected myself. The sad aura that it gave off made me feel as though they were not greeting each other, but instead, they were saying goodbye, unwillingly. My heart sympathized with them because somehow I saw me and Weston in that image, and as much as I told myself I could say goodbye to him, I knew from the sadness the thought brought me that it wasn't what I wanted.

I was relieved when Wes came in carrying two glasses of cranberry juice. It was my favorite drink to have with breakfast, so I started sipping on it right away. I was thirstier than I thought, and the sweet aroma of cinnamon, which was coming from the kitchen, was making me realize I was also hungrier than I thought.

A few minutes later, he brought in two plates, each with scrambled eggs, toast, and a half grapefruit that was oven-baked with butter, cinnamon, and brown sugar on top. My eyes widened.

"These are my favorites."

"Really," he said, not sounding too surprised.

I picked up my fork, beginning to think he was some sort of psychic. He sat on the side of the table, like my mom usually did, which made it feel more comfortable. We both started eating, and I was waiting for him to chime in. After a few minutes, he started talking.

"Thank you."

"Thank you for what?" I wasn't trying to be ignorant. I had a good idea that he was talking about me saving him for the last 24 hours, but I was curious to know if there was one thing in particular to which he was referring.

"Thank you for trusting me," he clarified.

"I don't trust you," I said, calm and collected.

He smiled.

"I suppose I deserve that right now. But you *did* trust me enough not to let the paramedics take me." He put his arms by his side. I kept eating because it was easier to keep focused.

"Well, then," I said, between bites, "I guess that would be a good place to start. Maybe you can tell me why you would rather die than let the paramedics take you to the hospital."

He casually replied, "I wasn't going to die."

I looked at him and let out a small laugh. "That's funny, because you looked like death to me. If you weren't dying, what do you call it?"

"Sleeping."

I looked at him and saw that he was serious. "Sleeping? Huh. It looked like hypothermia to me."

"It was normal."

"Normal how?" I shot back.

He took in a deep breath. "It's normal because I can't regulate my body temperature."

I raised an eyebrow. "Why not?"

"I'm not like you," he said quietly, studying my face for a reaction. I kept chewing, waiting all too eagerly for him to continue, but he was struggling to find the words.

"Why can't you regulate your body temperature?" I pressed.

"I'm not sure how to explain this to you."

"Try me."

"Well, when I was sixteen, I got very sick. I was taken to Dr. Oliver Thomas, and he took me in." I listened attentively, but feeling the agitation return at the mention of the doctor as he continued. "I was given a rare blood transfusion to try to save my life." His eyes met mine hesitantly. I raised my eyebrow, unsatisfied.

"Dr. Thomas died in 1959, so how is that possible?"

He was growing more uncomfortable by the second and starting to look around. "*How* is that possible?" I asked again.

He brought his eyes back to mine. "Because he gave me the transfusion in 1916."

My eyes narrowed. I was contemplating which looney bin to check him into.

"1916?" I wanted to make sure I'd heard him correctly.

He nodded. "Dr. Thomas gave me a rare cold-blood transfusion, which he mixed, and for some reason, I lived through it—and I have since only aged three years in the last ninety-one."

At that moment, I excused myself from the table and went to grab my things. My overnight bag was upstairs, and I was still in my pajamas. I decided I would leave the house in what I was wearing, and I started stuffing my clothes in my bag. He followed me into the study.

"Keep your distance," I warned.

He stopped in the doorway on command. I roughly grabbed my bag and went to leave. He was blocking me and made no indication that he was going to move.

"I'd like to leave now," I informed him, refusing to look him in the eye.

He stepped further into my path. "You wanted to know the truth."

I jerked my head up and saw that he was watching me. His eyes were warm and pained. His nonthreatening demeanor made me feel more confident and assertive.

"Yes, I did. The *truth*!" I clarified. I dropped my bag on the ground and walked over to the desk. "Not some fabricated nonsense that you could've taken right out of here!" I pointed to the journal on the desk.

He closed the distance between us before I realized what he was doing, and he captured me by the shoulders. I flinched.

"Do you really think I would tell you something like this, if it weren't true? Do you think I asked for this?"

"I don't know. Who knows why you would say something so crazy, but I'm not sticking around to find out. Now, please let me go."

He moved his hands to hold my face, forcing me to look at him.

"Think. Sophie. You took my temperature yourself. You *saw* it. It's 80 degrees. I wouldn't be standing here right now if what I said wasn't true. I wouldn't make this up."

I scrunched up my face, trying to shake the thought. "Please. Sophie. I swear to you. I'm not lying to you. I am what I say, and if you don't want to be with me because of it, I won't blame you. I'll let you walk out of here forever, but please, don't think I lied to you. I would never lie to you."

I felt my knees weaken beneath me as I melted to the floor. He knelt with me, never releasing his hold on my face. It was the only thing that kept me from completely falling over. I was weakened and mentally exhausted.

"Look at me, Sophie." His voice was soft. "You know I would never hurt you."

I could barely open my eyes wide enough to see him, and what little I could see was blurred by water-filled eyes. He leaned closer and put his forehead to mine.

"Why is this happening?" I moaned. "I can't believe any of this. I can't."

"Yes, you can. I know you can," he said softly.

I shook my head. "No, it's insane."

"Just tell me what I can do to make you see. I'll do it."

I closed my eyes and absorbed the touch of his hands. They were cool. The feeling sent a small chill down my spine, with images of his freezing body at the pier. Also flashing through my mind was the strange reflection in his eyes, along with images I couldn't decipher whether I'd made them up or actually remembered them.

"You have to show me something more concrete," I said, wiping away the tears. "You have to show me something real."

"Okay," he said. He lifted me by my elbows and walked me over to the sofa to sit, and then he made his way over to the bookshelf. His fingers gently traced across the bindings of several books, as he slowly walked along the shelves. When he found what he was looking for, he stopped and gently pulled it from the shelf.

It was a medical encyclopedia. He opened it to a page and sat beside me with the book resting partially on my thigh. I leaned over to see a captioned picture labeled, Dr. Oliver Thomas, 1934. He was a blond-haired man with round-rimmed glasses. The soft lines of his face, accompanied by a square jaw, made him look powerful, smart, and kind at the same time.

"Do you see this picture?" he asked. I nodded.

Then, flipping toward the very back, he pulled out a loose photograph. He handed it to me. "This is me with Dr. Thomas in 1939."

It was a very old but well-preserved photograph of Dr. Thomas, standing with his arm around a taller boy who looked more than similar to Wes. The hairstyle was different, but beyond that, the person in the photograph looked *exactly* like Wes.

"This was our last photograph together," Wes said. "He didn't want to take any more after that, because he worried about someone finding out about me."

I took my fingertip and traced it over the face of the boy in the photograph.

"The picture is taken on the empty lot where he built his home not too far from here. If you go there today, you can see these two mountain peaks from the back deck." He pointed to two very distinctly shaped peaks in the backdrop. "And if you stand in the front yard, you'll see these trees right here. He built the house that is there now in 1940." He was pointing to where they were standing.

I handed him the picture in silence. He gently placed the picture back in the book and returned it to the shelf. He moved farther down the shelf and pulled out another book. This time, it was a book of Walt Whitman poetry. He turned to the back of the book and pulled out another worn photograph.

"This is a picture of me and my mother." He handed it to me. "This was taken in front of a bookstore she owned in London in 1915."

I studied the photograph and was humbled by the history of it. The woman in the picture had a contagious smile. She had a look of happiness that exuberated off the page. Next to her was another mirror image of Wes. Again, the hairstyle and the clothes were completely different, but I would recognize those eyes and smile anywhere. It was him, only younger. It was comforting to see the obvious joy he gave the woman standing next to him, but it was also disturbing to fathom that the same person was now sitting next to me. I gave it back to him and stood up to leave.

"Where are you going?" he asked.

"I need to think. I'm not saying I don't believe you, but I need some time to make sense of it all."

He nodded in understanding as he closed the book.

"Sophie?" he called. I turned around. "No one else knows what I have told you, so please, if you don't mind…"

"Oh Wes," I said in defeat. "You don't have to worry. Even if I did tell someone this, they would never believe me."

"That's not necessarily true," he corrected. "There are people out there trying to uncover the mystery my uncle left. If they knew I existed…"

"Okay. I get it. I won't tell anyone." And with that promise, I accepted that I might actually believe him. The only question that remained was what I was going to do about it. All I knew at that moment was that I couldn't figure it out there. I needed time alone.

Chapter 9
Coming to Terms

By about 10:00 p.m., I decided I wanted to see Wes again. I had been thinking about what he'd said all day. Basically, the world as I knew it no longer existed if what he said was true. I had to make a decision as to what I believed.

Everything leading up to our move to California had been for my mother's purpose, and I always felt lost. But somehow, this last place, this last move, felt right to me. For the first time ever, I felt like I belonged somewhere. I was convinced that the comfort California brought me was happiness, but it wasn't until I met Wes that I realized it was something else.

For me, happiness had always been feeling content. Feeling good, having no complaints. But when I met Wes, I realized that happiness could be more—something that elevates from the inside. Butterflies in the stomach, a smile that won't go away, and it's like an addiction that makes a person yearn for more. It's not something one thinks about, it's something that's felt, involuntarily.

I had always been a thinker, trying to find happiness and comfort in thoughts and ideas. It was only now that I realized happiness begins in the heart, and on that evening, my heart was speaking to me and yearning for how I felt when I was with Wes.

Sure, what I'd learned was outrageous, and sure, I had questions that were still unanswered, but when it came down to it, this was someone who had never been anything less than kind, giving, and understanding. And in addition, simply stated, I yearned for him. Every single ounce of me, whether it made sense or not, yearned for him. So, on that evening, I dialed his number, without reserve. I knew I had made the right decision the moment I heard his voice.

"You called," he said softly, without the normal hello.

"Wes, I don't really want to talk about this over the phone. I think we should talk about this in person, but I can't come out. It's a school day tomorrow, and my mom will have a conniption if I go somewhere now."

"I'll come to you then," he offered earnestly.

"What about your car?"

"I had Curtis take me to get it this afternoon. I have it."

"Okay, well then you can come over now if you want."

Without delay, he replied, "I'm on my way." His voice was still soft, but more eager than I was used to. I gave him instructions to come around to the back deck, so he could enter through my terrace, and once we hung up, I simply started freaking. Suddenly, I grew self-conscious of my décor and neatness.

I assessed my room and decided upon straightening up around my desk area and smoothing out my comforter to make my room look neater. I also shoved my old Raggedy Ann doll under my bed and made sure I didn't have any clothes lying around. Once I felt satisfied, I sat nervously in my corner chair waiting for my visitor to arrive.

Quicker than I expected, I heard a rapping at my door. It startled me.

As casually as I could, I opened the door.

"You're nervous," he observed.

"A little," I admitted.

"I'm not going to hurt you," he whispered.

"I don't think that." I shook my head to reassure him.

He reached out slowly and placed his hand over my heart. I could feel the pounding ricochet off of his palm.

"Then why?" he inquired.

"I'm just nervous. I've never had anyone in my room before."

He smiled slightly. "Do you want me to leave?"

"No, of course not." I looked around. "You can just sit there." I pointed to the chair. He obliged soundlessly, and I sat on the edge of my bed with my legs crossed. We sat in silence for several moments. He was absolute perfection sitting there in the dim light, and his presence was inexplicably soothing. Eventually my heart rate slowed, and my nerves relaxed as I allowed myself to absorb the gladness I felt with having him there.

"You're better now," he observed.

I blushed. "Yes."

"Why is that?"

"I don't know. I guess I like having you here," I admitted. It was easier to say than I thought. For a moment, it seemed like he was contemplating the words I'd spoken when, unexpectedly, he stood and took two slow steps in my direction. He leaned down just shy of my face. Although my heart fluttered, I sat completely still as he paused for a reaction. When he was sure I wasn't going to shy away, he touched his lips to mine. He was gentle, but his kiss was compelling. I placed my hands on both sides of his face and pulled him closer to me. The force caused us to fall backward on my bed. He held his weight off of me effortlessly, but his kiss grew more intense. Like our first kiss, I was surprised by my own aggressiveness. Whatever he was didn't seem to matter to me. All I knew was that I wanted him in any way I could have him.

After several moments of our lips mingling in complete unison, he turned his face away to regulate his audible breathing. It gave me a chance to catch my own breath. After a few seconds, he shifted to the side and offered an unexpected apology.

"What for?" I asked, sitting up.

He was contemplating heavily. "I'm not sure what came over me," he said.

I sat quietly, unsure how to respond. I didn't want him feeling as if his advance hadn't been wanted. "What is it?" I asked.

After a moment of intense deliberation, he confided in me. "I was just so relieved that you wanted to see me again. I don't think I realized how *much* I wanted that."

He had always seemed so collected, and for the first time, he actually looked emotionally vulnerable. I sympathized, because I was feeling that way, too.

"I know exactly how you feel."

He studied my face for a few moments and then whispered, "You are truly amazing."

"Oh, I doubt that," I assured him. I was a lot of things: different, private, creative, independent, inquisitive, but amazing, no. Certainly not.

"You are," he insisted.

"You don't know me very well," I pointed out.

"I know you better than you think, and I can affirm that amazing is an accurate description."

I studied his expression. "Why is that?" I asked. "Because you've told me the most outlandish thing in the world and for some reason, I can't stay away?"

He let out a chuckle. "Yes, that's a big reason."

His admission reminded me that we did have a few very large, unresolved matters to discuss. It was hard to remember them with him sitting in my room.

"That reminds me, there *are* things I want to know."

"I'm sure there are. I'll tell you whatever you want."

I knew I didn't want to keep questioning him. I had questioned his intentions and even existence since the day I'd met him. I wanted answers without any prodding.

"I don't want to ask you questions. I want *you* to tell me."

He turned toward me. "Starting where?"

"I want you to tell me about your family and how you ended up like you are."

I scooted myself all the way to the head of the bed and lay on my pillow, signaling to him that I was planning to listen for a while. He took the cue, and although he remained closer to the foot of the bed, he extended himself so that he was lying across the bed as well. He propped himself up on one elbow and studied me intensely. I made sure that my expression was soft and inviting. He began his recollection as if it was a recent memory.

"I was born in London, January 12, 1900," he revealed.

I tried my best not to flinch or appear uncomfortable.

"I was my parents' second son. A couple of years before I was born, my parents lost my brother. He was two years old, and he was hemophilic. My parents didn't know until he fell down and hit his head pretty hard. It shook my mother up really bad, and she rarely ever talked about it. They traced the condition back to my mother's family, so when I was born, they expected me to carry the disease as well."

I could tell that the memory was extraordinarily painful for him.

"For as good of care as she took of me, no one would have ever suspected that my case was as severe as it was. Most kids with my condition would not have lived past their toddler years. She was an amazing woman. Only now do I realize how great of a job she did."

"What about your father?" I interjected.

"I don't remember my father much, but he was *not* Weston the second." He briefly glanced at me to be sure I'd heard. "His name was Charles Wilson. He mostly traveled, and he died when I was three. He left my mother a substantial amount of money, and she used some of it to buy a bookstore and a brownstone near the medical district in London, in case something happened to me."

I studied his face closely as he spoke, and before long, I could actually picture him in London. I could see him wearing the clothes similar to the ones in the photograph I had seen. He looked just as perfect then as he did now.

"So what happened to you?" I asked, refocusing.

"When I was about to be sixteen, I had an accident that should have killed me. As my mother planned, I was close enough to be taken to a nearby doctor, which happened to be Dr. Thomas. I was dying, and he administered an experimental serum mixed with cold-blood, and here I am."

"So how does something like that work?" I had positioned myself closer to him so that I could take in everything he was saying. He seemed undistracted by my closeness.

"Well," he said, "he was working on ways to cure sickness and prolong life. No human blood transfusion appeared to alter people's ability to fight illness at the time, in a way that was beneficial at least, so he came up with the idea of using cold-blood. He had acquired different samples and one worked on me."

"Were you the first?"

"No, he tried it on several people, and they all died. He had actually given up when I came in. My mother begged him to try anything to save me, and he did."

"So why did it work on you?"

"He believed it worked because I was hemophilic and my own blood wouldn't clot against it."

"So why do you not age normally, and why can't you regulate your body temperature?" I caught myself. I said I didn't want to be asking questions, but I couldn't help it. I was intrigued.

"Well I'm not exactly sure why I age so slowly. Dr. Thomas believed that the cold-blood transformed all of my cells and my metabolism. Everything is working slowly for me, and it seems that it causes my natural aging process to progress at a much slower pace. I can't regulate my temperature because of the cold-blood. It is a part of me now."

"So what exactly is in your blood?"

"I don't know—various mixes. All I know about for sure is the gator blood. It was what he found to fight against infections, but he destroyed any other notes he had. He wouldn't even tell me."

"Why would he do that?"

"Because he didn't want anyone else to be able to replicate it."

I didn't understand. "But if it cured you, why wouldn't he want others to know about it?"

"Because I wasn't *just* cured. My transformation was not something I would wish on anyone. It took me years to recover. *Years*. He didn't want to put anyone else through that again, and plus he wasn't even sure if it would work a second time."

"So, you are the only one?"

"As far as I know."

"So you think there could be others?"

He shook his head quickly. "No. Dr. Thomas made certain that no one knew about me or the particular serum he used, but there have been other doctors who studied his work. They knew he was close to finding a cure for sickness and that he hoped to prolong people's lives. Many others have tried to replicate previous experiments he did, but none of them have been successful, that I know of."

"So people are looking to replicate it?"

"Yes."

"What do you think they would do? What if they just want to find a cure, too?"

"What I have is not a cure." He dropped his eyes.

"Why? You have been the perfect age forever. Why wouldn't you be glad?"

He smiled lightly. "Didn't you notice what happened to me at the pier?"

Somehow, I'd almost forgotten the look of death he'd worn in my car that evening. I shuddered at the memory.

"Sorry," I said, frowning. "But, other than needing to stay warm all the time, what else is so bad?"

His mood shifted dolefully. "Well, it gets very lonely for one, and for another, it is *very* difficult for me to keep track of time."

I pondered that idea and couldn't see the downfall.

"What is so bad about managing your time?" I asked naively.

"Well, for me, time moves differently. I'm progressing slowly while everyone around me is progressing quickly. A year for you and a year for me are not the same. We figured out that I age one year for every thirty, and if I let it, thirty years will feel like a year to me.

"What do you mean, if you let it?"

"I have to concentrate very hard to slow down what is happening around me in my mind, so that it doesn't seem like a blur."

"A blur?"

"Yes, that is what it feels like. If you can imagine the headache that would give you, then you can have a pretty good idea of how I felt for a long time. It took me about two years to figure out how to manage it. If I don't force my mind to stay on pace with real time, then everything around me goes by too fast for me to focus."

"Is that why you were mumbling things about time and seeing me when you were passing out?"

"Was I?"

I nodded, and he rolled his eyes, trying to shake the thought. That brought them to my attention.

"And your eyes?" I asked.

"What about them?"

"Why do they have that glassy film on them sometimes? Almost like a faint shine on a lake at night."

He smiled. "You're very observant," he noted. "Well, apparently I've acquired transcendent eyesight also."

"What does that mean?"

"It means I can see *very* well. *All* the time."

"Interesting. What about now?" I asked. It was relatively dark in my room, and I wanted to know how well he could see my expressions.

"If I wanted to I could read you a book right now."

"Okay then. That's pretty good," I understated. "So what are you going to do now that you are like this?"

"Finish what Dr. Thomas started. I hope to make something good out of all of this."

"How so?"

"Well, there is something in my blood that definitely has the ability to cure people, and right now my goal is to help doctors find it without having to go through what I have had to deal with. No one would truly want this if they knew what it was like, so I hope to be able to take some of what I have and incorporate it into a medicine that doesn't alter people—just simply cures them. Labs that my uncle funded are close to a breakthrough. We have already found that proteins are great antibacterial fighting agents. Extracts have also been proven to help heal burns and other infections."

"So why can't people know about you then?"

"That's a good question. You would think people would take what I have and use it for the greater good, but unfortunately, that's not how the world works. We have encountered many different people looking for the missing pages to his journal, and many of them have bribed, stolen, extorted, and threatened my uncle. The people who want what I have are willing to kill for it, and I don't trust them. I can't trust anyone."

"Then why did you trust me? Why tell me?"

He snickered. "Well, you made me jump into cold water, and the rest is history."

I nudged him. "I didn't *make* you."

"Well, I wasn't going to let you do it."

"Okay, but you didn't have to tell me. You could have made up another reason."

"That would be lying, and I told you, I wouldn't lie to you."

I felt myself blush. "Why is that?" I asked.

"Because you saved me."

"You said you weren't going to die, remember? Sleeping, that's what you called it," I reminded him.

He raised an eyebrow in recognition. "True," he admitted. "I wasn't, but you saved me in other ways."

I moved my pillow closer to him and nestled up against his chest. He naturally began stroking my hair, and I closed my eyes in complete peace. Given my nature, I was surprised that I wasn't asking him a thousand other questions, but the truth was, I didn't want to. It was clear to me that he was something special. I had thought so from the moment I met him, only I couldn't figure out what it was. The truth was beyond my wildest imagination, but now that he'd told me, I could see it. I could see him being sick and dying. I could also see his mother begging for his life as if I were standing there pleading for it myself, and the fact that he was lying next to me brought me comfort no matter how impossible it was. I snuggled closer to him.

"I'm glad you came," I murmured.

"Does this mean that you are okay with this?"

I thought for a moment and soaked in the feelings that were going through me. "It appears that way." He stopped stroking my hair and I froze. "What's wrong?" I asked.

"You don't have to be okay with this. If you don't want—"

"No, I want this. I don't know what exactly *this* is, or why I don't think you're insane, but I believe you, and I like you, and that's all that matters."

"Are you sure?"

"Yes, I'm sure. Now if you don't mind." I pulled his hand back to my hair so he could continue. He chuckled and started softly rubbing my hair again.

After a few moments, a thought transpired. "Can I ask you something?"

"You can ask me anything."

"Why me?"

He pondered that question for a few moments, but he never ceased playing with my hair. "That is a question you will have to ask fate," he concluded.

"Fate? You think it was fate that brought us together?"

"I know it is," he replied.

It seemed as though I was missing part of a little secret. I can't say that I fully believed in fate at the time, but I did like the idea of putting my crashing into him episode off on something other than my stupidity. I liked the idea of believing that I was meant to run into him. I liked the idea so much that I reveled in it until my eyes got so heavy, I involuntarily slipped into a peaceful slumber.

I don't think I will forget a single moment of that night. It was the first time where there seemed to be no hesitation hovering in the air around either one of us. My nervousness with being near him had ceased, and any doubt I'd had of his feelings for me had faded away. The closeness between us was so right, and so natural, that there was no way for me to doubt it. I wanted him, and I was sure of it.

After that night, it became routine for Wes and me to spend time together every day. I accepted him for who he was and he, for whatever reason, wanted me, too. A day didn't go by that I didn't see him. During the week, he would come over and help me patiently with my homework. I knew he must have been bored, but he insisted that he got a kick out of watching me learn the material.

On occasion, I would ask him just to do it for me, but he kept saying I'd regret "compromising my integrity." I think he was completely wrong in that. My integrity would've been just fine. That much I knew, but he didn't seem to mind sitting with me while I did my work, and I found that I learned better with him there, so I couldn't complain. Plus, he was an excellent tutor, and I even grew to like government, a little. Getting firsthand accounts from someone who had actually lived through several presidencies made learning about it *much* more interesting.

My favorite moments were of the times we spent together at night. He stayed with me almost every night, and it was during those hours that I came to know more about him. Each new piece of knowledge made me hungry for more. Everything he revealed about himself was central to his character and survival.

For one, I learned that his body temperature range needed to be between 70 and 90 degrees. He was most comfortable when it was in the middle of that range, and once his body temperature went above or below, he would start to have problems functioning physically and mentally, like what I had seen at the pier.

His losing consciousness was a sight I never wanted to repeat, and given that it was wintertime, I found myself always monitoring the heat or checking to make sure he was adequately bundled when going out. I was a complete nag who was getting on my own nerves with it, but he didn't seem to mind, even though he was an expert on taking care of himself.

During one of our nights together, I also learned things about him that had to do with his mental and emotional survival. He opened up to me about how difficult some years had been for him. He said there was a period, after Dr. Thomas died, when he was so lonely and depressed that he couldn't see himself living. He had no one he could trust and had given up trying. He mentioned the word suicide, and I cringed. I eventually asked him what had stopped him from doing it, and he said it was two things. The first was a promise he'd made to his uncle to make sure good came out of his existence, and the second was the hope of finding me. He told me he was convinced I'd come into his life, and if he had to live a solitary existence until the day he met me, then he would do it.

My heart turned to absolute mush. It's not everyday that a girl is told by her boyfriend that he'd lived through forty years of solitude waiting for her to walk into his life. It made me feel wanted and needed. They were feelings I hoped would never go away, and I wanted to take the opportunity to tell him how I felt. It was simple: I *loved* him. Now, all I had to do was find the right time to say it, and I took a chance on the right time being then.

He had been lying on my bed with his body turned toward me, and I was nestled into his chest. Sometimes, it seemed like he was more open with me when I wasn't watching his every expression and on that particular night, I gave him privacy as he talked about the difficulties of his past by burying my face in his chest. Having granted him the absence of my stare also made it easier for me to murmur those binding words to him. I cleared my throat and released the words, "I love you."

Once I said them, I felt momentary stiffening in his muscles, as if he was surprised by my declaration. I braced for the rejection.

"You don't know how good hearing those words makes me feel," he whispered. His voice was reflective, but silence followed for several seconds. I waited as my pulse started picking up in concern for the lack of immediate reciprocation. I wondered if I had said it too soon. After moments that were probably shorter than I remembered, my trepidation was eased. He shifted himself lower so that his eyes were even with mine, and then he put my cheek in the palm of his hand.

"Sophie," he affirmed. "I love you more than anything else in this entire world. You have no idea how much."

Hearing him say those words solidified every sacrifice I had made by giving him a chance. Every ounce of sanity and rationality that I'd given up in order to trust and believe him was well worth the feeling I had at that moment. It all seemed so surreal that I wasn't sure if any of it was actually happening.

"What is it?" he asked.

"What?"

"Your face, I don't recognize that look."

I started thinking about my newfound fortune. "Well, I'm just thinking that this seems like a dream. It's too good to be true."

He chuckled. "Which part?"

"All of it, but especially the part about you loving me. Are you sure?" I asked.

"No."

I was about to open my mouth to protest when he covered it with his finger. "Yes," he said, chuckling. I giggled in return, but my chuckle was cut short when he placed his entire hand over my mouth. My eyes widened and then, super quickly, he just rolled off my bed without a sound. I was dumbfounded, until I heard her.

"Sophie?" my mom asked, knocking at my door. My mom *never* came up to my room, so I jumped up.

"Yes?"

She opened my door, which further shocked me.

"Mom? What is it? I was trying to sleep."

She came and sat on the foot of my bed. I almost had a heart attack right then and there. I situated myself between her and my hidden guest, who was lying on the floor next to my bed.

"Well, I was up having a late-night snack, and I wanted to see if you were awake."

"And…." I prodded.

"And I wanted to ask you something."

"All right, what is it?"

"Well, you know Tom, right?"

"Of course, Mom, what is it?" I was losing my patience and getting hot under the collar with guilt.

"Well, he would like to spend Christmas together, with you and me." She paused a moment. "What do you think about that?"

"I don't know. Spend Christmas where?"

"He wants to come here."

"I guess so," I replied. "This is what you came up here to ask me?"

"Well, yes. We've always spent Christmas together, just me and you, and I'm not sure how I would feel inviting him. It's been bothering me for days, but he really wants to."

"Why wouldn't you want to?"

She thought for a few minutes. "I'm just not sure if I'm as ready for family time like he is."

I didn't know what to say to that, and I really didn't want to have to come up with something. I just wanted her out of my room.

"Well, Mom, I'm sure it will be fine." I stood up to hint that I was ready for her to exit. She took the bait. I walked her over to my door, plotting to lock it behind her once she left. As she reached the door, she paused and turned around. I stiffened.

"How are things with you and Wes?" she asked.

A lump built in my throat. I cleared the airway. "Fine," I said, as casually as I could.

"Good," she countered. "Maybe you can invite him to dinner, too. I would rather have another guest. You know, it will take the pressure off."

"We'll see." I went to shut the door.

"Does he have somewhere else to go?" she asked, not satisfied with my lack of commitment.

"Um. I don't think so."

"Well, it's settled then. Invite him. It'll be nice to have him." She smiled and left the room, oblivious to the infringement. I shut the door and locked it for the first time since I'd moved in. Then, I let out a huge sigh.

"You can come out now," I said, turning around. He was back on my bed before I reached it myself. He was grinning widely.

"I don't know what you think is so funny," I spat.

"Just listening to you squirm in your socks."

"Not funny," I grumbled. "She could have caught you here, and then I would've had to deal with her completely freaking out."

"She wouldn't have caught me." He was so sure.

"Oh yeah, you might be able to hear well, but you can't get invisible."

He looked at me, raising his eyebrows. "Are you sure about that?" he smirked.

I looked at him in horror. "You can not! Can you?"

"No silly." He pulled me close to him and gave me a big, wet kiss right on my lips. I laughed and wiped my face with the back of my hand and kissed him again, neatly.

"So?" I whispered.

"So?" he countered, just as softly.

"Are you coming or what?"

"Coming where?" He feigned confusion.

I smacked him on his arm, which hurt my hand far more than his rock-hard bicep. "To Christmas!"

"Oh that," he said, rolling over so I was pinned beneath him. "Only if you ask nicely."

I tried to wriggle free. "My mom is the one that invited you, remember?"

He relaxed and released me. “Well in that case,” he said. “I’ll be here.”

I smiled and nestled myself up against him again. After a while, my blinks became slower and heavier. Before I let my eyelids win the battle, I thought I’d ask one more question.

“What do you want for Christmas?”

He gave me a gentle squeeze before whispering, “More time with you.”

Chapter 10
CHRISTMAS

I knew exactly what I was going to buy him for Christmas. The first thing would be inexpensive, but the second thing would require a little bit of savings. I couldn't imagine what I would do if I didn't have my own income. Asking my mom for money to shop for my boyfriend's Christmas present was absolutely unappealing.

I'd worked at Healey's for a few months, so I had acquired some savings that had virtually gone untouched. In the entire time we dated, Wes never let me pay for anything. And, I still owed him $500.00 for fixing my car, which he had yet to let me pay him back for. So I was more than willing to spend a good chunk of my savings on him. In fact, I welcomed Christmas with open arms. It was the first time I'd actually be able to spend money on him without him being able to refuse.

For the first present, I tricked Wes into visiting me at work one afternoon after I asked Dawn to "spontaneously" take our picture. It worked out perfectly. I met him in one of the aisles, and she acted as if she was taking pictures of the outside of the store while stumbling upon us on her way to the back. She casually suggested that we take a picture together. Wes was a great sport about it.

We were standing in front of shelves of books, and Wes put his arm around me, which led me to put my arms around his waist in return. He, to no surprise, took a great picture with the smile I love, and I was pretty pleased with the way I turned out. I looked happy and "in love," as Dawn described it, and given the fact that we both had connections with bookstores, I thought the picture was perfect.

I ended up getting two copies of the photograph made—one for me, and one to go in a picture frame for him. I figured since his house was so void of pictures, I could start to liven it up with memories for him.

The second gift was going to be harder to find. I wanted to see what kind of advance technology watches were out there. The watch I'd seen him wear was an older-looking watch that had the time, date, and an alarm, but that was it. I thought that surely the 21st century would bring in better technology than that, and I was right. I searched online and found a Suunto Stealth Watch. It was all black, and sleek looking. I thought it would look nice with everything he wore, but more importantly, I bought it for the functionality. It had time, of course, but it also had three different alarm settings, altimeter readings, barometer readings, a compass, and most importantly, current air temperature readings and temperature predictions. What I found amusing about it was that it was scratch-proof, waterproof, and had preprogrammed calendars up to the year 2089.

Since I'd already crashed into him via my Jeep, sent him diving into cold water to save a stranger, and since he would surely be around in 2089, it was perfect. And the best part about the whole thing was that it cost me almost what I owed him for fixing my car. I relished in that little detail. In fact, I smiled as I wrapped it.

I was so excited about giving him his present that I didn't even want to wait until Christmas Day. I had to work on Christmas Eve, and afterward, I went straight to his house hoping to surprise him. I rang the bell when I got there, and from his expression when he opened the door, it had worked. I walked in studying his face.

"What's going on?" I asked, as he shut the door behind me.

"Nothing, I just wasn't expecting you." He began punching in the code to the house alarm. I hadn't seen him use that before, so it struck me as odd. "I thought you were going to call me when you got home?" he said. "I was supposed to come to you tonight."

"I changed my mind. What's with the alarm?"

He leaned in to give me a kiss on the cheek. "Nothing, I'm just being cautious."

"Cautious about what?" I pressed.

"There was a break-in at one of the medical labs."

"What for?"

We were in the living room now, and he sat down casually on the chair. I followed suit on the couch.

"Someone was looking for something. They broke into one of the research facilities and took some trial notes and samples."

"So, why does that have you locking up your house?"

"Because they took some study results for some alligator plasma."

I sat up. "Why didn't you tell me?"

"I was going to once you called me when you got *home*," he smirked.

"Well, I wanted to surprise you. Do you think you should worry?"

"No, I'm not tied to that particular lab by name. Funding is anonymous, so there is no paper trail, but similar things like this have happened in the past. If my uncle taught me nothing else, it was to err on the side of caution. It's probably nothing."

I relaxed a little and leaned back on the sofa. "Are you sure?" I asked.

"Yes," he answered, moving next to me. "But," he added, touching my cheek with the back of his hand, "I *would* feel better if I knew where you were planning to be."

His touch felt so good that it was almost instant relief. In fact, I would've felt instantly at ease had I not been completely aware that he was heightening his home security as well as his concern for my whereabouts. It made me uneasy.

"Now, why did you come by here?" he asked, changing the subject.

My thoughts shifted to the contents of my handbag. "Well, I wanted to give you your present." He started to smile. "But, I don't feel very jolly right now."

"Why not?"

"Well, you have it like Fort Knox in here, and you're worried about where I go, and now you want me to pretend like everything is great."

He put his hand under my chin to hold my gaze to his. "Sophie, everything *is* great. It's fine. I'm just taking precautions. If I thought something was really wrong, I would've come to you, right away, to tell you in person. Plus, I would've escorted you home. I wouldn't have just waited for you to call me. I'm sorry to worry you. But everything is *fine.* And great," he assured me.

He kissed me so softly after that, that I couldn't detect one ounce of tension in his body. He was completely at ease and within a few moments, I was, too.

"Okay then," I said, softening. "I suppose I could give you your gifts."

"Gift*s*?" he asked, lingering on the *s*.

"Yes, and you can't refuse the gift*s*, because it's Christmas and that would be rude."

"Actually, I can refuse them, because it's not Christmas yet," he reminded me.

The smile disappeared from my face. "You can't be serious. I came all the way over here. I *want* you to open them."

"Hmmm," he said, as if he was pondering heavily.

"Fine, I'll take it home." I went to yank my bag up, and he grabbed my arm.

"I'm just kidding, Sophie. Calm down. I want your gifts. Please give them to me."

I grinned in victory at the fact that he hadn't called my bluff this time.

"Good," I said, pulling the watch out first. For some reason, I thought that would be the easier gift of the two. I loved our picture together, but I didn't want to seem too vain, so I saved that one for last.

I held out the small box and then tucked it back to my chest. "Now, I had no idea what I was going to get you," I lied, trying to set him up to accept my gift without a fight. "So, I hope you like it."

"Of course I'll like whatever you give me." He reached his hand out, taking the bait.

"Promise?"

"Promise." He ran his finger over his heart in a criss-cross fashion. I handed it over. He pulled back the paper slowly. I saw his eyes widen when he saw the name brand on the box. He looked up at me with narrow eyes.

"Open it," I said, smiling.

He pulled back the lid and then closed it just as smoothly as he had opened it.

"Sophie. This is too much."

"What? It's just a watch," I said innocently. "You said you would like it," I reminded him.

"Of course I like it. I just don't want you spending your money on me."

I reached over and covered his mouth.

"I want to. Besides, it's really for me anyway. I want you to have it so I can check it. You know, so I can make sure your surroundings are appropriate." I poked out my bottom lip a little. "But if you don't like it—"

He removed my hand. "No, I love it. I really do. Thank you," he said, leaning over to kiss me on my cheek.

"You're welcome," I said, satisfied. "I have another one for you." I pulled out the second gift. His expression hardened. "Relax, it didn't cost much at all, so don't freak out."

I handed him the second gift and watched him, hesitantly, as he opened it. I wanted him to like this one the most. When he opened the gift, his stare disappeared into some place that was beyond the picture he was looking at. After a few moments of silence, he touched the picture through the framed glass and traced our smiles.

"I thought you could use some pictures in your house. I hope you like it."

"I love it." He reached around the back of my neck and gently pulled me toward him until our lips met. His kiss was different from what I was used to. It wasn't urgent or soft. It was binding. I felt the necessity of it, and it made me feel closer to him than ever before.

"I love you," he uttered.

I smiled warmly. "I love you, too."

He put the picture on the fireplace mantel and then set out to leave the room.

"Where are you going?"

He looked back with a gentle smile. "To get your gift."

I hadn't even thought about a gift for myself. I was never one to look forward to presents. Maybe it was because it had always been me and my mom, and I felt bad thinking that she had to spend additional money on me.

He returned with a small, square box, which had clearly been professionally wrapped in silver and blue paper. I'm not sure if the bow was as complex to unwrap as I made it seem, or if it was my nervous fingers, but it took me longer than normal to unravel the gorgeous wrapping.

Once I was able to get my hands on the box itself, I wasted no time pulling off the top to reveal a stunning bracelet.

"Oh my gosh. It's *beautiful*." I lifted it and placed it in the palm of my hand. "It matches my necklace." The bracelet was classic. "Is it antique?" I asked.

"Yes. I had the clasp updated, but the beads are early 1900s."

The beads were in impeccable condition, but I could tell they were old. I put it on my wrist. It was lovely. The three larger stones were the exact same color as the stones in my necklace, and they were connected by alternating silver beads and blue stones, which were a perfect contrast.

"I love it." I smiled. It was the best gift I had ever received. I probably would've said that about anything he bought me, but that was not the point. The bracelet truly was my favorite, because it fit me perfectly. Aside from the fact that it matched my only other accessory besides a purse, it fit my style. It was original and nice looking without the impression of being brand new. It was something I could show off without being flashy, because it wasn't expensive looking. It was simply exquisite. I thanked him a few times over and gave him a gracious hug and kiss.

I wished I could've stayed the night, but unfortunately, my mother was expecting me, so I only got to stay for a few hours, which were fantastic. I was only reminded of the abnormal event preceding my arrival when I went to leave and he disabled the alarm.

"Are you going to be using this all the time now?"

"For a while," he said. "Until I can be sure the incident is isolated. In the meantime…" he continued, taking hold of my hand as he walked me to my car. "The code is 1663."

"Why are you telling it to me?" I wondered.

He smiled. "You never know when you'll have me jumping off a pier again."

"Very funny." We were at my car by then. He opened my door for me, and I reached up to kiss him before climbing into my Jeep.

Once I got home, it was hard for me to sleep. I kept running through the following day in my mind. Wes had never fully sat down and had a conversation with my mom for longer than five minutes, and I hadn't with my mom's new friend either. Imagining all of us around a dinner table was odd. What kinds of things do we talk about? *Hi Tom, this is Wes, my boyfriend. He was born before you, but he got a shot from the fountain of youth so he's still around.* No, I don't think so.

I shook my head, trying to shake the abnormality of the whole situation, and insisted upon going about the day just like any other. Wes was normal to me, and as far as the rest of the world knew, he was normal to them also.

The next day, my mom and I started cooking the turkey around noon, and dinner was set for 4:00. Wes arrived at 3:00, as I'd requested, but what I hadn't requested was that he come with a gift in tow. That was all his idea. My mother was pleasantly surprised when I escorted him into the kitchen with it.

"Hello, Ms. Slone," Wes said.

"You have to stop calling me that. Gayle, please," she countered, reaching out to give him a hug.

"Gayle," he obliged.

He handed her the beautifully wrapped box, and she paused to remove her apron. After setting the apron on the table, she took the gift and led us into the living room. We sat on each side of her, both watching as she unwrapped the paper. Since he hadn't even told me he was planning on getting her a gift, I had no idea what it was. I was just as eager as she was to see what was inside.

She pulled the top off of the box, gently, and revealed tissue paper. *It must be fragile,* I thought. She lifted the wrapped object out of the box and unraveled the tissue paper. It was a delicate blue and white antique teacup.

"That's Dr. Thomas'," I observed. Both she and Wes looked at me with wide eyes.

"It's beautiful," she said. "Who is Dr. Thomas?" I looked at Wes, whose eyes were locked on me. He was mute. I looked back at my mom, who was waiting for an answer.

"He was Wes' uncle," I said, looking at the cup as she finished unwrapping the matching saucer. "It's an heir-loom."

My mom whipped her head around to face Wes, who was still staring at me.

"Wes, I can't accept this. This is for you. I shouldn't have it," she said.

I cleared my throat to signal Wes to respond. He blinked and turned away from me.

"I want you to have it, Ms. Slone. It would mean a lot."

"Oh! Wow," she said, marveling in the fine details. "Thank you. I'll take great care of it." After a few mo-ments, she took the cup and saucer and walked back to the kitchen, still admiring the pattern. Wes shifted into her previous spot, making it so he was only a few inches from me.

"How did you know that?" he asked.

"Know what?"

"Know that the teacup was Dr. Thomas'." His expres-sion was intense.

I leaned back from the unexpected interrogation. "I don't know. I just figured it was old and just assumed it was his."

"Why wouldn't you assume it was my mother's?" he asked, which was a perfectly reasonable question.

I shrugged. "I don't know, lucky guess. Why?"

He examined my expression for a while before relaxing. Just then, the bell rang, and my mom practically flew out of the kitchen. "That's Tom," she said nervously, making her way toward the door. Like the gentleman he was, Wes stood up to welcome his arrival. My mother led Tom in. He was a handsome man, considering he was already gray. He was also much older than I would have pictured for my mom, but he was good looking and seemed good to her. He gave her anything she wanted, and it was nice to see someone spoiling her. She deserved it.

"Tom, you've met Sophie, and this is Weston," she said, motioning toward Wes. Tom walked around the sofa and Wes met him halfway, reaching out his hand for a shake.

"Wes. It's nice to meet you. I'm Tom Lawrence," he said.

"Nice to meet you, sir," Wes returned politely.

Both Tom and my mother were smiling, oddly, like proud parents.

"Mom, do you mind if we go for a walk?"

She exchanged a glance between us. "No, not at all, kids. Go right ahead. Tom can help me in the kitchen. Just don't be gone long. Dinner will be ready soon."

We both nodded in compliance and made our way to the exit. I grabbed his hand after he bundled himself up in his heavy coat and hat. I, too, bundled up more than I normally would have. I had grown accustomed to doing that, so as not to draw too much attention to Wes' overcompensation.

"I'm sorry," I said, as we started walking. "I just wanted to get out of there for a minute. It was too weird."

"Tell me about it."

It struck me as strange for him to agree. "Why is that?" I inquired.

"Because I know him."

I snapped my head up. "Know him how?"

"I went to school with him."

"When?" I shot back.

"When I went to Berkeley, the first time. Thirty years ago."

"Oh my goodness. I had no idea. I'm sorry. I never would've had you come." I was starting to freak. He stopped walking and turned toward me.

"No, it's okay. We had no way to know. There are a zillion and one Toms out there. Besides," he said, putting his hands on my face. "I'm used to running into people I knew before. They think they knew my father."

"Weird."

"I know." He smiled and leaned over to kiss me. His lips felt cooler than normal. He was getting cold. I went to move his hands back down to our sides so we could head back, and I felt his wrist. He was wearing the watch I'd bought him. I smiled.

"Let me see," I said, pulling his sleeve back to look at the weather reading. "Ah, it is 48 degrees out. Let's go." He smiled and took my hand as we headed back toward the house.

My mom and Tom were in the kitchen when we arrived.

"That was fast," she said.

"It was cold," I replied.

Dinner was about ready, and I started helping her transfer the food onto the dining room table. Tom was more than eager to help as well. He followed her around like she was a queen.

My mom set the place setting so she and I were opposite from each other. She wasn't ready to give Tom the position at the head of the table. I was just fine with that, because it meant I was sitting closer to Wes. My leg could reach his under the table.

Tom volunteered to ask blessing over the food, and then he carved the turkey as we passed the side dishes around. Once we all had our plates full, my mom wasted no time initiating the conversation.

"So, what are you studying at Berkeley, Wes?"

"Chemistry," he answered, softly, making eye contact with only her.

"Chemistry?" Tom interjected. "That's great. What do you plan to do with that?"

"I think I might go into medicine," he answered, not quite making complete eye contact with him.

"That's impressive. I teach at the medical school there," Tom noted. "I would be happy to put in a good word for you if you want."

Wes smiled kindly. "That would be nice. Thank you."

"Of course, if you have smarts like your father, you won't need my recommendation," he added.

I coughed, and everyone turned my way to make sure I was okay.

"I'm fine. It just went down the wrong pipe." I quickly took a drink.

Once my mom was satisfied with my well-being, she diverted her attention back to Tom.

"You knew Wes' father?" she asked.

We all looked at him attentively, including Wes.

"Yes, I did. We went to Berkeley together. We were study partners and friends. I thought he was going to go into medicine, too, but he went to flight school instead." He looked at Wes for a reaction.

Wes appeared very calm and unnerved. I suppose years of experience playing it cool paid off. He decided it was best to go along with it.

"You knew my father?" he asked.

"Yes, I did," Tom said, nodding. "He was a good man."

My mother was fascinated with the connection. I, on the other hand, was almost sick to my stomach.

"Thank you," Wes responded politely. They both started eating again, and for a few moments, it was silent.

"You look like him, you know?" Tom pointed out. I cringed.

"That's what people say," Wes responded casually.

"It's quite remarkable. You could pass for him, if you had different hair and the accent."

"Accent?" I questioned.

Tom looked at me. "Yes, his father had an English accent. It drove the girls crazy."

"Really?" I perked up, quite interested and jealous at the same time.

"Yes, really. He could've had any girl he wanted, but he was never interested." I relaxed. "I didn't even think he liked girls until he graduated. He ran off and married, and I never saw him again. I never met her, but I assume that was your mother." He motioned toward Wes, whose eyes were fixed on his food.

Tom sensed the awkwardness. "I was so sorry to hear about his accident," he offered.

Wes smiled softly. "Thanks."

"Okay," I interjected, taking the attention off of Wes. "So do you have any kids, Dr. Lawrence?"

His facial expression changed from sympathy for Wes to sadness of his own. "I had one son. He died a few years ago."

"Oh, I'm sorry."

He nodded in acceptance. My mom rescued me from the uncomfortable feeling by asking me to pass the potatoes. Gladly, the rest of the meal continued with just small talk. After dinner, I went to the kitchen to help her clean, but Tom was already helping. I offered anyway. "Do you need any help?" I asked.

"No sweetie. I'm fine. Thanks. You go entertain your guest."

"Okay. Let me know if we can help."

She never turned from the sink. "Okay, will do."

Tom turned to give me a soft smile. I nodded and went to Wes. He was on the living room sofa expecting my entrance.

"Wow," I said. "That was freaky." I plopped down on the sofa next to him.

"Agreed," he said, placing his arm around my shoulders.

"Married?" I asked.

He smirked. "No."

"But Tom said—"

"I had to give people a reason for me to disappear."

"Oh." That was satisfying enough. I leaned my head on his shoulder. "Did you really have an English accent?"

"Yes, I'm from London, remember?"

"Well, where is it?"

"Well, I can't very well get away with being English forever. I've Americanized myself over the years. Plus, I have to do anything I can to distance myself from…" He was searching for words.

"From yourself?"

He smiled.

"Can I hear it sometime?" I asked.

"Anytime you want."

"With the exception of Tom being around," I corrected. He chuckled. "Do you think he suspects anything?" I whispered.

"I don't think so," he answered. "He was attentive, but I didn't sense that he was bothered by my presence." There was something about the way he said *sense* that made me curious.

"How so? How can you tell?" I asked.

"I can get a pretty good vibe off of people."

"Vibe? Like a feeling?"

"Yes. I can sense the energy they give off, and he seemed more excited than anything. I think he likes your mother."

"So you think he's good for her?"

He pondered for a moment. "He was a good friend when I knew him, and he seems all right now. I'm not sure about the part about his son though."

"What do you mean?"

"I'm not sure. His heart rate picked up once you asked that."

"Hmm. Well, I bet yours did, too, when he started talking about you."

He laughed.

"Can you hear what they're saying now?" I asked.

He leaned his head back to listen. “Yes.”

“What are they talking about?”

“They like me,” he said, smirking.

“Good,” I replied. “Too bad we won’t be hanging around here though.”

“Why is that?”

“Because I can’t risk any more awkward exchanges between you and your *old* friend, and I really don’t want to watch him and my mother together, if you know what I mean.”

“That sounds good to me,” he agreed, before leaning down to kiss me gently. Of course, I took it a little further than that. After a few moments of clandestine making out, I snuggled in closer to him, all the while plotting on how I could spend more time with him *away* from home.

Chapter 11
THE NEW YEAR

After our holiday dinner, it got easier to spend more time with Wes without my mother prying too much. Of course, it helped that she had a new social life of her own. She had other things to do besides pry into the love life of her eighteen-year-old daughter.

Lucky for me, on New Year's Eve, it turned out my mother was going away with Tom for the night, so I was granted even more freedom. I wanted the night to be special, and I needed to feel completely alone with Wes, so I decided I wanted to spend the night at his house.

He ended up planning the rest of the details as a surprise. All he asked was that I wear a nice dress, and I, of course, didn't really have one. So, I ended up going shopping, and without knowing where we were going, it was hard. I settled on the classic knee-length black dress, because I remembered hearing that a little black dress is appropriate for just about any place and occasion. I also snagged some little black strappy shoes. I left my hair down, because it made me feel more like myself.

When I arrived at his house, I noticed a limo waiting in the driveway, and it piqued my interest. "What's this?" I asked.

"Just a car," he said, greeting me.

"No, not just a car. What's it for?"

"It's for me and you. I want to be able to focus on you tonight. Not the road."

I blushed. He carried my bag into his house and then escorted me to the limo.

The thinker in me wanted to press the secret of our destination, but the intuition in me concluded that it didn't matter. He could've been taking me to the end of the world, and for as handsome as he looked in his black shirt and slacks, I would've gone willingly. So, instead of interrogating him, I chose to nestle close to him and enjoy the ride.

Eventually, I realized we were going into San Francisco, and I anticipated dinner, but once again, he completely amazed me. We *were* going to have dinner, but it was going to be on a New Year's Eve cruise around the bay.

"You're kidding me," I said, when I saw the yacht. He grabbed my hand and led me from the limo. "This is ridiculous."

"You don't like it?"

"Of course I like it, but it's way over the top," I said. I mean, most girls my age were out at a party with a sparkly hat and a noisemaker for the night. Here I was about to step foot on a yacht on the bay with the hottest guy on the planet. I immediately thanked Kerry, telepathically, at that moment for simply causing me to smash into his car. I also remembered to give props to fate, since Wes seemed convinced that this was why we had met. Whatever the reason, I felt like the luckiest girl in the world.

Our dinner was delicious, but I noticed we were the youngest people on the yacht, or at least I was. There were countless couples, and many of them were much older. I didn't feel awkward. In fact, it felt very comfortable, but it made me start thinking about how long the other couples had been together.

It eventually hit me that we didn't seem to fit into that picture. I couldn't envision us like that. If he only aged one year for my thirty, I would eventually look like his mother. I shuddered at the thought. It was bothering me all through dinner, but I couldn't figure out how to discuss it without actually bringing my potential oldness to his attention. That certainly wasn't attractive, so I decided not to go there for the time being. Instead, I settled on a more subtle topic.

"What do you want to do for your birthday?" I asked.

He smiled softly. "Nothing."

"Well I'm getting you something whether you want me to or not, so you might as well tell me."

"Let me think about it," he replied, taking a sip of his drink.

"Well you better think fast. I'm a planner. I like to get things done early."

He set his glass down. "Good thing I have a few years."

I raised my eyebrows. "Your birthday is in less than two weeks," I reminded him.

"Not really. The last time I checked, I won't be twenty until 2036."

I leaned toward him. "You're joking."

He just looked at me with no change in his expression. "You're *no*t joking," I said, leaning back in my seat. He shrugged his shoulders innocently. "So you don't even want to pretend?" I asked.

"How would you feel if someone wanted to celebrate your birthday in March?"

"Okay, so you have a point, but you still have to make everyone else *think* you are having a birthday, and that means I can think it, too, right?"

Instead of answering, he scooted his chair back and put his hand out for me to take. "What?" I asked.

"I would like to dance with you," he said politely.

I thought about pressing him on the matter at hand, and then I realized it would be stupid to ruin the mood. Instead, I took his hand as we went to the dance floor. Although I was confident in my rhythm, my new shoes were hurting a little, so I was a bit apprehensive at first. Lucky for me, they were slow songs, and I had forgotten my scrunched up toes by the time he took me in his arms. Song after song went by, and I didn't think about my feet one time.

At 11:45, he led me outside and we sat on a bench where other couples were gathered. It was a cold evening, and I was worried about him keeping warm, but he insisted he was fine.

"I really would feel better if we went inside," I said.

"Sophie, I'm fine. We won't be out here much longer."

I tried to find other excuses to lure him in. "What about the ball dropping? How will we see it out here?"

"In case you didn't notice, we're on a boat. Not in New York," he said, teasing me.

"I know, but I meant, how will we know when it's time to kiss?"

"I didn't know we needed a *time* to kiss."

"Would you stop it? You know what I'm trying to say," I countered.

"Trust me, Sophie, you will know when it's time to kiss." It was clear to me that he was not going, so I sat there half-sulking and half-content. I sulked because I was worried about him keeping warm, and I was content because the view was beautiful. The water was pitch black, and I could see the reflection of the city lights across it. It was peaceful.

Within a few moments, my mouth dropped open when the entire bay was lit by an array of blue, red, and green hues shooting into the sky. Suddenly, I knew what he meant about us knowing when it was time.

As soon as the sound of the fireworks followed the initial lights, I turned to him and smiled. His eyes were welcoming, and his smile was utterly and completely captivating. I kissed him without thinking of anything else, other than the joy that was flowing as we rang in the New Year. The night couldn't have gotten any better. At least not until we got back to his house.

The ride home couldn't have gone fast enough. I was both nervous and excited about spending the evening with him. I made sure I'd packed my cutest pajamas. I wanted to feel like myself, so I didn't buy anything out of the ordinary. I just picked out a newer pair of cotton pants and a T-shirt.

Our arrival was a little awkward. Both of us were unsure how to handle the situation. By this time we were very comfortable with each other, but all of our experiences spending time together, through the night, had been in my room. This was different. This was his house, and his room. To help with the transition into the new surroundings, I settled on a familiar room to start.

"Mind if I change in the study?" I asked.

"No, of course not." He seemed a little bit more at ease at the idea of that as well.

I ended up changing in there while he went to his room. I quickly changed and pulled my hair back into a ponytail, then I went to wait for him downstairs. He followed shortly after wearing black sweatpants and a gray long-john shirt that clung to the curves of his muscles. Suddenly, my T-shirt selection felt inadequate because I was sure it didn't show off my assets like that.

"Are you tired?" he asked, as he entered the living room.

"No," I answered, without having to think about it.

He picked up the remote control and put on the remnants of televised New Year's celebrations. It felt like a first date, because there was obvious nervousness between us. I think both of us knew this evening would be cardinal in our relationship. The largest matter at hand was that I loved him and wanted him to be *the one* that night.

Instinctively, I rested my head on his shoulder, and he wrapped his arm around me. "Thank you for taking me to dinner. It was great," I said, softly.

He gave me a squeeze. "Thank *you* for coming."

We watched the television for a few more moments until I broke the silence.

"Can I ask you something?"

"You can ask me anything."

"Will you kiss me?"

He looked perplexed. "You don't have to *ask* me, Sophie."

"No, I mean. Will you really kiss me?" I could see the inference register in his mind. He knew what I wanted, and he put his palm to the side of my face and pressed his lips to mine. I closed my eyes and absorbed the heat coming over me. My body was on fire for him. I felt it from my toes all the way to the top of my head. I wanted to *be* one with him. So much that when I was absolutely sure every cell in my body wanted to move forward, I pressed my lips fully to his and pulled him toward me. His hand moved through my hair as he shifted his weight onto me.

He moved his lips down my neck in response and kissed me from one side to the other in a way that sent even more fire through my body. I turned my face to find his lips again. After a few moments, I moved my hands beneath his shirt and molded my hands against his cool back.

He gripped the back of my neck in response, only to release it as I pulled his shirt over his head. The firmness and coolness of his chest against the heat that was permeating through me, was about to send me into a frenzy.

"Are you sure you want to do this?" he whispered in my ear.

I nodded without hesitation. "Yes."

He returned his lips to mine and started moving down my neck again. After a few seconds, he let out a low, frustrated grumble and slid himself lower to rest his head on my chest. He squeezed me tighter, as if to signal that he didn't want to let me go, but I could see torment and frustration in his face. His eyes were closed tightly, and his jaw was clenched. It was completely unexpected. I lifted my head in reaction.

"Are you okay?"

"I'm fine."

"No you're not. What's wrong? What did I do?"

He still wouldn't open his eyes, and he continued to press his ear to my chest.

"Nothing," he uttered. "You didn't do anything. I'm fine. Just give me a minute."

I rested my head back on my pillow trying to run through the last moments and nothing seemed wrong to me. I didn't understand the disruption, unless it had to do with me.

"I'm sorry," I said. "If you don't want to..."

"Sophie . . ." He was burying his face into my shirt. "I don't know how to stay focused. I can't."

"Oh, you mean you *can't*, actually do that?" I looked down to read his expression.

"Yes, I can. I think anyway." He shook his head, dismissing my assessment. "But that's not the problem."

"Then what is it, Wes? You're killing me with suspense."

He sat up. "I have to concentrate really hard to keep my mind on pace with real time."

"Okay," I murmured, not quite understanding.

"When I'm close to you like that, it is virtually impossible for me to keep focused."

"So what are you saying?" I needed him to spell it out for me.

"An hour together with you could feel like a second to me if I'm not careful."

"Careful?"

"If I let myself lose concentration on time, which is exactly what happens when I'm that close to you, then I would virtually lose hours of time with you."

"Don't you think it would be worth it?" I asked. "You might lose one thing, but you gain another."

He pondered what I was offering for a few moments, then smiled and touched his cool hand to my still heated flesh. "Being close to you feels better than you can imagine."

"Then what's the problem?"

"I would rather be just like this with you for hours than the other way for minutes."

"So, it bothers you to be close to me?"

He shook his head. "No. Actually, when I'm around you, I'm the calmest. It's easiest to concentrate when I'm with you, until you get me like this." He smiled.

"So, does that mean we could never?" I asked.

"I don't know. But, I won't sacrifice my clarity for it. I don't want to miss a single moment of the time I have with you." He pulled me close to him and gave me a gentle kiss on the forehead. I had to take in a deep breath just to absorb it all.

"Well, I guess we have plenty of time to work on your clarity," I said, still hopeful. He didn't seem to find as much optimism in that idea as I did. He didn't reply.

"Speaking of time," I added, breaking the silence, "what will happen to us as time does go by and I get *older*?"

I could feel his chest and arm muscles contract around me with unease.

"I don't know," he answered.

I'm not sure if I was too tired to think about the unsure future or too afraid to let myself, but neither of us elected to consider the question further. Instead, silence took over until I nodded off to sleep.

He must have carried me upstairs, because the next thing I remembered was waking up to the splendid sunrise through his bedroom window. The question from the night before still lingered in the back of my mind, but it was only a fraction of my thoughts in comparison to the other memories of the night.

Chapter 12
THE TURNING POINT

That weekend, he was out of town for a racing event, so I didn't see him for a few days. It ended up working out well for me, because I had midterms to study for and it gave me time for that.

It also gave me time to work on a paper for English. Normally, I would've dreaded it, but this time, I was looking forward to it. It's not that I minded writing. I loved it. What I found difficult was getting out what I wanted to say without sounding too opinionated. Teachers always say they want students to express themselves and write about what they want, but when we do, it's like playing the lottery. You never know what the teacher is going to say. They may love it, or they may say it's all wrong, so I had always handed in my papers with apprehension. But the online school was different.

I appreciated the whole cyber student-teacher relationship. I didn't have to see my teacher's face when I turned something in, or better yet, I didn't have to see the reaction when it was passed back. This way, I sent it through the Internet without ever having to gauge the reception. It was great, and so with this paper, I was eager to get going. I was really planning to go over the top with this one.

Our topic was a motif in Othello. We had to identify a recurrent theme or element found in the play and write about it using supporting evidence. *Excellent*, I thought. I decided to write about blindness. Sure, it's argued that military valor, naivety, and jealousy are all portrayed, but I couldn't help but think about how Othello's blindness to what was real caused him to see what was not.

I wasn't sure where to begin, so I spun around in my computer chair and reached for my copy of *Othello*, which was on the end of my bed. I thought about how easily Othello loses faith in those he trusted based on stories and fabrications. I was flipping through the pages to find a good quote when I heard the taps at my door. It scared me at first, because I wasn't expecting Wes, but I relaxed when I saw him. I turned off the light at my desk, as if I was afraid someone was watching us from the darkness, and then I opened the door.

"Hey, what are you doing here?" I asked happily.

"I just wanted to talk to you." He eyed my blank computer screen. "Oh, were you trying to get some work done?"

"Yes, but I don't want to do it now. I'll do it tomorrow. It'll be easy." I was distracted by his presence. Realizing how much I had missed him, I reached up on my toes to give him a kiss, and he leaned down just enough to meet my lips in the darkness.

"What is it?" he asked, reaching for the book.

"Othello paper," I answered, plopping down on my bed. "I'm going to write about how stupid he was. I mean not stupid, per se, just…blind."

"Othello wasn't blind," he said, sitting at the foot of my bed, flipping through the pages. "I think he saw everything so clearly from the beginning."

"You think he saw that he was going to kill Desdemona?"

"No, I don't think he saw *that*. I think he just knew true happiness was unattainable to him from the beginning. He subconsciously believed their love was too good to be true."

"That's interesting, but I think it means exactly what I said. He was blind. It *was* attainable."

"You've always been so hopeful about life."

"Well then," I said, moving over to him. "Since you know so much, I guess you know how much I missed you." I climbed up on my knees and leaned over his back with my arms around his waist.

He gently cupped one of my forearms in his hands. "Well that's what I came to talk to you about."

"Okay, talk." I leaned my head down so it was resting on the back of his neck. He smelled so good. I nestled my cheek further into the comfort of his cotton, hooded sweatshirt.

"Sophie," he said, softly, while tilting his head toward me until his temple was touching my forehead. "You have no idea how happy I was to see you that day we met."

"Really? I couldn't tell. You looked like you'd seen a ghost." I giggled.

He turned away, and I squeezed him tighter, so my forehead was touching the back of his neck, just to let him know I preferred less distance.

"Sophie, I was living in the darkest abyss possible until you came back into my life."

I nestled closer to him. He turned his head back toward me, which suited me just fine. Then, he softly said, "Which is why I don't think this is such a good idea."

I wasn't sure I'd heard him, so I lifted my head and was about to ask him to repeat what he'd said when he continued.

"You are so young, Sophie. I have a lot of experience here, and I admit that you make me happy, but I don't think it's enough."

"What does that mean?"

"It means that I know where this is going, and it's not good, so I want to do us both a favor and spare us any more pain before we get too close."

"I have no idea what you're talking about." I shook my head in disbelief. "What are you saying?" It was all so sudden.

He stood up and took two steps toward the door. Without turning around, he quietly murmured, "I can't do this with you. I just can't."

Hopping up, I lurched forward and moved in front of him. "What do you mean, you can't do this? You're confusing me."

He remained just a few inches from me, but he looked away. "I'm sorry. I don't mean to confuse you. I just can't go through this again."

I was losing my patience with him. I felt my chest tighten. One minute, everything felt so right, so perfect. And now, I'm not exactly sure what was going on, but it felt very wrong. "Stop it," I snapped. "Again? What do you mean by again? We've never been through anything like this. Please just tell me what's going on."

I was almost embarrassed. I'd never begged anyone for anything before. I'd always gone out of my way to distance myself from someone, and yet there I was clinging to every word he said. I took a deep breath and let out a sigh. We stood there in the darkness of my room facing each other, although I was the only one trying to make eye contact.

I studied the perfect angles of his face, which were illuminated by the glow of my computer. I examined the crease between his eyebrows and wondered why he looked so troubled. More like pained. It made no sense. I reached for his face, and in the same motion, he leaned away from me.

Rejection and anger were building in me. Before I had a chance to get one word out, he cleared his throat and said, "I'm sorry, Sophie, I just can't be with you anymore. Not now. Not ever." Then, he turned and looked at me, as if trying to see if I understood.

I shook my head, and then he whispered, "I'm sorry. I really am."

"Wait!" I gasped, and just like that he was gone. I lurched to the door and cried out, "Wait!" Only this time, it was raspy and barely audible. Not that it mattered because there was nothing out there. No one to hear me anyway. He was gone, and only the darkness remained; yet I couldn't bring myself to turn back into my room. I stood there trying to understand, trying to make sense of this. I had no idea what had happened.

My eyes searched the darkness while my mind frantically ran through the last twenty minutes in my head. I tried to pinpoint exactly what had gone wrong.

Thinking back twenty minutes wasn't far enough. Once I thought about it, I knew right away. The look on his face when he arrived had been distant. I *had* noticed something was off, only I'd ignored it.

With that last thought, the realization of what just happened gathered together in a lump in my throat. I had not imagined this. It was real. He was gone. Whatever happened, whatever the change in him, it happened prior to these last moments with him sitting in my room. He had come over specifically to break things off. I blinked, and with that last revelation, the first tear spilled over.

When I woke up the next morning, my eyes stung in the sunlight. I must have literally cried every last tear I had, because my eyes felt dry and sore. I rolled back over and covered my head with the pillow in an effort to drown out each thought. The memories of the night before wouldn't go away. I remembered the butterflies I'd had in my stomach as I leaned against his back. I felt the warm sensation when my arms wrapped around his waist. And then I felt the gravitational pull that yanked my heart out of the door into the darkness. I had nothing left, and all I could do was curl up into a little ball with the pillow still over my head. I didn't cry. I'm not sure if I was out of tears, or if crying and cringing in anger didn't mix.

I had no idea where any of this had come from. We had been going out for almost five months. I saw him just about every day. He had opened my eyes to things I hadn't known existed. There was nothing else in this world like him. He was magnificent. He was caring. He was nothing I would ever find again. And that did it. The cringing turned to crying again.

I think I cried for about an hour more and slept for another two hours, because it was lunchtime by the time I woke, and I hadn't eaten anything. My stomach was growling. I blinked away the sunlight again and was greeted by more stinging in my eyes. I sat up in my bed and waited for the blood to catch up to my head. Once I felt I was capable of holding my head up, I walked myself to the bathroom to brush my teeth. It wasn't a pretty sight.

My hair was all over the place. Part of the top was laying to the left, part of the top was laying to the right, and the back was sticking out. What was most shocking was that my eyes were bloodshot, with red circles under each of them. Seeing myself in such a state made me angry. I brushed my teeth without looking in the mirror again, and when I finished, I wiped my mouth on my towel and headed downstairs to get something to eat.

I grabbed a bowl, the milk, a spoon, and the box of cereal in one trip and plopped down at the table and began eating. *Oh crap*, I thought. *It's Monday, and Mom is off today.* If I had been coherent enough to have remembered that, I would've stayed in my room starving, but it was too late; she came around the corner as soon as the thought crossed my mind.

"Hey honey," she said, entering the kitchen.

"Hey." I had a mouthful of cereal, and I kept my head down, hoping she'd pick up on the idea that I was too busy eating to talk.

"You look terrible," she said.

"Thanks."

"No, I mean it. Look at me."

I decided I had eaten enough breakfast, so I tilted my head down, grabbed my bowl, and began making my way to the sink. "No, I am fine."

"Sophie, I know you well enough to know you are not fine. I am your mother, you know. You can at least tell me what is bothering you. I won't pry."

"You're prying now," I pointed out, as I put away the milk.

"Just tell me what happened."

"Fine. Wes broke up with me last night. Okay?"

"Oh," she said, nodding her head in understanding. "Do you want to talk about it?"

"No," I answered, making a quick exit from the kitchen.

"His loss," she called out.

Although I didn't reply to her, I liked the sound of it. He *did* say that I was the one who brought him out of the abyss. I mean, he was the one living the miserable, empty life all alone, feeling like a freak, and being bored out of his mind. My mother was exactly right. It was his loss. At least that was what I told myself.

When I reached my room, I saw the copy of *Othello* on my desk, and it reminded me that I had a paper due at midnight. I sat down at my computer to log onto my class so I could confirm how many pages the paper needed to be. When I logged on, I could see that almost the whole class was online, too. We were probably all working on this thing, procrastinating together.

I clicked on the assignment link and saw that it had to be three to five pages. That was nothing. I could easily write five pages on being stupid. This paper was going to be especially easy and bitter after what had happened last night.

I pulled up an empty Word document and sat there staring at my screen, a crease developing in my forehead. After a few minutes of thinking, I began typing my title: "*Othello: Too Blind to See What Could Have Been.*" It was one of the best papers I had ever written, and although I got an A, it was little compensation for how I felt.

By Wednesday night, I hadn't heard from Wes at all, and I couldn't stand the distance between us. I called him, but I was only greeted by his voice mail. After several calls and unanswered messages, it became clear to me that he'd meant what he'd said. There was no mistake that he'd take back the next day. I felt completely hurt, frustrated, and angry all at the same time.

I didn't understand how everything could be fine one day and then the next, my whole world could be turned upside down. I tried to convince myself that he was an evil person, but that didn't fly. He wasn't evil. I almost wished he had been incredibly mean and awful to me, then it would've made it that much easier for me to get over him. But, he wasn't mean at all. He had managed to break my heart as nicely as possible. I even remembered the pain in his eyes when he'd said it, and he did sound sorry about breaking it off, so it still didn't make sense. *Then why?* I kept asking myself. What was it that had him backpedaling?

I found myself just as confused, then, as I had been the day I'd first met him. Everything was a mystery when it came to him, and that both bothered me and motivated me to try one more time to reach out to him. I was tired of leaving messages and not getting a response, so I tried sending an email hoping he would give me something. If he didn't want to talk to me, he could perhaps reply in writing. I opened my email and began my message:

Wes,

I'm not sure what I did, but I'm sorry.
I truly am. You're making it clear that

you don't want to talk to me, but I refuse to believe this is how we end. Please give me some answers. Please give me *something*. I miss you.

Love,
Sophie

By Thursday, there was still no response from him, and I was falling into a minor state of depression. I lay around on my bed practically doing nothing all day, every day. I was a zombie. I did my schoolwork, and as soon as I was done, I went to bed. I was miserable. I lost track of how many times I cried in my room, but I did a pretty good job of not letting my mother know how bad it was. She left me to my privacy. I suspect she knew I was not myself, but when I was around her, I did a decent job of carrying on her theme that it was his loss. I pulled myself together long enough to go downstairs for food and to have enough conversation with her that she didn't need to feel worried. Maintaining that was going to be difficult while I was on campus, but I had to try.

Driving to lunch that week, I was fine. I knew he wouldn't be there before my lunch, so I could concentrate on having a somewhat relaxing lunch. It was the leaving that I was worried about.

I had almost gotten used to the idea of not seeing him, so I was afraid a fresh image in my brain would make me ache more. However, on the other hand, I worried about not seeing him, because it would mean he was purposely avoiding me. I largely considered what would be the worse of the two, but never anticipated the true ache I was about to feel.

After lunch with my mom, I headed back toward my car. It was rather chilly that afternoon, so I put my hands in my pockets as I walked. It helped calm the nerves, but it didn't help with the pounding in my chest as I neared the wooded path that took me straight to the parking lot. My heart was beating so hard, I thought it would jump out of my chest. I tried to regulate it by pacing my breathing, and that was when I saw him.

He was about fifty yards down the path, but I knew it was him right away. He had on his large, wool zip-up gray coat and his navy hat pulled over his ears. No one else would've been dressed that warmly in fifty-degree weather. It was definitely him. I started to perk up a little as I realized he wasn't going out of his way to ignore me.

Just as I was about to veer toward his side of the path to cut him off, he began smiling and laughing. It took just a few seconds after that for it to register in my brain that he was walking with someone. My eyes diverted to a petite blonde walking beside him. When he laughed, she laughed. At one point, she seemed so tickled with him that she leaned in toward his body and patted his chest with her hand.

I was furious. I had only a minute or so before we would pass each other on the path. Several things shot through my mind. One of them being to pull out every last strand of the girl's long hair, and the other was to shove both of them off the path. I couldn't believe it. It was so unbelievably tacky and hurtful. I knew if I said anything at all, it would only come out in a bunch of gibberish, because I was so dumbstruck and hurt at the same time. I feared my words would betray me in the form of rambling nonsense, so I tightened my lips. I couldn't bear anymore embarrassment. As they drew closer, I looked toward the ground. I turned my head down and away so neither one could see my face. She was still giggling as they walked by. After they passed, I managed to mumble the word, "Thanks." And I knew he could hear me.

It took everything I had not to break into a sob when I got into my Jeep. I found myself wanting to ram into another innocent car, but I decided against it. I went to the overlook instead. Thankfully, no one else was there. I stayed in my car, leaned over my steering wheel, and cried. I felt like a complete idiot. I was both sad and angry with myself for believing in him. I'd convinced myself that he was interested in me. I had fallen for him, without a doubt, and I was stupid to believe it was reciprocated. Kerry was right. She always tried to be so supportive, but I could tell in her tone that she didn't even believe it was possible for him to be that perfect. We were just high school girls, and he was a college boy, magnificent, a wonder. I was foolish to think that a girl like me could hold him.

It took me about twenty minutes to pull myself together. I promised myself, as I looked out over the hills that day, that he would not be the cause of any more sad or angry tears of mine. If that was what he wanted to do, then I wasn't going to stop him. I wasn't going to be *that girl* and let a guy ruin me.

I revamped my thinking that afternoon. I missed him, and I wasn't going to lie to myself and say I didn't, but I wasn't going to let the idea of him control my life anymore. I had no choice but to pick myself up and move on. I had been fine before I met him, and I was convinced I would be fine afterward. I had to be.

I worked really hard that afternoon at the bookstore. I asked Dawn to switch the stacking for the register. I wanted to be doing something hands-on that required me to concentrate on more than just waiting to ring someone up. I managed to stack two whole carts of books before Dawn walked back and asked me what pills I was on.

"Nothing," I told her, laughing. "Just trying to keep busy."

"Let me guess. Something with Wes?"

"Whatever would give you that idea?" I replied, still stacking.

"Well, he's driven by here about three times."

"He did what?" I asked, turning to look at her.

"Yeah, I think he was looking for you at the register."

"Are you sure?" I asked back, quickly heading toward the front with the cart.

She was following me now. "Yeah, but that was about a half-hour ago. What's going on?"

"Well, if you really want to know, he broke up with me on Sunday, and today I saw him with another girl. Interesting, huh?" I'm not sure she was expecting that much drama.

"Are you serious?" she said, tightening her lips.

"Very."

"Then why the drive-by?" She seemed to be talking to herself out loud, so I didn't reply. "He has a lot of nerve," she said.

You're right about that, I thought, as I headed to the counter to grab another set of books.

"He probably feels bad," she added.

"As he should," I said, between pounding stacks of books on my cart. I was not one to feel sorry for myself, so if he was checking to see whether I'd killed myself, he was wasting his time. "I don't really care," I said, wheeling the cart back to an aisle. It gave me no comfort whatsoever that he had driven by. He could've driven in circles a hundred times and it wouldn't have made up for the hurt I felt.

I finished putting all the books on the shelves and was sitting behind the counter with Dawn. We were both bored, so I started thinking about something to do. I really didn't want to go home and be alone. Dawn and I got along well at the store, but we'd never really hung out beyond that. I was always with Wes, and it never really came up, but now, I thought it might be a good time to start.

"Hey, Dawn, what are you doing later?" I asked.

"Nothing, why?"

"Do you want to do something? Like maybe a movie?"

She smiled and leaned her elbows on the counter. "Oh, I see, you need to get your mind off of Wes."

"Is it that obvious?"

"Yes, but I don't mind. We can go out. It'll be fun. Who needs him?" She said, smiling.

Chapter 13
GRAVITY

I hadn't been out with a friend in a long time, and I was glad to be doing it again. I threw on a pair of jeans and a sweatshirt and pulled my hair up in a loose ponytail before heading out the door for a girls' night. When I arrived at her house, she was already coming out to greet me.

"Hey, I have an idea," she said, as soon as she got in.

"Shoot," I replied, giving her my full attention.

"Let's go to a party instead."

"What party?" I was ready to go out, but I didn't have a party in mind. I wasn't so sure about that. I really just wanted to go to a good old-fashioned movie with a lot of popcorn and chocolate.

"Some friends I know are having one. It'll be fun for you to get out. Come on. We can do a movie anytime."

I didn't want to go to a party at all, but at that point, I would've been open to trying anything. I just wanted to keep from thinking about Wes.

The party was at a huge house on the hillside. There was an outdoor pool in which kids were actually swimming. I didn't know anyone, but Dawn took me by the hand and introduced me to a few girls she knew. I didn't remember their names, but I tried to be polite. There were several people lounging around the pool area, and there were more inside dancing. None of them looked younger than eighteen.

"How do you know these people?" I asked over the music.

"Oh, they're Danny's friends. This is his friend Jared's house." They were not people she knew from school. They were older kids. I felt so out of place. Danny was twenty-one. I looked around some more and noticed guys and girls drinking, and it was very uncomfortable.

"Are these all college kids?"

She laughed. "If you call taking one class and living with your parents a college kid, then yeah." She rolled her eyes. "Stay here. I'll be right back." She disappeared through the crowd too fast for me to object. Perfect. Here I was standing in the middle of a room with a bunch of people I didn't know. It felt like the first day of school all over again. Everything I hated. It was awful.

I decided I needed some air, so I went out to the patio. Most people were having fun and nobody really paid attention to me, which was good. I watched some guys jump in the pool. It must have been heated, because they were shiver-free and having a great time.

There were also several girls giggling around the edge, sitting with their legs in the water. I watched as two boys swam over and pulled them in, fully clothed. They each let out an ear-piercing scream, and it made me laugh a little.

Dawn found me, bringing us two cups full of punch, and we sat down on a stone ledge. I took one whiff of the cup and knew it wasn't just punch, so I passed. I set the cup beside me on the ledge and listened as Dawn pointed out more faces to me.

"See those two?" She was pointing to a girl who looked about our age, and an older-looking guy wearing a mint green polo shirt with the collar flipped up. "They're supposed to be dating, but he calls me all the time. Scum bag. And that guy." She pointed to a different guy who had messy chestnut hair and a scruffy face. "His name is Quinn. He's twenty. I have his number in my pocket. I'm so not going to call him. He's so lame. They all are," she added confidently.

"Then why are we here?"

"Because I'm waiting to see Jackson. He's Jared's younger brother. He may not be here though. He doesn't really hang with his brother's crew."

"Why didn't you just call him to see if he was going to be here before we came all the way out here?"

"Because I'm too much of a frickin' coward to do that. I'll use you as my excuse. I'll tell him Danny invited you." She smiled and continued. "Besides, I'll take my chances. If he doesn't show up soon, we'll leave."

That sounded just fine to me. I was already eager to leave.

Just as I was about to stand and try to find something regular to drink, the one identified as Quinn came over to Dawn and offered her another cup of punch. She looked down at the one she was sipping on and it was just about empty, so she said, "Sure, why not?"

"I'll be right back, Dawn. I want to see if they have water or something."

Quinn took no time sitting in my spot, and I looked back to see Dawn scooting away from him. I figured I should hurry so I could come back and spare her from Mr. Scruff.

I went into the house in search of a drink, but the only thing I found was a big bowl of the same bitter punch everyone else was drinking. I was about to give up when a friendly voice interrupted my retreat.

"Can I help you find something?" he asked.

"Danny!" I said, all too happy to see him. Finally, there was someone I knew. "I was just looking for a water or something."

"Come on, I'll find you one in the kitchen." I followed him as he maneuvered his way through the crowded room, constantly looking back to make sure I was right with him. He was naturally good looking, like Dawn, but he was always dressed a little too grungy. Tonight he looked nice. It was the first time I'd seen him away from the store. I was so used to him wearing the same pair of jeans and flannel shirt all week that his choice of a white T-shirt took me by surprise. It screamed clean. "What are you doing here?" he asked, looking back.

"Dawn brought me. She wanted to stop by."

"Oh great. Tell her she'd better get home before I find her myself and tell her. She's too young to be here."

"Yeah sure," I said, as we entered the kitchen. I guess it was embarrassing for your little sister to show up at your friend's party, and she was only seventeen, but she seemed to know a lot of people there. I thanked him for the water and maneuvered my way back toward the patio.

My path was intercepted by a tall, sandy-haired guy. He wasn't bad looking, but he was not at all my type, if I even had a type.

"Hey, I'm Chase," he said, leaning in to be sure I heard him over the noise.

I had to tilt my head back to keep his breath off of my ear. "You have pretty eyes," he said.

I wouldn't have been interested anyway, but his lack of creativity really disappointed me. "Thanks," I replied, stepping aside.

He was back in my path. "Can I get you something to drink?"

"No thanks. My friend is waiting," I said, trying to be polite. He put his arm up on the door hinge to block my way. I looked up and noticed his sleeve pulled back. There were several needle marks in his arm. His eyes were also wet looking, almost resembling the shine in Wes' but blue and not nearly as pretty. In fact, his looked like he was on something, and by the look of his arm, I was willing to bet he was. *Thanks, but no thanks,* I thought.

"Are you sure?" he asked.

"Yes. I am sure," I said, shoving my way through to the patio.

I headed back over to the stone ledge in time to see Dawn walking away with the Quinn guy. He had his arm around her, and I thought that was strange. She hadn't sounded too interested in him before, but I didn't want to be a third wheel, so I sat back down on the ledge sipping my water.

I was a little irritated sitting there by myself. I scowled after her in the darkness, and I noticed her tripping over her own feet as she walked. Quinn had his arm firmly around her waist, holding her up. That was odd. She was practically falling over, which made me think she wasn't coherent enough to make the decision to go off into the woods with a stranger. I followed after them. The path led along the street and up into a little grassy wooded area.

I stepped onto the trail they had taken and saw her lying on the ground completely out of it. Her eyes were rolled into the back of her head, and he was bending over her copping a feel.

"Hey! What are you doing to her? Leave her alone," I shouted, moving in.

He stumbled to his feet clumsily and grabbed me by my sweatshirt. "Mind your business, little girl," he said, slurring his words. I was pushing to get past him, but he was too heavy, and he shoved me backward instead. I lost my balance, and my heels rocked backward. I was falling until I hit a rock-hard figure behind me. I was grabbed under my armpits, and I started to shout, but a hand was clamped over my mouth. I started kicking. Arms quickly turned me around, and I saw that it was Wes.

He looked at me, staring into my eyes, and then he set me aside. I watched as he grabbed the Quinn person by his collar and asked if he liked picking on girls. Quinn's slurred reply was barely understandable. From what I could make of it, he said, "Hey man, I'm trying, just hangin' out; this chick was into me. That's all."

"I don't think so," Wes said, as he gave him a gigantic shove back toward the street. Quinn lost his balance and fell over. He stumbled back to his feet and clumsily turned around and walked toward the party in a zigzag fashion. I was momentarily relieved. Then, Wes turned around and zeroed in on me.

"You need to go home," he ordered, leaning to within a few inches of my face. He grabbed my elbow and began to steer me toward the street as well. "This is no place for you." He was pulling me, and I had to yank my arm free to stop moving.

"I'm not leaving without her," I shouted. I didn't want to stay anyway, but I wasn't about to leave Dawn lying in a dark, grassy area by herself.

"She'll be fine. She needs some time," he said.

I didn't care what she needed. I was not leaving her.

He looked at her lying on the ground.

"I'm *not* leaving her alone," I said. My eyes narrowed. His shoulders dropped as he realized I had a very valid point. He went over to her and scooped her up effortlessly. Then he turned around and motioned toward the street, waiting for me to go. I walked out first, and when we reached the sidewalk, I headed away from the house and toward my car.

A guy was walking from that direction, and he looked at Dawn with a scrutinizing glare. "Is that Dawn?" he asked. He looked a little younger than most of the other guys there, so I figured it must have been Jackson.

"I think someone put something in her punch. I'm taking her home," I said, hoping to calm his suspicions. He looked annoyed at the idea of someone doing that to her.

"I can take her," he offered. Wes was not slowing his walk in the least.

I interjected. "No, it's okay, I'll take her. Her parents think she's with me." It seemed to be enough, and he nodded and left us alone.

We reached my car, and Wes placed her in the passenger seat and buckled her up. She was out of it. When he closed the door, I asked him what he was doing there, but he just walked off across the street without answering or even looking at me. The rudeness was extremely unsettling. I walked around to my side and slammed my door as

I got in. I started the engine, threw it in gear, and bolted as fast as I could down the street.

My night out to the movies had turned into a bizarre evening from hell. I had Dawn in my passenger seat, half-asleep and incoherent, and I didn't know what I was going to do with her. To make matters worse, Wes had showed up, treating me like some child. I was angry.

When we reached the road beyond the neighborhood, I noticed headlights right on my tail. It was him. He was following way too close, and I thought about slamming on my brakes for a moment to send him a message. It turned out I didn't have to. As soon as the road straightened out from a long bend, the little black sports car passed me on a double line with ease and then disappeared around the next bend. I let out a big sigh and shook my head.

It was about 10:00 by then, and I couldn't take her home in that state. She was starting to come around some, so I decided to stop and grab some ice cream to make me feel better as I passed the time. I ordered a double scoop of cookies 'n cream with chocolate syrup and ate it in my car while I waited for her to recover. I concentrated really hard, with each bite, trying to remove the image of Wes from my mind. It wasn't working.

"What the hell?" Dawn said, sounding groggy, when I was down to my last few bites.

"You're asking me?" I said, still eating.

"Where are we? How did I get here?"

"I think someone put something in your punch. You passed out."

"Jerk," she said.

"Tell me about it."

"What happened?" she asked, rubbing her temples.

"Well, that Quinn guy tried to molest you in the woods and then Wes came out of nowhere and stopped him. He put you in my car."

"Wes? I don't remember a thing."

"And I think your Jackson guy saw you. He offered to take you home when he saw Wes carrying you, but Wes wouldn't let him. I don't think he trusted him. I can't say I blame him with the state you were in."

She sank lower into the seat and covered her face. "I'm so embarrassed. I want to die."

"No you don't. You'll be fine," I assured her. "Just don't drink the Kool-Aid anymore."

"Oh my gosh. This is the most embarrassing moment of my life."

"You'll be okay."

"Sophie, I don't know what I would've done if you weren't there. Thanks."

"Don't thank me. Thank Wes. I was no match for that guy."

"What was he doing there?" she asked.

"Don't know. He wouldn't say. Maybe he was attending the party."

"Doubt it," she said. "Most of those guys are losers."

I took her home around midnight, and she seemed okay. She said she had a little headache, but nothing that would alarm her parents. I wanted to drive around some more to wind down, but I decided against it. My eyes were getting heavy.

I attempted to run through the whole evening in my head when I got home. I tried to start from the beginning of the party, but I kept seeing Wes' face. Frustrated, I went to bed. I was both physically and mentally tired.

I went to work the next day as usual. For the first part of my day, it was just me and Mr. Healey. It was very awkward. I couldn't go stack books because that would've left the register unmanned. I was stuck behind the counter, just hoping that he wouldn't ask me what movie Dawn and I had seen the night before. I was never very good at lying, so I thought if I directed the conversation, then maybe he wouldn't go there.

"Mr. Healey, do we have any books on reptiles?"

"Uh, yeah, I believe we have a few in aisle two," he said, not looking away from his cataloging. I still felt guilty.

"Do you mind if I go grab one? I'd like to do some research."

"No, not at all."

I walked back to the aisle and started looking through the selections. I ran my finger over several titles on dinosaurs, birds, tigers, and whales before I came across a book titled, *Understanding the Cold-Blooded Creature*. I thought that would be appropriate. I had an idea that I was going about things the wrong way. I was trying to figure out why he was doing things, but I was thinking in terms of human behavior. He wasn't totally human.

I took it back to the counter and started reading through it. Mainly, I was looking for temperament, mental capacity, and anything that would explain the phenom's behavior. I read through some passages about the need to regulate body temperature, but I already knew that. Something else that stood out was a paragraph about how their nerves and muscle tissues function better in warmer temperatures. That could've explained his mood swings. Maybe it was the cold weather that had him acting all weird and moody. I kept reading. I came to a chapter titled, "Reptile Behavior." It talked about motivation. I was very curious to learn what makes a cold-blood tick. The chapter described the difference between the warm-blooded and cold-blooded needs. It said that humans do things because they have a natural motivation to do so. It said we eat because we're hungry; we sleep because we're tired; and we exercise to remain healthy.

Reptiles, on the other hand, operate on a more basic level. It said that their main motivation in life is to survive day to day. It said their very basic needs were food and shelter, but they really don't need things beyond that, like companionship. It said to understand them, one must realize that the only way to provide for their needs is to keep it as happy and unstressed as possible. It also said they do not like feeling pressured or cornered.

I knew Wes had cold-blood in him, and his life was dominated by it, so I had to believe these could be true about him also. His number one motivation, naturally, was to live day to day. His basic need was survival, and he didn't need companionship. I was different. I needed food and shelter to survive as well, but mentally my main motivation was happiness. His wasn't. I needed him, and I had let him see that. According to the book, he didn't like to feel cornered, and that was exactly what I must have been doing.

I wasn't sure if that was accurate, but it did provide me with a momentary explanation. I closed the book and returned it to the shelf. It really didn't make me miss him any less, but it did answer some of my questions, and had I not just seen him with a cute blonde, I might have tried to figure him out some more.

I heard Dawn's voice at the front as I walked back to the counter. I was glad she'd made it in. She looked like hell, but I wasn't about to tell her that. She said she'd woken up with a horrible headache. She asked me to stack for her, so she could rest at the counter, and I was glad to oblige. I rolled the full cart toward the aisles and started putting the books in the appropriate sections. When I had the time, I even tried to alphabetize them so the customers could find certain titles easier. Mr. Healey didn't really like that, because he said the customers would start asking for the whole store to be like that. But I did it on occasion anyway.

About halfway through my first cart, Dawn came back pretending to be looking for a book.

"I feel like crap," she whispered.

"Man, I'm sorry to hear that," I offered.

"I want to wring that guy's neck," she said, leaning close.

"Well, you have his name and number."

"I already tried that. It was a bogus number, and Jackson said he hadn't ever heard of a Quinn."

"Yikes. That's scary." It really was—to think something like that could happen so quickly. I shook off the thought. "Did you say Jackson? You talked to him?"

Her demeanor lightened up a bit. "Yes. He called me last night to see how I was doing. He said he would've taken me home himself, but some tall guy wouldn't let him."

We both laughed.

"Did you talk to Wes yet?"

I looked at her as if she had two heads. "What for?"

"To thank him."

"Oh, no. He's not interested in talking to me, and really, I am tired of calling him. He's moved on." I didn't like the sound of that, but it was the truth.

"Well, I think we should thank him."

"You can go right ahead," I told her.

"Can you call him now?" she asked. "I really owe him."

"I'm not calling him. He won't answer." I was certain. "You can call though."

She pulled out her phone and asked for his number. I dialed it for her and gave her the phone. It couldn't have been two rings before he picked up the phone. *Jerk*, I thought. So he wasn't making it a habit to avoid *everyone's* phone call, just the ones coming from my number.

"Hi Wes?...Yes, this is Dawn. Sophie's friend. I just wanted to call and thank you for saving my ass last night. I really appreciate it....Yeah, well thanks anyway, really. Okay, bye." She hit the off button and slid the phone back into her pocket. "He seemed nice." I let out a grumble in my chest and went back to stacking. "Well, he was," she said, walking back to the front.

I felt like I was living in some sort of nightmare. What are the odds that I would move to a new state and meet a guy who was the result of some transfusion gone wrong, but right, making him a miraculous being. And what are the odds I would be the only one who knew his secret only to be tormented by being made an outcast? It could've easily been a nightmare except for the fact that if it was, I wouldn't have felt like I loved him, and he wouldn't have had so many weaknesses. No, I was certain I was not in a nightmare. It only felt like one.

Chapter 14
THE SECOND REVEAL

By the time Wes' birthday came around, I hadn't seen or heard from him. I wasn't sure whether I should contact him, and the thought bothered me all day. He really didn't deserve a well-wishing in my mind, but I couldn't stop thinking about it. Then, I remembered that he didn't want me to acknowledge it, and that was enough to motivate the oppositional defiance in me. I wasn't going to call him, but I was going to bring it up, so I settled on a simple text. HAPPY BIRTHDAY was all I wrote and, of course, he never replied.

One would think that time made things better, but it didn't. I only grew to miss him more. It didn't help that every time Tom came over he would say, "So, where is Wes? You know, that boy is going to be something someday." I had to tell him that we were not hanging out anymore. Then, it didn't help that my mom would ask me every few days, "Has Wes called?" As my stares grew more hostile in reaction to the question, she eventually knew to stop asking, but his absence was constantly hovering in my house.

I decided that what I needed was a break and some fresh air. One night, I drove to the overlook. Even though it was where Wes and I had first decided to start seeing each other, it didn't matter. The view was unmatchable and instantly calming.

I pulled right up to the ledge and sat in my car, just thinking about how things began to spiral out of control. Our relationship seemed so perfect, all the way through New Year's. I thought we loved each other so much that I wanted to take things to a deeper level with him.

I guess I had reason to be happy. He could've very well taken my innocence that night, and then turned around and broken up with me. I suppose I had good reason to be thankful, but I wasn't. It made things all the more confusing. He had been so loving to me in every single moment we were together, and then just like that, it was gone. I felt so lonely, and I couldn't shake the feeling.

I was staring off over the city in deep thought when lights flashed in my rearview mirror. I turned to see an SUV pull in. It parked about thirty feet down and was as close to the edge as I was. Within a few moments, I heard laughing as some guys got out of the truck. They walked around to the front end of their vehicle and leaned against the hood smoking cigarettes. I checked to make sure I had my doors locked, even though there was no indication that they'd noticed me.

After they finished their puffing, they hopped back into their truck and backed out. I leaned my head onto my headrest to return to my previous thoughts. Just then, the SUV turned in my direction and rolled to a stop behind my car. I was pinned in, with nowhere to go except over the cliff, and that made me feel very nervous.

The driver rolled down his window, and I could hear laughter.

"Hey. You got a name?" he said, laughing.

My entire body tensed. Before my brain and mouth met up with each other to offer a reply, another set of lights pulled in. This time, the vehicle pulled in right up to my door, so the lights were blinding me. I started reaching around for my cell phone in a panic.

"There you are," a familiar voice said. I looked up to see Wes standing at my door with his hands casually in his pockets.

"She's taken fellas. Let's go," I heard from the truck as they drove off.

"Oh my gosh, you scared me," I said, covering my heart with my hand.

"You're out here, by yourself at night, and a car full of strange men pin you in, and *I* scare you?"

"You know what I meant."

"Right," he said, backing toward his car.

"So that's it?"

"That's it," he confirmed.

"Thanks," I said, sarcastically.

He turned around. "Don't thank me. Just go home. Please."

Ugh! I wanted to scream. I was so angry, steam could've been seeping out of my ears. What was with this guy? I drove home in complete irritation, and the feeling only worsened as the night went on. I was furious, and to make matters worse, I couldn't sleep at all, because I was thinking about him.

The next morning, I decided to drive up to his house and demand an explanation for his behavior. I didn't care if I was cornering him or not. When I got there, his car was parked outside, so I knew he was home.

When I got out of my car, my eyes narrowed as I marched up to his front door. I knocked as hard as I could. He had a doorbell, but I thought the knock would allow me to channel some energy as well as let him know I was serious about whatever game it was he was playing. I waited and there was nothing. I knew he was home, so I kept knocking. After a few minutes, he cracked the door open wide enough for me to see his hair dripping wet and a white pool towel around his waist. My eyes traveled back upward, trying to ignore his six-pack long enough to refocus.

"Umm." Was all that came out. *Oh my God. What was I going to say?* It finally came to me. I cleared my throat. "What's your problem?" I asked, firmly, enunciating each word.

He opened the door a bit wider and casually pulled a dry T-shirt over his head. "I can't seem to get away from you, and that's a problem."

Suddenly, his cuteness wasn't so cute anymore. Irritated, I stepped closer. "You *refuse* to talk to me, then you *stalk* me, and now *I'm* your problem. You know, you really know how to make someone want to drive off a cliff."

The smirk immediately disappeared from his face, and he grabbed me by my shoulders. "Don't say that," he said, half shaking me. "Do you hear me, Sophie? Don't say that." I stared at him in shock and watched as his flash of anger turned into that look of torment again. "Just please don't say things like that." He let me go.

He was staring off into space like he was thinking about something, so I said, "Listen, I just wanted to come here to try to figure out why you keep going back and forth. One minute you're talking to me and the next you're not, and the next you're following me everywhere. I want to know why." It was like he wasn't even listening to me. "Hello?" I said.

His head jerked in my direction. "Can you just leave please?" he asked. I thought about that option for a minute, and I decided against it. I knew what I wanted.

"No, I can't," I told him. "I want some answers." I pushed my way past him into his house. He followed me into his living room until we were both standing in front of the large window. This is what I'd been waiting for since the night he'd left me in my room. I had wanted an explanation so badly for so long, and here was my chance. Now, all I had to do was figure out how not to let it go all wrong.

For several moments, I just looked at him, and he looked at me. He was so beautiful. Looking at him, I felt every single moment we had ever shared come back to me. The laughing and talking, just the talking for hours, was something I'd missed. I wanted it so bad, and the rush of the emotions coming back to me made my shoulders feel heavy.

"Tell me what you want," he demanded, sharply enough for me to pull myself out of the recollections. His tone made it clear that he was agitated. I tried to reassure him that I meant no ill will towards him.

"Look, I know it's not in your nature to feel cornered or attached, but I need some answers anyway."

He looked at me, confused. "My nature? What is that supposed to mean?"

"Nothing, I just read some things."

"Wait a minute, what did you read?"

I thought it was my turn to ask questions and somehow he had flipped the script.

"Just forget it."

He was curious now. "No, tell me. What did you read?"

I wished I hadn't said anything. I sifted through the best possible responses before settling on a mediocre one. "I just read a book on the behavior of cold-blooded creatures is all." I tried to dismiss it. It did sound stupid. He started laughing, which made me angry. "What's so funny?" I growled.

"You think I'm acting this way because I'm a cold-blooded creature?"

I stood there without commenting. He shook his head in disbelief. "Sophie, you are way off-base."

"Well then, tell me why," I demanded.

He let out a deep sigh and looked at me. "You don't want to know."

"Maybe I don't, but I do deserve some answers."

"Fine." He stood there, motionless, and I took it as an opportunity to get what I needed.

"Why won't you talk to me anymore?" I asked.

"Because I'm trying to stay away from you," he said, more easily than I appreciated.

"Why?"

"To change the future," he said, flatly.

"How is staying away from me changing the future?"

"I don't know," he answered quickly.

"Then why are you doing it?"

"I don't know," he gritted through his teeth.

I felt like I was grasping at straws, and I didn't have enough experience in this matter to pick the right one. I wanted real answers. I needed a question that required him to give me a real explanation. I thought of one quickly, because I was running out of room on this one-way street. "Okay, why are you so distant and mean one minute, and the next, you're popping up out of nowhere?"

He thought about that for a few moments and answered, "I want to stay away from you, so that's why I'm distant. And if you took better care of yourself, then I wouldn't need to keep popping up."

I was fuming. "Well, don't do me any favors," I said, taking a step around him. He was back in my path in an instant.

He gently grabbed my arm. "Sophie, please don't leave like this. Calm down first."

"Calm down? Two weeks ago you were telling me you loved me and then you went AWOL, and you want me to calm down?"

He was frustrated now. "What do you want from me?" he asked, glaring into my eyes.

"I want you!" I shouted. I was shocked at how easily I'd blurted that out. "But . . . you know that already, and it doesn't matter." I hung my head for a moment.

"It does matter to me," he said softly.

"Well, I can't tell it! You're doing a pretty good job of making me feel like crap."

"I'm sorry," he said, realizing the truth in it.

"I don't want apologies, I just want an explanation."

He turned away from me. "Why is this happening to me again?" He seemed to be talking to himself, but I took it upon myself to chime in.

"You keep saying again. What do I keep doing?"

He turned back around. "You keep finding me. And I don't know how or why."

"You're the one who showed me where you live," I reminded him.

"That's not what I mean. You know where I live *now*, but how did you know what states, what towns?"

"Listen, you're not making any sense. I didn't know what town you were in until I saw you that day." I was truly confused now, but I tried my best to keep up with him.

"No," he said. "You just appear in my life over and over and over and on one hand I'm so happy to know you, to see you. I feel so alive, so strong when you're near me. I feel like I can do anything I want when I have you with me, but then there is that other part. There is that day where I know you will leave again."

"Why do you keep saying again over and over?"

He tilted his head up toward the ceiling, and he let out a deep breath. Slowly, he opened his eyes and turned toward me.

"Please, just tell me the truth. What is going on with you?"

"You want an explanation for what is going on? Fine, I'll give it to you. I have loved you already, in *two* lifetimes. Two lifetimes cut way too short, because you died in both of them. And I can't stop thinking about it happening again."

I wasn't sure how to react to that, so I looked at him for a few seconds and asked, "Are you serious?"

"Yes."

"Okay um, so, give me just a minute here. I need a moment." I sat down on the couch and stared at my feet. He took a step toward me like he wanted to help me, but he decided against it. Instead, he just watched me closely, waiting for a response.

I was finally getting the chance to stare him in the eyes and get the answers I wanted, and I was staring at my feet. I knew I looked like an idiot, but I didn't care. I wanted to get this right, so I needed a minute to think, and I used every second of that minute. I didn't want to lie to him and act as if I believed this, but I didn't want to insult him either. I wanted to choose my words very carefully. "Okay…what makes you think this?" I asked. He looked at me and sat beside me on the couch. Now, he was the one staring at the ground.

"Sophie," he said, "I've been around for a long time, and there are a lot of things that I don't know, but what I do know is that I've been with you before, and each time you go away."

"I haven't gone anywhere. I've always been right here. You've been the one not wanting me. I am—"

"You don't understand, Sophie," he said. "What I'm telling you is that I have loved you three separate times. Once in 1916, then again in 1963, and now…so that makes three."

I looked in his eyes and then back at my shoes again. My right foot started to tap in a constant rhythm while I was trying to go over what he was saying.

There must have been someone I reminded him of, someone he'd loved in 1916. "I'm sorry," I said. "I had no idea that you loved someone so much from your past. It was selfish of me not to realize—"

"Aren't you listening?" He sighed. "I didn't love someone from my past. I loved *you. You* were the one I loved then. I do not expect you to understand or believe me, which is why I've never tried to explain it to you, but I can only assure you that for whatever reason, and by whatever power, you lived then and you live now. *You.*" I could tell he was concentrating very hard to stay focused. "What I don't understand," he added, "is how to change the outcome. I can't get away from this…." He quieted, searching for his words. "Hell," he finished.

Now the tear I was holding back finally escaped with one blink. He reached over with his hand and gently wiped it away. "Why are you crying?" he asked.

"I don't know," I replied. "I think it makes me sad to hear you describe being with me as hell for you."

"No, Sophie. That's not what I meant at all. It's not being with you that is my hell. It's losing you that is, and I don't want to go through it again."

"You're not going to lose me," I said. He didn't seem convinced, but he was more at ease. There was still that sense of hesitation and apprehension between us, but I felt my heart swelling again, and I wasn't sure if that was a good thing. I needed more information.

"So how do you know it's me? How do you know I'm the one you knew?" I asked gently.

He paused. "Well, you are different, but you're also the same," he said. "When you ran into me that day, I had this feeling inside of me that bolted to life when I saw you. You look strikingly similar. I suspected it was you. Then I saw your necklace, and—"

"My necklace?"

"Yes, how many people do you know who wear Axinite crystal jewelry? It's a very rare choice, you know."

"No, I didn't know that." I looked down at my necklace. "I found this in a consignment shop, and I liked it."

"I know you like them. You used to collect Axinite jewelry."

"I did?" I asked, sounding surprised, but a little convinced.

"Yes, you did, and it is no coincidence that you picked that one."

"So you had a feeling and then you saw my necklace, and that's how you knew it was me?" I recapped.

"Well, I was pretty sure, but to be certain, I waited for you to show up again on campus. That's when I asked you all those questions about yourself, and then I knew for sure. I have very good senses." He paused for a moment to gather his words. "I can sense when people are happy, angry, afraid, and I can tell people apart with my eyes closed. I would remember you anywhere."

"So why did you start dating me and then change your mind? What did I do?"

"You didn't do anything," he said. "I was just too selfish to walk away from you. The closer we got, the stronger the memories got. When I almost lost control on New Year's, I realized how precious the time was with you. Then, I couldn't shake the images of losing you again, and I figured it would be best for both of us to try to break the cycle."

"And by the cycle, you mean I—"

"You die," he answered absently.

My eyes widened at the jolt I felt in hearing the last word.

"When?"

"You died when you were nineteen. Both times." All of a sudden, a cold chill went up my spine, and I shuddered.

"I never grow old?" I started to feel mournful about never getting married or having kids. What would be the point of falling for Wes if it was for nothing?

"I'm sorry," he said. "I didn't want to have to tell you."

"It's okay. I wanted to know." As soon as I said it, I wasn't sure if I meant it. I think I did. I did want to know what he was thinking. I had no idea any of this was going on in his head. It was all so bizarre.

I thought there was no way it could be true. I'm Sophie. I'm eighteen, and I've just met this boy this year. Well actually, he was not a boy. He is practically immortal. That was all so true, and I knew it. So if that was all true, then maybe, just maybe he was right when he said I'd lived before. I must have shaken my head a little at my thoughts, because he squeezed me tight and asked me what I was thinking.

I told him I was wondering if what he'd said about me was true. I turned to look at him, trying to gauge his response, and his dark eyes looked deep into mine. It felt as though his mind was writhing in defeat. He touched his forehead to mine and murmured, "I wish it wasn't."

"Is that really why you've been acting so erratic and irrational?" I asked.

"I was *not* being erratic and irrational."

"Yes, you were."

"How so?"

"Well, you were being erratic by being with me one second, dating other people the next, and then following me around the next."

"Is that what this is about?" he asked.

Ignoring his question, I continued. "I want to know how you can say you were so scared of losing me while you were taking walks with Blondie."

He shook off the accusation. "I was just trying to make you think I was over you. It wasn't real."

"Right."

"It wasn't. I'm telling you. There was no interest in that girl whatsoever. I just borrowed her."

I rolled my eyes. "Borrowed her? What is she, a car?"

"*No*, she has a boyfriend. I'm study partners with both of them. I asked her one day if she would walk with me, so I could show someone I wasn't interested."

"That's great. Well, it did more than that. It hurt my feelings."

"I'm sorry. I thought that was the only way to make you think I'd moved on. I thought if you stayed away from me, you might have a chance at a different life and maybe a different outcome."

"So then why follow me places?"

"To make sure you were all right."

"Well, that's erratic," I pointed out.

"Fair enough," he said. "But what about irrational? You called me irrational, too."

"You're irrational because you think I'd be better off without you," I said flatly.

"Well, you're more irrational than I am by far," he countered.

"No, I'm not."

"Well, you know I'm not normal, to say the least, and I've just told you that you died twice already, and you're still sitting here. I say you are."

"Fair enough," I said, thinking he might be right.

"What *are* you thinking anyway?" he asked.

"I don't know what to think. I'm just happy that you're talking to me again. I'll pinch myself later and decide if any of this is real. Why does all this worry you now anyway? I'm only eighteen," I said, trying to lighten the mood.

"Because I don't know how to save you."

That took the light out of the mood. "Well, that makes two of us, because I don't know how to save myself either. It's a good thing we don't have to think about it for another year," I added.

"You don't have to pretend here."

"I'm not pretending. If what you're saying is true, we'll figure something out together."

He sat there without moving away from me, and I took that as a good sign. He offered to take me home that evening, and there was no way I was about to let him out of my sight after that revelation, so I quickly accepted. "What about your car?" he countered.

"Maybe you can pick me up tomorrow and we can hang out. I can get it then." I tried to sound hopeful.

He considered the idea and wrapped his arm around my shoulder as we walked to his car. I took that as a yes.

I had some time to think in the car while he was driving. There were certain things I needed to know in order for any of Wes' explanation to make sense. One, what was the cause of this? Was it some sort of reincarnation? Two, if it was a reincarnation, how did it work? Three, why did I keep dying? And four, how come I couldn't remember any of it?

The more I thought about this, the more I started to feel confident that this was not such a bad thing. I mean, I know Wes just told me I wouldn't live to see twenty. That was frightening, but I was trying to look at this like the glass was half full. If he knew all of this, then that meant we had been together. He must have loved me, and I must love him for us to keep finding each other. If that was true, then it seemed we were given more than one chance to be together. How many people could say they had more than one chance at first love? And not just their first love, but their only love.

If I could only make him see that he didn't have to look at this so negatively. There was nothing to fear. We could change this, and if we couldn't, I was going to come back if history repeated itself. Right? All I had to do was make him see this. It sounded good to me. Then again, I wasn't the one living through my death over and over. I wasn't sure if it was fair to ask him to just deal with whatever was to come, only to have to wait however many years for me to find him again. *If* I even found him at all. Maybe he was right. Maybe it would be better if I left him alone. He could experience a love that could last longer than what I had to give. I could release him from this hell, as he described it. I had no idea what I wanted. On one hand, I wanted to be with him more than anything, and on the other, I didn't want to be the cause of his hell on earth. These were my two options, and I would have to decide.

We pulled up to my house around 8:00. My mom's car was in the driveway, so I needed to come back to reality. She would ask me all the normal questions: How was your day? Where have you been? Do you have any homework? I wasn't sure I was up to putting on the façade, as if I'd had a normal day. Wes had just informed me that I was some sort of walking ghost. Yeah, Mom, I'm great!

Wes opened my car door and walked me to my front steps. I invited him in, but he declined. "I need to take care of something," he said. I let out a small, involuntary sigh of disappointment, and he stroked my cheek. "I'll come back later, and we can talk about whatever you want."

I nodded.

As I turned, I heard him say, "I love you."

I looked back at him, wanting to return the sentiment, but hesitated. He tilted his head forward and said, "I don't know what to do about it, but I can't deny it."

All I could say in return was, "I love you, too."

"I know," he said, with a half smile. "I'll see you later."

I watched him get into his car and drive off. All of a sudden, my swelling heart went idle. I took a deep breath, turned around, and put the key in the door.

I wasn't in the doorway two seconds before my mom asked me who I had been talking to. She was in the kitchen cleaning the dishes, but she took a break to peek around the doorway so she could see me. I hung my jacket on the coat rack, trying to prolong the silence as long as I could.

"Weston," I replied.

"Really?" she asked, in record time.

"Um yeah," I said, as I turned around to head straight for the stairs.

"Where did that come from?"

"I went to his house today to talk."

"And?" she asked.

"And we talked." I knew my mother well enough to know that she wasn't going to give up easily. She was nosy, and I couldn't blame her this time. We'd moved to a new city, and the only friend I'd had for six months was a boy who had the power to dictate my mood from day to day. After he broke things off with me, she never knew whether I was going to lie in bed all day or bury myself in my homework. Now she finds out I'm talking to him again. This wasn't going to go over well.

"Why don't you come in here and talk to me? I'm cleaning the dishes. I made spaghetti." I wanted to make a mad dash to my room and evaluate what I had learned today, but something in me felt sorry for her. I'd gotten a glance of her looking like she was lonely, and that triggered a whole new realization.

If I was going to die in a year or two, then she would be left alone. She had only me, and all of a sudden, I felt this feeling of guilt for trying, purposely, to stay off her radar. I didn't have it in me to turn my back on her, or put the barrier of my bedroom door between us. Instead, I turned around and told her that sounded like a good idea.

"Perfect," she said, as she turned to heat a plate she had already prepared for me in the microwave. I sat at the kitchen table while the microwave hummed. "So what did you guys talk about?" she asked, while she was working on the dishes again. Privacy 101 said that I should lie, but I had this strange longing to have someone else help me with this. I had to figure out how to get advice. He certainly wasn't objective, and I didn't have any close friends here. I suppose I could've called Kerry, but she really didn't know how much I loved him. She wouldn't have understood if I sprung it all on her at once. Plus, I was dealing with the fact that I couldn't very well tell her I had fallen madly in love with an immortal science experiment, could I? And I definitely couldn't tell her I was a living ghost, so she was out. That left my mother. At least she knew I really liked him. So, I decided to test the water. Right about then, the microwave beeped, and I jumped up to get it.

"Um, we talked about why he freaked out last month and wanted to stop seeing me." I grabbed a fork from the drawer and returned to the table while she continued transferring dishes to the dishwasher. She didn't comment on what I'd said, and I took that as a good thing. She was listening before making any premature suggestions. “Then we talked about why he’s been acting so strange, like following me around and stuff.” I took the first bite.

“He was following you around?”

Oops. I forgot she didn’t know that. “Well, sort of. He just seemed to pop up in places I was. I thought he was following me,” I added. The spaghetti was really good. It’s one of my favorites. I was glad I’d decided to eat instead of sequestering myself in my room. I had plenty of time for that later. Besides, it felt good to get some of the weight off of my chest.

“Anyway,” I continued. “I drove out to his house today to ask him why he was going back and forth all of time. I wanted him to make up his mind. Either be nice to me or leave me alone. No back and forth stuff.”

“That makes sense. What did he say?” she asked, working on the pots now. Her back was to me, and that could’ve been why I felt so comfortable having my first real boy talk with her. Only I had to be careful about how to word this. I didn’t want to just make something up completely. I really did want to get some advice. The problem was, I couldn’t very well tell her that my dilemma revolved around the fact that I was going to die in a year or so, and he didn’t want to have to hang around for the third time. I had to come up with something else.

“He said he liked me a lot, but since he’s had a lot of loss in his life, it made him think he shouldn’t get attached, in case something happened to me.” That was perfect. I smiled as soon as I said it.

“That’s right. He lost both of his parents. That is so sad,” she said. “Poor boy.”

“Yeah, I know.”

"So does he want to be friends or not?" she asked.

"I'm not sure. I think so." This wasn't working. She was being nice, but I needed some advice I could use. I needed to figure out how to make this a little more clear without her thinking I was nuts.

"Mom, I think he's closed himself off, so he doesn't ever have to deal with death again."

"Well honey, you can't live your life thinking death is going to come all the time. You have to live life, and if it comes, then we can only hope we were able to do all the things we wanted. He has to want to do something. Everyone does."

"So what should I do?"

"Well, what did he say he wanted?"

I stopped eating at this point, because I didn't seem to have the same appetite. I looked down at my plate. "He said he didn't think he could handle losing someone he loved again."

"Did he actually say the word loved?"

"Yes. Why?"

"Well, I had no idea you guys were that serious. I'm not sure what to say about that." She turned around and leaned her back against the sink. "All of this talk about death is making me gloomy. You guys are too young to think about these things."

"So what do I do?" I was almost desperate for an answer. I had no idea how to handle this situation. I loved him. That much I knew, but I also didn't want to be the cause of his everlasting pain. And that is exactly what it was. Gosh, I was starting to feel sick.

"Honey, you guys can't think about that. You have to think about things you want to do. Not things that you fear.

Everyone is going to die. You can't change it. You just have to make the best with what time you have. If you don't do things that make you happy while you're living, then what's the point of what time you have at all?"

I was actually beginning to see what she was getting at, and it made sense. At least it did for now. "Thanks, Mom. I appreciate it." I stood up to rinse my plate and put it in the dishwasher. "I have a lot of homework to do."

"All right sweetheart," she said. "I'll be in my room if you need anything."

By the time I reached my room, I felt better. My mom had actually given me a lot of things to consider, and I was glad we'd talked. I looked at the clock and realized it was getting late enough for me to take a shower and get into bed. I knew Wes was coming back tonight, so I wanted time to curl up in my bed and think about all of it first.

Chapter 15
1916

Anyone wondering how an eighteen-year-old handles the news that they're going to die young? It's very simple. They numb themselves up to the actual reality of it and then, when they force themselves to acknowledge the possibility, they cry. At least that's what I did.

As soon as I got in my bed that evening, I started thinking. *Is this true? Is Wes crazy? Am I really insane for considering this? How could he know?* All of these things passed through my mind, and the only answer that came out on top was that I believed it. I knew, somewhere deep within me, that what he was saying was true. I felt it. It was almost as if I'd never been able to plan too far ahead, because I knew there was no future for me.

Whatever was going to happen was unknown, but I did know that whether or not I was going to die in one year or in fifty years, I didn't want to live it without Wes. My mother was right. People shouldn't live their lives being afraid of something. They should do what they want while they can, and with that, I made my decision. Selfish or not, that's what I wanted. If he wanted to use fear of losing me as an excuse to stay away from me, then that was his choice, but I'd made mine. If it was too difficult for him to handle, then I wouldn't blame him, but I would at least have an explanation for his decision.

By the time he came back to my house, I was ready to hash things out. When he entered my room, he immediately sensed my distress.

"You've been crying," he said.

"Yes," I admitted, moving aside to let him in.

He sighed. "It's because of me."

Yeah it was, I thought, but I didn't reply because I wasn't sure how to.

"Sophie, I'm sorry that I only seem to cause you—"

That's when I cut him off, hoping to come to a resolution quickly.

"Listen Wes, you're going to have to stop with the sorry stuff and decide what you want to do. I can accept if you don't want to be with me, but you can't have it both ways."

He looked at me, perplexed. I was even surprised by my abrasiveness, but there was no way to get around it. I wasn't about to take the high road and sacrifice what I wanted in order to spare him pain or *hell,* as he put it. It was like my mother said: I can't live fearing death, so I wasn't going to. I'd made my decision, and now he needed to make his. So, I gave him the choice.

"I love you, but the point is, you have to decide whether you're going to be with me all of the time or not. No staying away and then coming around." I could tell my offensive attack was unexpected.

"What do *you* want?" he asked.

"I already told you what I want. This is about what you want," I replied.

He moved over to the bed and sat, pondering the choice. "Can we talk about this first, let you hear everything, and then decide?"

"No we can't," I countered. "You decide before we go any further. You either want to be with me or you don't."

He turned away and dropped his head. "How can you say what you want when you don't even know the whole story?"

I repositioned myself. "I know Sophie and Wes' story. I don't know or remember Weston the first or second, so I can't base what I want on that. I can only base it on how I feel now, when I'm with you."

"Sophie and Wes' story," he whispered back. He looked at me again. "What happens when Weston can't save Sophie?"

"You've already saved me," I said, patting my hand over my heart. His face softened at the line I'd stolen. "I love you, Wes. But I need to know what you want to do."

He moved so he was sitting beside me on the bed. He shook his head slowly, with his eyes closed, and I was waiting anxiously for his answer.

"I want you," he murmured.

"Are you sure?" I asked.

He nodded, and I let out a soft sigh of relief. It felt right to be close to him again. That made me feel so good, but I also knew that we couldn't get past all of the doubt without being fully open with each other from that point on. "I need to hear it all. I want to know what you know."

"Where do you want me to begin?"

"At the beginning, where it all started. Tell me everything." I scooted over to make room for him to lie down. He situated himself so he was turned toward me, and I was lying on my back, staring at the darkness of the ceiling, preparing myself for my forgotten past.

"Are you sure you want to hear it?" he asked.

"I'm positive." There was no way I could turn back now.

He took a deep breath and gathered his thoughts. "I was sixteen years old, about to be seventeen, but to all accounts, I was a child. I had lived a very sheltered life to say the least. Rarely did my mother allow me to go outside and do what normal boys my age did, and when she did, she was with me, making sure I didn't hurt myself.

"Finally, when I was sixteen, she allowed me to go to the bookstore once a week by myself. I was old enough to have my own interests, and the books she brought home no longer held my attention. So, once a week, I would venture out to the store to pick up a few I liked.

"On that particular day, I saw a girl who stopped my entire world. She was walking toward me on the sidewalk, and she had this demeanor like she was headed somewhere important, so I watched her curiously as she neared. The closer she got, the more I could see of her. She had the most transparent green eyes, contrasted by remarkably dark hair. I couldn't take my eyes off of her as she passed. I was so intrigued that I actually turned and followed her. I could tell she was a few years older than I was, but I didn't care. I was mesmerized. I followed her for a long time. It was difficult to keep up with her because she was walking quickly, and my knees were achy."

"Was that from the hemophilia?"

"Yes, the blood would often gather in my joints, and if I overexerted myself, they got very sore and painful. Today, they compare it to arthritis." I nodded in understanding, and he continued. "I was able to follow her long enough to notice she was wearing a nursing uniform and was headed into a brownstone in the medical district.

"I thought about her every day after that. Over the next two weeks, I took it upon myself to walk around that street as often as I could in hopes of running into her again, but I had no luck. My knees got worse every day, but to me, the ache was worth it, just to have been able to see her again. She was that beautiful.

"By the week of Christmas, I hadn't seen her and had given up. My joints ached tremendously, and I wanted to lie in bed all day, but it occurred to me that I hadn't gotten my mother a gift yet. So, I decided to venture out one more time.

"My mother hadn't received a nice present since my father died, so I wanted to get her something special." He paused in thought. "That's when I bought the bracelet you're wearing now."

I pulled my arm up to see my Christmas present. "This? This is the exact bracelet?" I asked.

He nodded. "Yes, I bought that in a London shop for her and was on my way home when I saw the girl again. She was across the street, headed in the opposite direction. My eyes were locked on her with every step she took. Looking so content and driven, she walked like no one else was around her. That's what made her so intriguing.

"The next thing I remember was my feet being tripped up by an alley cat. It happened so quickly I don't think I could've prevented it, even if I had been paying attention. When I realized I was losing my footing, I tried to untangle my feet, and I might have been able to if it weren't for the force of an Irish Wolfhound colliding into me in pursuit of the cat. The sheer size and strength of the dog forced me backward. All I remember, about the fall, was my feet completely coming out from under me and a hard hit to my back and head on the cobblestone.

"I knew it was bad. I felt the back of my rib cage thrust into the ground, followed by a cracking sound from the back of my head. To make matters worse, the hound fell on top of me and scratched my neck and face with his claws trying to get up.

"I heard people scream at the commotion as the hound ran between the crowd. I just lay there, motionless. I hadn't suffered anything like that before. I was shocked. I tried to roll over to pull myself up, and that's when the ringing in my head started. I immediately lay back down. I tried to focus, but my concentration was broken by a pain filling in my abdomen and the flow of blood coming from my deep scratches.

"At some point, I felt a warm hand touch my forehead. My vision was starting to go, but I could see clearly enough to know it was the nurse I'd been watching. All I remember her saying is, 'I'm going to help you. You'll be okay. You hit your head, and I need to get you some help.' She tried her best to lift me, but she couldn't. I heard her ask bystanders to help her, but no one would. At the time, there was a malaria outbreak, and no one wanted to risk getting sick themselves. The sight of blood literally sent people walking in the opposite direction."

I snorted. It made me angry to hear about people not helping. I refocused, still irritated. He continued. "By then, blood was flowing freely from the stinging scratches on my neck and face. I can only imagine the awful sight. It didn't bother me that no one wanted to help me, but it made me angry that no one helped her. It gave me enough strength to stand myself up.

"She wrapped my arm around her, not caring that my blood was smearing on her and her coat. She just kept promising to get me help. The next thing I knew, she walked me into Dr. Thomas' office, where I collapsed."

"Amelia." I remembered from the journal in his study. "It was Amelia who took you in." He surveyed my expression, and then I realized. "It was me. *I* took you to Dr. Thomas, didn't I?"

His nod confirmed my assessment. I let out a long, deep sigh. I felt the closeness of her, and I wasn't sure if it was because I *was* her, or if it was because I liked what she had done for Wes. Either way, it made me very curious. "What happened next?" I asked.

"I woke up in extreme pain. I was bleeding internally in my chest and abdomen, and my head was pounding like you couldn't imagine. You had given me some of your blood, but it wasn't enough to help mine clot. My case of hemophilia was severe. I was in and out of consciousness, but I heard your voice. You kept asking me for my name and where I lived. I remembered mumbling Weston and bookstore and then I blacked out again."

I could see that he would've preferred to stop talking about it, but he continued. I closed the space between us and rested my head on his chest to offer comfort to both him and me. With his arm around me, he began to tell me what happened next.

"Once I blacked out for the second time," he continued, "Dr. Thomas told you the news wasn't good. You had offered to give me more of your blood to help, but Dr. Thomas insisted that it wasn't going to work and that you needed to find my family right away.

"You ended up returning to the street where the incident happened and began walking around. You found a small bookstore with a closed sign in the window. It should've been open, so you asked the shops nearby when the owner would be back. They told you she was searching for her son. You obtained her address and immediately headed to her home."

Listening to Wes tell the story made me sympathize with what Amelia had to do, and once I pictured her in my head, I started to see the story unfold. The images were so vivid, I could see them. I could see Wes' frantic mother, just as if I were there. Amelia's story *was* my story. I closed my eyes and listened as I saw more detailed images in my head.

I saw myself knocking on Mrs. Wilson's door. As soon as she opened the door and saw me in my nurse's uniform, she took hold of my arms and pleaded with me. "You know where he is, don't you? Please, *please* tell me he's all right."

I could see the trepidation pouring out of her, and I couldn't bring myself to answer her. Instead, I offered, "I can take you to him." That was all I managed to say, and it was enough to send his mother quickly snatching her coat. She followed me, heavy on my heels, back to Dr. Thomas' house.

By the time we arrived, Dr. Thomas had covered Weston with a blanket up to his neck, so his mother couldn't see the blood pooling under his skin in various places. He had also re-wrapped the wounds to his neck and face, but we could still see the blood seeping through. When I walked her into the room, she broke out into sobs.

"No!" she cried. She rested her head gently on his chest and then she knew. She knew why he was covered. She peeled back the blanket slowly and saw the bruises on his elbows, wrists, and torso. They were spreading into a horrible array of hues all over him. "What happened? What happened to him?" She was shaking. "Please somebody tell me!" she cried.

At the sight of Mrs. Wilson's agony, I took a step forward and instinctively hugged her. She sobbed in my arms. I softly tried to explain the accident.

"What? A dog? All of this for a dog?" She dropped to her knees. "What was he doing out walking? Where was he going?" I remembered the box we'd taken from his pocket and retrieved it, hoping it would provide an answer for her.

"Mrs. Wilson, I think he was buying this," I informed her, handing over the box. She slowly pulled back the top, and at the sight of the bracelet, she broke into hysterics. She stood up and zeroed in on Dr. Thomas, who was standing in the back corner.

"Doctor, you have to help him. He needs blood. You have blood, right? I can give him mine. He needs it!"

Dr. Thomas rested his hand on her shoulder. "Amelia here, has already given him some of her blood. His internal bleeding is too severe. I'm sorry."

She was determined, pleading, and unfazed. "No, you can't just let him die. You're a *doctor*. Please, you can't just let him die!"

"I'm sorry, there is nothing I can do." His shoulders drooped, and I saw his eyes were tearing up. He had watched so many patients die that year, and this incident was taking its toll on him.

"Don't tell me that!" she snapped. "Please doctor, I've already had one son die from this, and that's what his doctors told me. Please don't tell me that. Weston is *all* I have now. I have no one else. Please."

"Mrs. Wilson, more blood will not help him."

She cut him off. "Then give him something else. You have to have something. Anything. *Please.* I can't live if he dies like this. Please help him."

I started to flinch at the startling memory, and Wes steadied me. "Sophie, what's the matter?" he asked.

I didn't want to tell him about the images that were flashing before me, because my images were much more detailed than what he was saying. I was afraid to tell him how bad the scene was, because I feared it would cause him to hold back, and I wanted him to tell me everything he knew. Instead, I took my palm and placed it on his cheek. "Nothing," I said. "What happened after I brought your mother back?"

"Are you sure you're okay?"

"I'm fine." I smiled. He settled back down onto the pillow and started rubbing my hair.

"After you brought my mother back, I could hear her pleading with Dr. Thomas to save my life. I was in and out of consciousness, but I could hear that she was frantic. Dr. Thomas eventually realized I was going to die regardless, and if he did nothing, my mother would never forgive him. He explained to her that he'd been working on an experimental serum that had been unsuccessful, and she insisted he try it anyway.

"Dr. Thomas agreed to perform the procedure that evening. But, before he started, he insisted that my mother wait outside, given the complexity and risk of making a mistake. Once she was out of the room, he put wrist and ankle restraints on me and strapped me to the bed." As I concentrated, Wes' voice slowly started to fade again, and it was replaced by even more frightening, clear images.

In my mind, I saw Dr. Thomas injecting the serum into Wes' arm. I saw the blood making its way through the vein. I could see Wes' muscles tighten. Dr. Thomas kept filling the vein with so much blood, and I was concerned. "What are you doing?" I asked.

"It's taking it with ease. The serum is flowing freely. I'm not forcing it," he said.

He kept emptying the blood into his arm until Wes' eyes snapped open, and he started jerking his arms. It looked like he was going to tear the leather restraints, he was pulling so hard.

Eventually both arms, followed by his legs, began convulsing, and he shouted for us to stop. I closed my eyes and turned away. The tears started spilling over. I couldn't handle it. I went to leave, but Dr. Thomas called out to me.

"Amelia, look!"

I turned, but remained distant.

He called again. "*Amelia*, get over here. Look at this!"

I walked over to him, slowly, flinching with every one of Wes' shouts of agony. His arms and legs were still fighting to free themselves from the restraints. I almost turned away again, but then I saw what Dr. Thomas was pointing out. The bruises on the arm, where Dr. Thomas initiated the serum, began to recede toward the vein.

"Do you see that, Amelia?"

I nodded.

He was bewildered. "I've never seen anything like it."

It was amazing to watch the bruises begin to get smaller and smaller, but the shouting was ear-piercing. It wasn't worth the pain. "Dr. Thomas, he's in pain, make it stop," I said.

"I can't."

"I can't watch it. I won't stand here and wait for it to reach the heart."

"Amelia, *please*. I don't want this any more than you do, but his mother insisted. Now, stay. You can't leave a patient."

He was right. As much internal sadness as I was feeling, I couldn't leave him. He hadn't asked for this. I took a deep breath and refocused. He was still convulsing, and the only thing I could do was talk to him. "Weston," I said in his ear. He stopped hollering and clenched his jaw in response to my voice. "Dr. Thomas has given you special blood to make you better. It's the only way to save you. I know it hurts, but it's the only way." He started breathing heavily to hold back more screams. I stroked his forehead with my hand and kept talking to him. "Your mother is downstairs. She begged Dr. Thomas to save you, and this is the only way he can. You have to hang on. The new blood is working its way through your body."

He started shaking his head. "Make it stop, make it stop."

I rested my cheek beside his. "I can't make it stop, but I promise you, it will be over soon. Your bruises are already fading. It's fixing you. You'll be better soon."

He was still shaking, and our heads started to rock slowly in unison. I didn't leave him. I wanted him to know that someone was there with him. After a while, I tried to stand to go get his mother and he grunted a clear, "No! Don't…leave…me."

"I want to get your mother for you," I murmured.

He was panting. "No, please…don't let….her see…me like…this."

"All right, all right," I said.

Dr. Thomas was assessing Weston like a mad scientist. He was checking his fingers, his toes, every inch of him, and taking notes.

"Incredible," he observed. I didn't see anything incredible with the torture Wes was enduring. "I can see the blood traveling through the veins. It's amazing," he said.

I closed my eyes to ignore the momentary optimism and focused on keeping close to Wes' face so he could feel my presence. Wes' transfusion was worse than the other patients' had been. With them, I remembered the pain only lasting about ten minutes, and then there were a few hours of silence before the screaming picked up again. With Wes, it was a constant pain and fighting the restraints for three whole hours. Even when that stopped, he started shivering uncontrollably.

"What's happening, doctor?" I asked.

He looked just as perplexed as I did. "I don't know," he reported. "This is odd." He was feeling his pulse. "His pulse is slowing down, but this is remarkable. The bruises are gone." He looked around, assessing Wes' needs. "Get him some more blankets."

I hurried out and came back with several blankets. Wes was cold and needed several layers just to manage the chills.

Wes abruptly interrupted my trance with a light nudge. "Sophie, I think we should pick this up later."

"What? Why?" I asked, realizing I was breathing hard.

"You're getting all worked up, and you seem distant. I don't want to frighten you."

I turned toward him and nestled closer. "No, I'm okay. I think I was just remembering. Please. Tell me more." He remained quiet for a few moments and during that time, my mind was blank. I couldn't picture anything. I was eager for him to start talking again. "Tell me what happened after I brought you the blankets."

He pulled his head back. "I didn't say you brought me blankets. I'm not there yet. How did you know that?" His eyes were fixed on me in the darkness.

"I told you. I think I'm remembering some things. Now, please keep talking."

"Are you serious?"

"Yes. Now tell me what happened next."

"Sophie, this is a really big deal, if you're remembering this."

"I know, but I can't see anything else. It's all gone. I need you to keep going."

He studied me for a few more minutes and then started reciting his memory, but I could tell he was assessing my every expression.

"By the second day, I was kept warm with the help of the blankets. Dr. Thomas had also moved me into his study because there was a large fireplace in there. I was made comfortable enough for my mother to visit." He paused to check for my reaction. I gave him nothing other than an indication that I was listening attentively, so he continued.

"Dr. Thomas was ecstatic that I had made it past the first twenty-four hours, and so was my mother." He started to taper off in deep thought.

"What's wrong?" I asked.

He gave me a gentle squeeze. "Nothing. That's the story. That's how I was made into what I am."

"That's it?" I asked, knowing there was more.

"That's all they told me."

He was avoiding something, and I wasn't going to let him off the hook that easily.

"Wes, you have to tell me everything. We can't have any more secrets."

"What else do you want to know?"

"I want to know it all. What happened to you after that? What happened to Amelia? How did we fall in love?"

He laughed gently. "In case you hadn't noticed, I loved you the very first time I saw you."

"Well, I want to know everything. You have to tell me the rest. All of it," I urged.

He took another deep breath and began again. "Well, when I woke up, the room was spinning, and it got worse with every day that passed. The only way I could function was to keep my eyes closed. You ended up tying a blindfold around my eyes to make it easier for me. Dr. Thomas was convinced that it would pass as I recovered. Neither he nor my mother noticed my true transformation at first, but you did.

"You were actually the one to figure out that my temperature was off. Dr. Thomas would put me in front of the fire and within minutes, you could tell I was getting too hot. Dr. Thomas first attributed it to a fever caused by something internal, and you brought it to his attention that it was my surroundings that were making me hot or cold. That's when he started suspecting the cold-blood was changing me.

"You also recognized that my time perception was off. I couldn't see you, but I could feel you with me all the time. One day, I apparently kept thanking you because it seemed like you were constantly giving me things. You would try to give me food or drink, and I insisted that you'd already given it to me. That's when you knew something wasn't right.

"You had Dr. Thomas look into my sanity. It was then that we realized I was seeing days go by in minutes. He immediately stopped his research on the cold-blood and filled my mother in on what was happening to me. Neither of them knew what was going on, and she agreed to let him keep me in his care to monitor me."

He began to taper off again, and I could tell he was growing hesitant to continue. I started rubbing his arm in hopes of encouraging him. "What happened next?" I asked.

"Next, is when my mother caught the Spanish Influenza. I wasn't even able to say goodbye to her. All I remember is that you brought in a letter from her that told me how much she loved me, and that was it. She wouldn't even come near me, because she was afraid I would catch it from her. The worst part was that it happened so fast. I couldn't even tell her I loved her because the whole sickness was a blur to me. It was over before I knew it began. I was going to lose my sanity altogether, but…"

"But what?" I asked.

"You saved me again. After that, I wouldn't eat or drink. I just kept my eyes closed and blocked everything out. After awhile, you started reading Whitman poetry to me. Your voice was like a song in my ear. I focused on nothing else, and eventually I was able to slow down your voice. That's the first time I realized I could stop the blur if I concentrated hard enough. The sound of your voice became the only thing I looked forward to. It kept me sane for a while."

"What do you mean 'for a while'?"

He started to get tense. "I went insane anyway. Dr. Thomas brought me a letter from you, in what felt like minutes after you had been reading to me one day. You wrote that you were happy that I was saved and that it was the greatest accomplishment you'd ever had. You thanked me for my graciousness, and you asked me to always remember to do what is right, because the transformation worked on me for a reason. And you signed it, 'Love, Amelia.'"

"Why did that make you crazy?"

"Because I knew it meant you were sick, too. You had caught what my mother had and you, also, stayed away so I wouldn't get sick. I called for you and tried my best to focus, but the next thing I knew, Dr. Thomas told me you had died. The news sent me into a delirium. Sophie, you spent a year and a half taking care of me, and I wasn't coherent enough to reciprocate the least bit of courtesy to you when you were sick."

"Wes, do you know how many people died from that epidemic? It was bound to happen, and it would've happened to you, too, if you hadn't been kept away. Then where would we be now?"

"Sophie, I don't get sick. I'm immune to everything that I know of."

I started to feel a sense of his withdrawing from me, and I wanted it to stop. I wanted to change the subject.

"Well, the point is that I'm here now, right?"

He pulled me up against his chest and kissed my head tenderly. We lay there in the darkness for a while, and then I became curious.

"What am I, some sort of reincarnation?"

"I've asked myself that many times. But I don't know. I haven't encountered anyone else from the past. I don't understand it."

"Then how did you know for sure that I was Amelia?"

He answered with ease. "Sophie, let's just say I went away and you stayed the same age for thirty years. Then let's say you saw me again, and I was roughly the same age as I am now. Wouldn't you know for sure if it was me?"

I thought about it for a second. "I would never forget you."

"Exactly. I would know you anywhere."

"So then, I must be reincarnated. Why do you think I keep coming back and not remembering?"

He started rubbing my hair again, and I was glad to feel him relax a little. "Well, you seem to be remembering some things."

"Yes, but only when you give me something to picture."

"Well, I've read a lot of books on people who think they've lived before, and the only thing I gather is those people believe their life's purpose was not completed. They believe they've returned to finish something they were meant to do, and the actual memories are not what's important—it's their purpose that is."

I pondered that idea. *What could I have been meant to do? How could I even know that if I couldn't even remember what I was doing in the first place?* I tried to think really hard about what my purpose could be. I was never good at figuring it out in my current life, never mind one I didn't remember. I lay there thinking about everything I did that made me feel as if I'd accomplished something.

I had won a spelling bee in the third grade. I'd won an art show in the ninth grade. I passed my driver's test on the first try. I had been on the honor roll for the last two years. Those were trivial things. I had to think deeper. *What had I done that made me feel like I made a difference?*

Every answer I came up with led back to Wes. The pier, trusting him, and just being with him. It all led back to him, and when I compared it to Amelia, it also led back to him. She was the only one who had helped him when he needed it. If it hadn't been for her taking him to Dr. Thomas, he would've died.

The only significant common denominator between my accomplishments and hers was Wes. I sat up in complete understanding.

"You," I whispered.

"What about me?" he said, sitting up as well.

"It's you. I'm here for you. Think about it. You, technically, aren't supposed to be here, but you are. And maybe you need me to come back for you."

"What are you saying, Sophie?"

I shifted closer to him. "You said you loved me two times prior. The first time, you said I saved your life. When was the second time?"

He thought about it for a moment. "It was a few years after Dr. Thomas died."

"What were you doing? Were you hurt?"

"Not yet, but I was going to be soon, had you not returned."

"Don't you see it, Wes?"

His eyes narrowed in thought. I touched his shoulder. "Why would I come back and just happen to run into you? You said it yourself. You believe in fate."

He looked at me, considering the idea. "So what does that mean exactly?" he asked.

I turned so I was completely square to him. "It means I'm here for you."

I meant what I said. I felt it in every bone of my body. Weston was mine, and I was his. We were meant to be together in this world, so much that not even death could keep us apart. I knew it, and if I knew that, then I must also know there is a greater power that controls my destiny. In order for my soul to leave this place and come back to Wes, I had to believe there was an even greater purpose. We just needed to wait for it to be revealed.

No matter how much Wes feared the future, I couldn't deny the gifts of the past. It gave true meaning to the term soul mate. I went to sleep in Wes' arms that night, and despite the fact that he still believed my death was approaching, I slept in perfect peace. I knew I had existed before. Our love was timeless, and it couldn't be replicated.

When I woke up the next morning, Wes was already gone, which wasn't unusual. What was unusual was the small box sitting on my nightstand with a note attached. It read:

Sophie,

You are as beautiful now as you were the day I met you.

Love,

Wes

I smiled as I read the words. I slowly opened the box, wondering what timeless gift he had in store for me. Resting in the bottom of the box was a faded picture of Wes sitting between a young Dr. Thomas and a nurse who was the mirror image of me.

Chapter 16

REUNITED

Once I realized there was a past deeper than what I could've dreamed, I began to want to know everything about it—the good, the bad, and the ugly—but I couldn't remember anything. Thankfully, Wes was willing to fill me in on it without too much reserve.

For the other part of our history together, Wes actually chose to show me where we'd met. On a weekday afternoon, when I wasn't working, Wes took me up north, and while he was driving, he gave me an overview of what his life had been like after his transformation.

It took Wes a long time to function after the loss of his mother and Amelia, but he was eventually mentally, and physically, stable enough to be transported. In 1920, Dr. Thomas brought him to America and raised him as his nephew. It was through Wes' recovery that they discovered he was stronger, faster, his vision and hearing were unmatched, and most of all, the cold-blood had created a protective layer under his skin, so he was virtually impenetrable.

By 1921, Wes was getting restless, and Dr. Thomas purchased the Ford that still sits in his garage. Wes had never been freely able to roam the street before his transfusion, and that car was the beginning of him learning his limitless boundaries. When he got the car, he said he experienced exhilaration for the first time in his entire life. He lived without fear of getting hurt. He raced cars, he rode motorcycles, he did everything he could to test his limits and to distract himself from the fact that he was lonely.

It wasn't until Dr. Thomas' house was broken into, in 1940, that Wes went into hiding. Dr. Thomas' house was ransacked, and the only thing the thieves stole were some of his journals dated prior to 1916—the only ones that documented his early cold-blood experiments and serums.

Dr. Thomas convinced Wes that remaining out of sight was the best thing to do. He told Wes that the world would change for the worse if people found out his experiment had been successful. That's when they planned for Wes to disappear and emerge as Weston II.

At this point, we had arrived at an old road. It was a peculiar setup. It looked like a flattened runway, but it disappeared toward the edge of a huge drop-off. We got out of the car, and I looked around, quite confused.

"Does this look familiar?" he asked.

I gave the property a panoramic viewing and there was nothing. "No."

"Come on, I want to show you something." He took my hand as we walked along the rundown road until we couldn't go any farther. I stopped a good fifteen feet before the drop-off.

"That's far enough," I said. I could see it was a *long* way down, and I didn't need to go any farther. He took a few more steps toward the cliff and turned around.

"Do you see this cliff?"

I nodded. "What's going on, Wes?"

"I planned to drive off of it."

"You what?"

His voice was as calm as ever. "Yeah. After my uncle died, I secluded myself from the rest of the world. By 1963, I decided I'd rather die than live alone. I started coming out here to drag race with a bunch of college kids on the weekends."

"Let me guess. You drove a black Mustang?"

"Very good," he said, praising me. He smiled and then resumed his story. "We would start way back there." He pointed over my shoulder. "And we would race this way. The loser would be whoever hit the brakes first." He paused in reflection. "Anyway, on one of the nights, I just planned to keep on going."

"Wes!" I said a little too loudly.

He closed the gap between us. "Sophie, relax. I didn't do it, obviously."

I was relieved, but I still didn't like hearing his plan. "What made you stop?"

"I stopped because I saw you." He took hold of my hand and started walking me back toward our car. "You see. I was in my car, right over there." He pointed to where we had parked. "And the car I was racing against was right there." He pointed to the empty space to the right of his car. "And the crowd was lined up on both sides coming all the way down to here." Now, he pointed to where we were standing. "Anyway, when the flag was dropped, I accelerated without hesitation. *But, then* I looked out of the passenger window for just a second, and I saw you. You looked like an angel. It was pitch-black outside, and you had on a white sundress." He was smiling at the memory. I followed his stare into the darkness, trying to envision what he was seeing.

"So what happened?" I asked, feeling anxious.

"Well, I slammed on the brakes and spun the car completely around. Then, I catapulted myself out of the car and walked over to you."

"What did you do?"

"I called you Amelia." He was chuckling now, and I missed the joke.

"And?" I prodded.

"And you had no idea what I was talking about. You looked at me like I was insane and said, 'No, I'm Lenny.'" He laughed.

"What's so funny?"

"Well, then your boyfriend jumped in front of me and asked me if I wanted something."

I jerked my head around. "My boyfriend?" He was getting a kick out of it. I didn't believe him. "How do you know he was my boyfriend?"

"Because he told me that I was bothering his girlfriend, and he was referring to you."

I rolled my eyes. "Then what?"

"Then I left."

"That's it?"

"Until the next time I saw you. I asked around and found out where I could find you. At the time, I wasn't sure if seeing you was my imagination or not. I had to find you again to be sure."

He led me back to the car and opened the passenger door for me. I took the cue that he was ready to go. We headed back to town, and he was driving at complete ease.

I was glad to see him in such good spirits, but I was ridiculously curious about this boyfriend thing. I sat with a slight pout on my face.

"What's the matter?" he asked, resting his hand on my leg.

"I don't like the story about the boyfriend. I don't get it."

"Don't worry, sweetheart, he wasn't your boyfriend for long." I looked over to see his melting smile. He was completely tickled with himself.

"I still don't like it." I pouted.

"Neither did I," he admitted.

"So what did you do about it?"

He started reflecting again. "I followed you one evening to a carnival."

"Interesting," I observed.

He ignored the notation. "You were with a group of friends *and* your little boyfriend."

He looked over to see my reaction. I glared back. "Get to the point."

"So I followed you guys around. You were just as breathtaking as you always are.

"I watched you play a couple of games and of course, you didn't win anything. Then again, you didn't get to play much before your boyfriend lost patience with you. Either that or he was too cheap to let you continue. Regardless, I saw you were disappointed when you didn't win anything, and I didn't like it. Needless to say, your boyfriend was getting on my nerves.

"The final straw was when your friends wanted to ride the Ferris wheel. You were terrified. I could see it in your face and hear it in the rapid acceleration of your heart. You weren't going to get on that ride. So, your friends *and* your boyfriend got on it without you." He squeezed my leg and looked over at me. I could see his expression in the reflection of his lighted console. "I would never have gotten on a ride without you. I wouldn't have left you standing there by yourself," he added.

I blushed.

"So what next?" I was softening up to his chivalry.

"Well, I used the opportunity to talk to you. I walked up behind you and said, 'Lenny, right?' and you turned around biting your bottom lip, like you often do. 'Yes?' you replied. I was studying you intensely, and you plainly asked, 'Can I help you?' I snapped out of my reverie and asked you where you had gotten your name. I found it *strange*."

I agreed. It was sort of an odd name, but I had thought about it since I first heard him say it, and I was starting to own up to it. "Well, where did it come from?" I asked, curious.

"You said it was short for Lenore."

"As in Poe? Are you kidding me?" I asked.

He started laughing. "No, I swear. It's ironic, isn't it?"

"I don't think that's funny. I think you're making this up."

"Sophie, I wouldn't make this up. That was your name."

I shook off the irony. "So what did you say?"

"Well, I told you I was glad there was no such thing as Nevermore." He chuckled. "It made you smile, and that's when I was certain I had to have you. Then, your boy-friend came back and was not happy to say the least. 'Lenny, what is going on here?' he demanded, rather rudely, I might add.

"You tried to assure him that we were just talking, but then he went to take you by the elbow and you stepped back from him. He obviously wasn't used to not getting his way. He quickly became irritated. 'Lenny, let's go,' he ordered.

"I was pleased to see that you didn't appreciate his domineering personality. You just looked at me and then looked at him and said, 'Andy, I'm going home with *him*.' You pointed at me without even knowing my name. Andy looked completely insulted. 'You're joking, right?' he asked you. 'No, I'm not,' you said, and then you walked toward me. Even your friends were in shock. He was furious. He grabbed your arm, quite hard, and yanked you back."

"What did I do?" I asked, completely absorbed.

"You didn't do anything. But *I* broke his hand, taking it off of you."

"Wes!"

"Well, I wasn't about to let him manhandle you like that. I had to do something." He stopped, then added, "I didn't mean to break it." I could tell he wasn't very sorry.

"You broke his hand, and I still went with you?"

"Yes, you were just as irrational then as you are now."

I smacked his shoulder. He chuckled. "Actually, you said you would've walked home as tired as you were of him."

I rested my head on the back of the seat and thought about the encounter. I felt exhilarated at the idea of Wes rescuing me from some jerk. "Were you jealous?" I asked.

"No." He looked out the window and then quickly retracted his denial. "Yes."

I smiled. "Good. That means you're not perfect after all. You have at least one flaw." I leaned over to kiss his cheek before he could protest. We drove for a little longer before I broke the silence with my all too familiar curiosity. "So how did I find out about you? You know, your secret."

His demeanor changed a little then. "You only knew I was different. You never knew about our past."

"Why not?"

He let out a deep sigh. "Well, I didn't know how to tell you. Plus, I had no idea that it would repeat itself. You never questioned my past since the dates added up back then, and I *thought* we had been given another chance."

I braced for what I knew he was thinking. I figured there was no need to prolong it. "Tell me how it happened. What happened to me?"

He pulled over to the side of the road and put the car in neutral. He turned toward me and assessed me seriously. I raised my eyebrows waiting for the news. "You died in a car accident on the way to my house." He stared past me as he told me, so I shifted my head so that I was in his line of sight.

"That's it?" I asked.

He was bewildered by my relief.

"That's enough," he answered.

"Wes," I said calmly. "What you're telling me is that I died once during the biggest flu epidemic in history and then in a fluke accident. That hardly qualifies as a guarantee that I won't see twenty." He didn't seem relieved. The lines of his face were still hardened. I reached up and touched his face. "Wes, you've convinced yourself that I'm going to die based on things that can be prevented today. Those things don't have to happen again."

"Sophie, you can't expect me to pretend that it can't happen." He leaned his cheek into the palm of my hand.

"I'm not asking you to pretend that it can't happen. I'm just asking you not to be convinced that it will." I studied his face closely, and I could still sense the tension. I leaned forward and kissed him softly. His reciprocation was harder than usual, almost conflicted. I pulled away. "You have to relax. Everything will be okay."

He offered a small, unconvinced smile, and then he leaned in and kissed me gently on the cheek. "All right," he whispered, before putting the car back in motion.

I didn't take my eyes off of him the entire way back to town. I couldn't tell what he was thinking, but I could definitely tell he was deep in thought. I left him to ruminate without interruption while he drove.

Once we got back to my house, I couldn't stand the silence anymore. He met me in my room and I cornered him. "If something extraneous doesn't kill me then your silence will." He didn't find that funny. I immediately realized it was a bad choice of words. "Okay, okay, sorry. I didn't mean that. I just don't like your silence."

He finally yielded. "I'm sorry. I'm just thinking."

"Thinking about what?"

"About the possibility of me being wrong."

I smiled.

"Just *thinking*," he clarified, before I could get too excited. "You could be right, but I'm not going to risk it. I'm going to do what I can to make sure it doesn't happen."

"Fair enough," I said.

I was about to pull him toward my bed, so I could wrap myself up in his arms, when his cell phone rang. He looked at the number and his eyes narrowed.

"Hello?" he answered. "No, I'm not home. What's going on?... Which one?... What did they take? I see. I'll be right there." He hung up.

"What is it?" I queried.

He tucked his phone in his pocket. “Another break-in. This time at one of my labs.”

“What did they take this time?”

“Some more cold-blood serum. A lot of it,” he added.

I sat on the bed trying to consider the meaning. He leaned down and kissed me on my forehead. “I have to go.”

I stood up. “Where?” I didn’t like the whole idea. I wanted him to stay with me.

“I’ll be back in a few hours. I promise. I need to check it out.”

He kissed me again, and it was noticeably more relaxed than the first one had been.

“I still don’t like it,” I informed him.

He smiled. “I’ll be back before you know it.”

“But what if you’re not? What if something happens to you, after all this?”

He shook his head at the thought. “Sophie, nothing could keep me from returning to you.”

“Are you sure?”

“I wouldn’t leave you if I wasn’t.”

Although I felt better knowing he’d be back, it didn’t completely take away my apprehension. I paced every inch of my floor in his absence before I realized it was doing no good to worry. I had to believe that he would be all right. He’d managed to keep himself out of danger this long. I decided to take a long shower, go to bed, and wait.

The only way I could stop thinking about him was to try to think about something else. I shifted toward what I had learned about Amelia and Lenny and tried to pick out similarities. I was very much like Amelia in her instinct to help others in need and her interest in medicine. Plus, I imagined her to be very independent in order to go after such an innovative job during that time.

In Lenny, I saw toughness. She wasn't going to take being mistreated from any guy, and she wasn't afraid to go out on a limb. She also didn't get sucked into what the crowd was doing. I liked her, and I could definitely see myself in her.

I lay there for a long time thinking about what had made me who I was in each of these time periods. I always thought my personality was a result of my upbringing, and all of a sudden, I was pondering the nature vs. nurture concept. I wondered if I was the way I was simply because it was my nature or if it was the nurture of my parents. That's when I realized Wes hadn't told me about my "other" parents before. Why hadn't he mentioned them? Were they the same souls, too? That idea was very weird.

My thoughts drifted until I fell asleep. Within a few moments, the blackness behind my eyelids was replaced by a very vivid nightmare. I was being screamed at by an unfamiliar man. He kept shouting that I was gonna be sorry. I was shouting back that he didn't know what he was talking about. Then he violently shook me. "He's a misfit!" he shouted. "He doesn't deserve you!"

"You don't know what you're talking about!" I kept yelling. Then another unfamiliar face appeared. This time it was a woman who came up behind the man and touched his shoulder.

"Please, Frank. Stop," she pleaded, in tears.

He was so irate he shoved her to the floor. I tried to help her, but he stepped in my path. "You are not welcome here as long as you defy me!" He grabbed me and shook me by the shoulders again. "You will not be welcome in this house if you defy me!"

"Fine! I'm leaving!" I shouted. I ran, hysterically, out of the house, got into my car, and sped shakily down the highway. I was crying and between the tears and the rain pounding on my windshield, I could hardly see the road.

The next thing I heard was an overwhelming screeching sound followed by headlights shining brightly in my windshield. I swerved and lost complete control of my car. The car I was driving went right over the cliff, and my heart felt like it exploded. I woke up and screamed.

Chapter 17
THE NURTURER

Arms were unexpectedly wrapped around me as I gasped for air. "Sophie, it's okay. You were dreaming." I recognized the voice instantly.

"Wes," I whispered, still out of breath.

"Yes. I'm here."

I pressed myself closer to him. He naturally started rubbing my hair to soothe me, and then I remembered his absence. "You're back."

"I told you I would be."

I took a deep breath. "I had an awful dream."

"About what?"

"It was an accident. Someone was shouting at me." I paused, trying to remember. "Someone named Frank. He was yelling at me, and he shoved a woman and told me to leave." Wes immediately tensed up. I recognized the tightening of his muscles.

"And that scared you?" he asked.

"No, but the storm and driving off of the cliff did."

He sat up instantly. "Sophie, that was not a dream. You were remembering."

"Remembering what?"

"Your car accident. It was raining that night, and you were coming to see me. Frank was your father."

I was shocked. So much for the nurturing aspect. "Why would I fight with my father?"

"Because he forbade you to see me. He thought I was no good. I didn't have a prestigious reputation at the time, and to all accounts, my father was always 'traveling.' He didn't like my lack of parental guidance, and that's putting it nicely."

"That doesn't justify him screaming at me."

"You're right, and your mother never forgave him for sending you out in the storm like that. She never forgave me either."

I kept thinking about how she'd tried to stop him. It made me angry to think about him shoving her. "What happened to Frank?"

"He eventually left your mother penniless and then he remarried. He died a few years ago."

I was really bitter now. "And what happened to her?"

He paused for a long time.

"Wes, what happened to her?" I repeated.

He looked at me and very hesitantly whispered, "She's still living."

I gasped. "Where?"

"Sophie, I'm not sure it's a good idea."

"Where, Wes?" I countered.

"She's at an assisted living facility outside of town."

I was flabbergasted. That was completely unexpected. "You weren't going to tell me?"

He leaned closer to my face. "Sophie, this is all new to me. I don't know what I'm doing. What was I supposed to say?"

He had a point. "I'm sorry. That was rude. This is just too weird." I rested my head back on his chest as a peace offering, and he resumed softly stroking my hair as I took it all in.

I felt very secure with myself after that night. It was as if I carried the accomplishments of Amelia and Lenny inside me. I felt more confident than ever. The best part about everything was that things had returned to normal between Wes and me. We were back to spending every day together, and although he wasn't yet willing to sacrifice his clarity, he was very much loving and affectionate. I was as happy as I could've been.

I had all the answers I wanted, and the only unknown still hovering in my mind was the fact that Lenny's mother was still alive. I was very curious to meet her, but I was also hesitant that it would freak her out. She was ninety-one years old, and I didn't want to send her into shock at the sight of her dead daughter. It was not something I took lightly.

After heavy deliberation, I came to the conclusion that if I was her, I would want to know. So, I made up my mind to go visit her. Wes wanted to come with me, but I insisted on going alone.

One Saturday after work, I drove up to the facility. It was about an hour drive, and it gave me plenty of time to think about what I might say. I eventually concluded that there was no way to rehearse the conversation. Plus, I didn't know how alert she would be. I was going to play it by ear.

When I arrived at the nursing home, I was amazed. It was a beautiful complex located on a lake. The main building was yellow, with huge white columns, and it looked like a resort. I went into the main entrance and, despite the outside, I was still expecting it to look like a hospital. It had a sanitary feel to it, but it was much homier than I'd expected.

I walked up to the counter and asked the nurse, "Can I see Maria Emerson, please?"

She looked at me, surprised, above her reading glasses. "Who's visiting?"

"My name is Sophie Slone."

She looked me over from head to toe. "Ms. Emerson doesn't usually have visitors."

I didn't understand her point. "Why not?"

"She just doesn't have any family. Unless you're family."

I looked around at the reception area. The place was very nice. I couldn't understand who would be taking care of her. "If she doesn't have any family, who pays for her to stay here?" I inquired.

She smiled softly. "I wouldn't be able to provide you with that information." I took a deep breath. "But since there is no name to provide you with, I guess I won't be breaking any rules. Her stay is paid for by an anonymous donor."

"Interesting," I said, louder than I'd planned. She looked surprised. I refocused. "May I see her please?"

"Sure, you can find her in Suite 2036. Down the hall, up the elevator, and to the left."

"Thank you." I followed her instructions until I reached a private suite. I stood at the door in hesitation. All of a sudden, I wished that I had Wes with me, but it was too late. I had to do this alone. I took a deep breath and lightly tapped at her door. After getting no response, I slowly peeked in the doorway.

Ms. Emerson was lying in her bed facing a large open window overlooking the lake. "Ms. Emerson?" I whispered, as I tiptoed across the room. She didn't respond. I slowly approached her and quietly sat in the chair next to her bed. She was completely still. So still that I searched for breathing movements to make sure she wasn't dead. Thankfully, she was just sleeping. I studied her for any sort of recollection, and I didn't notice any physical connections, but I did feel an odd energy flowing between us.

I took the opportunity to examine her bedroom while she was resting.

There were several fresh flower arrangements throughout her room, as well as books, magazines, and notepads. It looked like there were plenty of things to keep her busy, including a piano. Sitting there, I could almost hear the sound of it playing. It made me smile. As I turned my attention back to her, I noticed a little round table and chair. The table held a very specific item from the past. Sitting on the table was a teacup and saucer that matched the set my mother now had.

A movement on the bed startled me as the woman turned to face me.

"I'm sorry. I didn't mean to wake you," I whispered, dropping my hair in my face.

"Lenore?" she whispered, in a feeble but hopeful voice.

I kept my head down, unsure as to whether I'd made the right decision in coming. I was frozen.

"Lenore, is that you?"

She held her hand open as an invitation for mine. Her hand was extremely wrinkled, but when I placed my hand in it, I was surprised at the softness of it. I still couldn't bring myself to look her in the eye. I was afraid she would see a difference between me and Lenny, and that would be worse than if I hadn't come at all.

She squeezed my hand with as much strength as she could, and then whispered, "He was right. He told me you would return. I didn't believe him." She struggled to turn her body so she could place her other hand on top of mine. "Lenore, let me see you. I've waited forty-five years."

I squeezed my eyes shut and took a deep breath. There was no turning back. I lifted my head in reluctance and moved the hair out of my eyes. I could feel her piercing stare even with my eyes closed. When I built up enough nerve, I slowly opened my eyes to reveal a mirror image of the green in hers. Even I was stunned. She instantly closed her eyes and released a tear.

"Thank you," she whispered. After repeating it a few times, it became clear she wasn't thanking me. Her gratitude was beyond anything I could've offered her. After a few minutes, I expected her to open her eyes and talk to me, but she just lay there holding onto my hand. She seemed content, and at peace, with just my presence.

After a while, I realized she had fallen back asleep. She was lying there so peacefully, and I noticed her hair had recently been brushed, and her nails were manicured and painted a light pink color. It was obvious to me that she was being well taken care of.

Once I was content with the time I'd spent there, I slowly pulled my hand from hers and gathered my things quietly, so as not to wake her. I didn't want to leave with her thinking I was a figment of her imagination, so I removed the cross necklace from around my neck and placed it into her hand. I hoped it would be enough to convince her that I'd been there.

I couldn't say what it felt like being there with her, because I didn't have anything to which I could compare it. But, I did know I was glad I had come. Whatever sort of comfort I offered her, I'm certain she offered it to me in equal amounts. Seeing her, and her reaction to me, made me realize that my existence was greater than anything I had known before.

I headed back through the lobby with a smile on my face, virtually proud of what I had done. Unexpectedly, a nurse stopped me as I walked by the desk.

"Excuse me, miss." I turned attentively toward her. "A gentleman was by here looking for you."

"For me?" I was surprised.

"Yes. He asked if he could see the person you were visiting. Once we told him where you were, he said he had an emergency and left."

"What was his name?"

"He didn't say."

That was strange. "What did he look like?"

"Older gentleman, gray hair."

That had to be some sort of mistake. I thanked her anyway.

When I got into my Jeep, I had two missed calls. They were both from Wes. I checked the time and realized I had been gone longer than expected. I called him back before I even left the parking lot. The first question I asked him was if he was the one who paid for her stay. As I suspected, he was. I wasn't surprised in the least.

"Thank you," I said.

"You don't need to thank me." His voice was earnest.

"Yes, I do. She's being well taken care of, and if it weren't for you, who knows where she would be." I thanked him again for loving me in a way I couldn't begin to comprehend. It made me miss him even more than usual. I couldn't wait to get home, and I'd only been out of town a few hours.

As I drove, I gave him the recap of my visit, and I also told him about the strange man who had supposedly asked about me. It sent him into worry overdrive. I couldn't get two words out during his interrogation. I finally cut him off. "Wes, calm down. I don't know anybody. I'm sure they had the wrong person." Either way, he insisted upon talking to me until I got home safely. I couldn't complain. His voice still sent butterflies through my stomach. I could listen to him talk for hours. He probably could've read the phone book, and I wouldn't have complained. Even so, I thought I'd use my time more wisely.

"Tell me something else about us," I asked, trying to lighten the mood.

"Like what?"

"I don't know. Something else about me—something about my past."

He paused for a minute. "Well, I could tell you about the time I bailed you out of jail."

"What? Shut up!"

He laughed. "I'm serious."

"You are not."

"Sophie, would I lie to you?"

I could tell he was smiling through the phone. I rolled my eyes, but I knew he wouldn't lie. "Go ahead. Spill it, what did I do?" I switched hands with the phone and propped my elbow up on my window ledge so I could drive more comfortably. Plus, I wanted to make sure I could listen to this closely. He continued, unusually amused.

"Well, right after I met you in 1963, you invited me to a Free Speech Movement Rally. I hadn't ever protested before, since I usually tried to lay low, but I wanted to be wherever you were, so I agreed. I picked you up, and you had a bandana tied around your head. It was very cute."

I couldn't help but smile as I pictured it. I could only imagine. I was starting to see why reincarnated souls didn't remember everything. They would be tortured by having to relive the completely embarrassing moments.

"Keep going," I prodded.

He chuckled softly. "You also had on a tie-dyed T-shirt."

"Okay, I've heard enough."

He laughed. "I'm just kidding. But you did have on a pink T-shirt that read, 'Free Speech!' in big, bold, black letters."

I rolled my eyes. "Well that's better, I suppose."

"Anyway, we went to this rally, and I have to say, you brought out the protester in me. It was no surprise how passionate you were about other people's rights. Your care for others is infectious. Being there with you made me want to hold up a sign."

"So, how did I manage to get arrested and you didn't?"

"Well, we protested for about an hour, and then you had to go to the bathroom. You went and never came back."

"What, did I fall in?"

"No, Sophie." He laughed. "But you did get mixed up with a crowd of girls who started throwing tomatoes at police officers. The officers didn't appreciate it, so they took you in."

"So, I didn't even get arrested on my own?"

"Nope."

I grunted. "So what happened?" I could tell he was grinning.

"Once I heard the commotion, I went over there in time to see you being handcuffed and guided into the back of a paddy wagon. So, I bailed you out. End of story."

"How embarrassing."

"It was cute."

"I bet."

"It was. Tomatoes in your hair and all."

"Oh my gosh."

"What? I like tomatoes," he said, laughing.

I shifted in my seat. "You'd better be glad I can't remember you. I bet you had long hair and bell-bottom jeans."

He was silent for a second.

"Hah! You did!" I said triumphantly.

"No. Not long hair, but maybe the jeans," he admitted.

I laughed out loud. At least I wasn't the only victim of the 60s. I smiled until I realized my cheeks were getting achy and even then, I couldn't stop.

Chapter 18
PAYBACK

About forty-five minutes into my hour-long drive home, I was so wrapped up in my conversation with Wes that I didn't realize I had been speeding. "Oh no," I said out loud, as I saw the flashing lights on my tail. I didn't even know what the speed limit was, but I didn't feel like I had been going *that* fast. "Dang it," I said, disappointed at my lack of awareness.

"What is it?" Wes asked.

"I'm getting pulled over. What do I do?"

He steadied my focus. "Is there a shoulder on the road for you to pull off onto?"

"No. Let me call you back." Crashing on top of it all was the last thing I needed.

"No," he interjected. "I'll wait."

I was having trouble multitasking with the blue light flashing in my rearview, but I managed to pull over at the next straightaway.

"I pulled over. What now?" I asked.

His voice was experienced and very specific. "You need to get your license out. He's going to ask you for your car registration and driver's license."

"Okay, I think I have those." I leaned over to open the glove compartment to find the registration and a bunch of papers fell out onto the floor. I could see the shadow approaching with a flashlight, and I couldn't fumble through my purse, the glove compartment mess, and talk to Wes at the same time.

"Hang on, Wes, I have to set the phone down." Without waiting for his reply, I set it down on the passenger seat and leaned over to find my registration card. I saw the insurance card still sitting in the glove box. I sat back up, and even though I had been expecting the officer's arrival, his tap on my window startled me. I jumped and then blinked away the blinding glare of his flashlight. I put my window down, so he could talk to me. He wasted no time scolding me.

"Do you know how fast you were going, miss?"

"Uh, no officer, I don't. I'm sorry."

He leaned in, toward my window, and flashed the light closer to my eyes. I squinted until I had to look away. He took a few steps back.

"I'm going to need you to step out of the car." The voice was deep and authoritative, but his demand was not what I'd expected.

"What?" I asked, for clarification.

"You need to step out of the vehicle."

I'd seen enough television to know this didn't happen for speeding, and I hadn't been doing anything else. "What for?" I asked, trying to block the light from my eyes.

The officer let out a sigh of impatience, but I refused to move until I was sure I'd heard him correctly. After a few seconds of not answering me, the officer very slowly and calmly, uttered, "Lenny, Lenny, Lenny. You are still *so* defiant."

I leaned my head to the side in an effort to see around the light. I tried to get a visual of the shadow, and that's when I saw a white cloth zeroing in on me. My face was aggressively overtaken as the fabric was shoved over my mouth and nose. I was forced to inhale a sweet, burning scent. I naturally flinched away, but the hand holding the cloth pushed harder. Once I realized this was no ordinary pullover, I made the decision to scream, but my vocal cords were numb. I started to panic and instinctively went to put my Jeep in drive, but my wrist was restrained by the grip of the stranger's much stronger hand.

Tightness permeated through my lungs. Within seconds, my eyelids started to close. I struggled as best as I could to push away my attacker. I reached for the eyes and scratched at his arms, but nothing worked. I only got weaker and weaker with each passing second.

As I slipped into an involuntary slumber, I could tell I was being pulled out of my car. My heels were scraping the ground, and I tried to kick my legs, but they were too heavy to follow my command. Instead, I could feel the grinding of gravel under my heels as I was being dragged. I tried to scream, but nothing came out. The cloth was still smothering my face. My eyes were closed, so I couldn't see, but I was coherent enough to feel myself being lifted and roughly shoved into the back of a trunk. Complete blackness came over me.

By the time I woke up, I was in a windowless room. I couldn't tell if it was day or night, but the air was close. I felt claustrophobic. My first pain was a major crick in my neck. I tried to rub it with my hand, but I couldn't, because my wrists were bolted to the arms of my chair. That's when the horror struck.

I realized I wasn't hearing the sound of Wes' voice anymore. I wasn't laughing. I wasn't about to see him. I had been *kidnapped*. What the heck happened? The last thing I could remember was being pulled over and then being suffocated with a rag. Where was I? I didn't know. My heart began to race.

I instantly regretted not letting Wes take the trip with me. My overconfidence in my safety had put me in the most feared position any young girl could think of. Yet, somehow, at that moment, I couldn't bring myself to fear for my own well-being. Instead, I felt anguish for the frenzy I was sure Wes was going through at that very moment.

I had just convinced him to relax and to be optimistic, that I wasn't going to die on him, and there I was in a strange room waiting for a stranger to return, with a sentence I was sure would be death.

I cringed as I heard a door to my right open. A dimmed light spread across the floor. The stretch of light was overtaken by a dark silhouette heading my direction. I instantly looked away and without a doubt, that was the exact moment when I began to fear for my life. The figure approached me slowly. "I see you're awake now, Lenny," he observed.

I kept my head down, too terrified to see the face of my captor.

With a tone of arrogance, the voice responded to my silence. "What's the matter? Don't you have something to say?"

I shook my head and kept my eyes closed, trying to block out thoughts of what was going to happen to me. My captor knelt down in front of me. He moved the hair away from my eyes, but I still kept them closed. He chuckled in amusement.

"Maybe you don't answer to Lenny. Hmm…maybe you prefer something else?"

I closed my eyes tight and pressed my chin to my chest trying to block out the stench of the nicotine coming off of his breath. My stomach felt sick. What was going on? Who was this guy? I decided I didn't want to know. I kept trying to drown him out.

"Still no response? That's okay. I'm sure you'll have something to say soon."

He started walking around my chair, being sure to stay close enough so that some part of his body was rubbing past me at all times. I don't think I exhaled the entire time he circled.

"You see, you think you have fooled everyone, but I'm on to you." He circled the chair one more time. "You think that you can do whatever you want in this world and not have to suffer the consequences." He stopped in front of my chair. "And the worst part about it is that you don't think anyone else has a right to your little 'discovery.' That's not very nice, Lenny."

He reached under my chin with his rough hand. I pulled away.

"Oh, come on, Lenny. Don't you want to make amends?"

I started trying to block out every horrible thought that was running through my mind. I tried to pretend he would go away if I ignored him long enough. He bent down to my level.

"Come on, Lenny. You're not making this very fun for me. I would appreciate it if you said something. You know? Like leave me alone, don't hurt me, or at the very least, who are you?"

I blocked it out. I tried to think about driving in my car again, like this never happened. I could tell he was losing patience. Shockingly, he took one deep breath and on the exhale, he yelled in my face, "How about, 'Who are you?'" I was literally shaking by then, and I was doing everything I could to hold back uncontrollable sobs. Taking it even one step louder he shouted, "Ask it!"

I flinched, and with a hoarse and weak voice I asked, "Who are you?"

He stood up, excited. "That's better!" He started walking around my chair again. After he circled a few times, he said, "I'm insulted that you do not remember me. Let me see if I can help you." He walked over and turned on the light. My eyes were still closed, but it was enough of a difference in lighting for me to notice.

"Oh now now, Lenny, don't be shy. Open your eyes. This is the important part." I was still too terrified to oblige, so he hustled back over to my chair and yanked my head back so I was looking up. "Now open your eyes!" he commanded.

I wanted to cry, and at that point, I knew he was going to get even more violent if I didn't cooperate. I blinked my eyes open, giving them proper time to adjust to the light, and that's when my heart skipped a beat. There were several pictures of Wes and me on the wall. I saw myself eating a funnel cake with Wes at the carnival; I saw a picture of us eating at the sandwich shop; and I saw several zoomed-in shots of us separately. It was an odd, creepy obsession.

"Do you like them?" he asked. I shifted my eyes toward him in hopes of recognizing the face. I was instantly sure I hadn't run into him before. He was older, I would've put him in his 60s, but he was muscular and very intimidating. He had a wide neck and a large, square jaw that was covered in sandy-gray stubble. His hair was a darker, greasy-gray color. I turned away quickly. "Oh, don't do that, Lenny; you haven't answered the question yet. Who am I?"

I closed my eyes again, trying to drown out the sicko. He got angry again. "Who am I?" he shouted in my ear.

"I don't know!" I shouted back.

"Ah, feisty as ever," he said, seeming pleased. He started walking around me again, and when he reached the front of my chair, he bent down again. "Take one good look and try to guess."

I inhaled, taking a slow, deep breath, and opened my eyes. I took another glimpse at his face for as long as I could tolerate, which was about two milliseconds, and then closed them again. "I don't know," I croaked.

He stood up, but remained standing right in front of me. "Understandable," he said. "But let me see if I can refresh your memory." He took a step closer and grabbed the index and middle fingers on my right hand. With a stomach-turning twist, he snapped my fingers back at the joints. I let out an ear-piercing shriek. The pain shot through my arm. Instinctively, I tried to grab them with my other hand, but my arm was still bolted to the other armrest.

"Does that refresh your memory?" he asked. I was cringing in pain as I felt the throbbing in my deformed fingers. "No? Well, how about this then?" He grabbed the last two fingers on the same hand and bent them back with even more force than the first. I screamed again and started crying in pain, fear, and anger.

"Why are you doing this to me?" I cried out.

He leaned right in my face and said, with an eerily deep voice, "Because your boyfriend owes me a broken hand, Lenny."

Chapter 19
THE PLAN

I opened my eyes, trying to put together the accusation. With the stare of his fiery, ruthless, egotistical eyes, I made the connection. "Andy," I whispered.

"You *do* remember me," he said, standing up again, completely pleased with himself.

"No," I said, building up nerve at the thought of this washed-out man ruining my life.

"What was that?" he asked.

"No, I don't remember you. How would I? You're *old.* The only reason I remember you is because of your hand."

He leaned over me and scrunched up my broken fingers. "Is there anything else you'd like to say?" He squeezed harder with each passing second, and I could hear awful crunching sounds.

"No," I yelled, through my tightened jaws. He released my mangled fingers.

"Good, now we can get to the point of all this. You have something that I want."

My breathing was labored as the panic built up. I dropped my head and closed my eyes again, hoping to push the reality of my situation out of my head.

"You see, Lenny, I was not too happy that you embarrassed me like you did. And I was *really* not happy, when your friend broke my hand. I had plans for us. Well, actually, not us—me. You were my ticket out of town. See, my parents didn't have money like yours, and I was hoping to cash in on you, but then you had to go and ruin it."

By then my breathing had steadied, but my nerves were going haywire. It felt like little bugs were crawling all over me, and I was bolted to a chair with no way to get them off. The guy was giving me the creeps, and his insanity was making me want to crawl out of my own skin.

"But that's okay, Lenny. See, I was upset at first, but then I got to thinking about Wes. That's his name, correct? Yes. *Wes* had barely touched me, and yet my hand was broken in fourteen places. Pretty remarkable, huh?"

I hadn't moved an inch, nor had I answered any of his questions, but he was going along as I had. "Yes. It was quite remarkable. So it got me curious. *Who was this guy? Where did he come from?* That's when I stumbled upon the great Dr. Oliver Thomas' accomplishments. Well, I'm sure I'm boring you with this, so I'll get to the point. There were a lot of rumors that he'd found a cure for diseases, while increasing strength and bodily performance through the use of alligator serum.

"Well, I figured there was something shady about Wes back then, but then you died in your little accident and he went off to Europe. I ended up joining the Army, and I thought that was the last of it. But, then the Army started a covert operation experimenting with various ways to increase performance in their soldiers. Much to my surprise, one of the trials included extracted proteins and cells from alligator blood. It was supposed to make us strong and immune to diseases that we could catch in other countries.

"As you can imagine, I was one of the soldiers who instantly volunteered to participate in the study. We found it *did* make us strong. It was exhilarating. The only problem was that it was temporary, and the withdrawal symptoms were painful. Soldiers started going haywire during withdrawal periods. The government pulled the plug on the whole thing.

"Then they sent us to a special facility so we could be weaned off of it like addicts. And just like that, they released us back into society with an honorable discharge." I could hear the bitterness in his voice. He started rubbing the top of my head, and I could feel the filth reach all the way down to my toes.

"After that, I spent twenty years being a security guard at Berkeley. That's when I saw you. You were just walking the campus like you were out for a Sunday stroll. Like you didn't have a care in the world. I was stunned. I thought I was seeing things." He stopped rubbing my hair and walked a few feet away. I couldn't tell what he was doing, and I didn't want to look.

"Anyway, I thought you might just resemble Lenny, but one day I followed you to the parking lot and that's when I saw him. Mr. Wilson himself was leaning up against your car as arrogant as I remembered. Imagine my shock to watch you and him take a stroll on the path.

"That's when I started following you two. I figured out you were up to something. I researched Mr. Wilson, and what do you know? He, or his father, or is it he? Well, we both know who it was. *He* had started research projects throughout various medical facilities focusing on, guess what? Alligator plasma.

"So little old me decided to cash in on your secret. You could say I relapsed. I started injecting the serum again, and I can't tell you how good it feels. I'm untouchable when I'm on it. But you see, Lenny, there is just one thing missing. I want to know how you and Weston have managed not to age a day since 1963." He paused. "It has *really* been bothering me, so I've decided you are going to tell me."

That's when I felt his presence close to me again. He positioned himself behind my chair, grabbed a handful of my hair, and lifted my head back. Still holding my hair in a solid grip, he placed a cool, hard object up against my throat.

"Now, Lenny. I do not have patience here. So if you value your life, I suggest you start talking."

"I can't help you."

"That's not the answer that I wanted." The object pushed deeper into my skin, and I was able to identify it as a knife. I felt a stinging sensation as the blade began to pierce the skin.

"Okay," I said, folding.

"Start talking."

"Okay, I'll tell you, but I can't concentrate with the knife at my throat."

"Well, you'd better try."

"Please Andy, where am I going to go?"

He let out an amused sigh. "I suppose you're right." He pulled the knife away and left the room. I started to feel momentary relief until he came back in, noisily dragging a chair. The screeching sound gave the effect of magnified nails on a chalkboard. I shuddered. He positioned the chair right in front of me and sat down, casually waving the knife.

"Okay, let's begin."

"What do you want to know?" I asked naively.

He leaned in, just inches from my face. "Have you not been listening? I want to know how you and Mr. Wilson are not aging. What do you have that I don't?"

"I *am* aging, Andy."

He studied me for a few seconds, then looked at his finger nails. Without warning, he gave me a bitter back-hand across my face.

"Try again," he ordered.

"I swear," I said truthfully. He went to reach for the fingers on my left hand, and I flinched. "Okay. Please, just listen. I'll tell you how, but you have to hear it all." He retracted his advance. "I'm aging, *but* Wes isn't. I'm some sort of reincarnation." I saw that he was about to cock his hand again. "Wait, Wes doesn't age, because he uses the serum. It only works on males." He was considering the explanation.

"Then why are you still here?"

"Lenny is not still here. I'm Sophie." That is when I received the second backhand across my other cheek. I spit out blood that time. I was really getting mad. "Since you know everything then you don't need me."

He called my bluff. "All right, I see this isn't working." He pulled out the knife again. "You have exactly thirty seconds to tell me what I want to know or you can say goodbye, Lenny, Sophie, and whoever else you want to go by." He pressed the knife under my chin and forced me to look him in the eyes. All I kept thinking was that I didn't want to die like that. I knew I had to tell him something.

"You can check the records. Lenny died. And I was actually born Sophie in 1991. I keep coming back for Wes. He needs me."

"Why?" he said, gritting his teeth. He was psychotic. I believed he was on something then, and I was afraid that no matter what I said, he was going to kill me anyway. I thought about just giving up, but I knew I had to try to stay alive. I had to think of something that would buy me time.

"Because I'm the missing piece," I blurted out. He rolled his eyes, and I knew I needed to give him more to go on quickly, whether it was the truth or not. I only hoped it would work. "Because he needs my blood." He raised his eyebrows in consideration. "My blood is the missing part of your serum. It's what keeps him young. Don't ask me why, because I don't know. All I know is I donated my blood to him in 1916. He has been young ever since, and every so often, I return to replenish him." I wanted to say take it or leave it, but I decided not to take my chances. Instead, I dropped my head and began to pray that he would believe it.

I knew my blood wasn't the key. Amelia's blood hadn't cured Wes. Only Dr. Thomas knew what he'd put in the serum. I wouldn't know. But what I did know, from Wes' recollection, was that all of the previous patients died from trying it. I was confident that it was not the true answer that Andy wanted, but if I could just get him to try it on himself, then I might be able to make it out of there. "There's one more thing," I added, closing my eyes, as if ashamed to give up the rest of the information.

"What is it?" he said, sounding eager.

"It's not the extracts the labs use. It's the raw form of the cold-blood itself, mixed with my warm blood. You have to inject the whole blood. It won't change you without it."

He smiled. "It's brilliant, of course," he said, standing up.

"Well, if you want to be changed. You'll need to go get real cold-blood."

"Oh, lucky for me, Lenny, I have it here. I've acquired many things over these past few months. Your Weston has quite a collection at his labs. Please excuse me for a second." He left the room, and I began to realize what I had done. I was pretty sure it would kill him if he tried it, but I realized in his absence that he was going to want my blood next. I hadn't thought it completely through. I was too busy thinking of a way to save myself and trick him. I didn't realize I was actually giving him a reason to kill me.

I let out a deep sigh. As I tried to hold it together, I started praying for more time. Just then, Andy came back in with a syringe, and then my praying turned to negotiating. "What do you plan to do with it?" I asked. He didn't answer. "You have already aged," I added. Then I wished I hadn't said that. That was really not a good way to start. I was expecting another blow, but he chuckled instead.

"Ah, I'll be happy with staying like this forever. But it's not about me. See, I have a grandson. His father died serving our ungrateful government in battle, and his mother died from cancer a few years ago. He's all I have left. He's about your age, and he already reaps the benefits of the extracts. He'll be very pleased to be the new Wes."

"The new Wes?"

"Oh, your Wes is going to die, right after you."

I was very angry now. "Just get on with it."

"Now, now, Lenny. Slow down. Your time will come." He started digging through a medical bag and pulled out an alcohol swab. He pulled back my sleeve and started tapping for a vein. I closed my eyes and made a fist. "I see you have experience with this," he falsely presumed.

I started thinking of Wes at that moment. I wanted to be with him so badly, and I regretted stupidly placing myself in this situation. I just wanted Andy to get what he needed and get away from me. I felt him place a band above my elbow, and I flinched as he pulled it tight. He carefully put the needle in and began to extract my blood. "How much do I need?" he asked.

I shook my head, trying to think of an answer quickly. "Not much. Just a little bit." I could sense he doubted me. "The blood won't go easily into your vein. It doesn't take much. You'll see." He continued to take more than I was sure he needed, and when he was finished, he started packing up.

"Now, you stay put, and I'll be back in a little while. I need to find someone to test this on, in case you're lying." If he did that, I was sure it would be the end of me, and for another innocent victim. I had to stop him.

"Once you do that, you can't kill the person. He will be unstoppable."

He turned, very interested in my threat. "What do you mean unstoppable?"

"After ten minutes, you won't be able to just kill him. He will be impenetrable. There will be more than one Wes. I hope you know what you're doing."

He stood there, studying me for a few minutes without saying or doing anything. I took it as another opportunity to add even more doubt in his mind. "Plus, you'd better hurry, because once *Wes* finds you, and you're not changed, he *will* kill you, and you will have a lot more than fourteen broken bones."

He smirked. "It's a good thing that he has no idea where to find me, isn't it?"

I started laughing. He swooped in and grabbed my throat. "What is so funny?" he asked. I tried to talk, but nothing would come out. He let up his grip a little. "What is so funny?" he repeated.

"I was talking to Wes when you pulled me over. I had him on hold when you came to my window."

"So?" he said, not understanding.

"So, you called me Lenny," I croaked. His eyes got wide. "It's only a matter of time before he figures it out, and when he does, he *will* be coming for you," I assured him. "And if you are not ready…"

"Shut up," he yelled, shoving my neck back. He snatched up my blood and stormed out of the room. I let out a huge sigh of relief and started to think about the possibility of what I had said. Wes *had* heard it. At least, I hoped he had. And if he had, then I was sure he'd be able to figure it out.

I wasn't sure how much time had gone by. I didn't know how long I was unconscious, and I had no natural light in the room to go by. The only thing that made me feel like too much time hadn't gone by was the fact that I hadn't gone to the bathroom. I pinched my knees together and tried to think about something else.

After a while, my mind drifted and my eyes grew heavy. The next thing I remember was dreaming about Dr. Thomas. He was young, like the picture I had seen of him with Wes and me. He was wearing a white lab coat, and I was looking over his shoulder while he was writing. "Amelia," he said. "I think I found it. I think this is going to work. The bloods are similar, and they complement each other in so many ways. I think this is the key to making the transfusions work." I leaned over his shoulder so I could see. He held up his journal with a list and what looked like numbers and formulas.

As I tried to focus on the paper, I heard an awful scream coming from above. It was the sounds of a person crying out. I opened my eyes as I tried to adjust them to the light, but it was still complete darkness. I listened, and I could tell the yelling was definitely coming from a man. Whoever it was, he was in excruciating pain. I heard a thumping sound, like someone pounding on the floor and rolling around.

The noise reminded me of how Wes described his transformation. *That's it*, I thought. Andy had tried it on someone. No, not someone. If he were going to try it on someone else, he probably would've restrained them, as he had me. He must have tried it on himself. *Perfect,* I thought, unless it was going to work.

A heightened sense of worry began working its way through me, until I started tracing back through my dream. My eyes widened in the darkness, as I began to consider that it might not have been a dream. It very well could've been a memory. A memory like the one I'd had the night Lenny died. And if it was a memory, what was it exactly that I was remembering? Dr. Thomas had called me Amelia, so I was remembering something that occurred between Dr. Thomas and Amelia. He said something about it working, and the bloods matching, and it was a list—not a list, a formula. I gasped. It was the serum. *The serum*, the missing pages to his journal.

It was difficult for me to concentrate on the memory over the screaming above, but I did remember that Dr. Thomas was showing me his discovery. He was showing me that he believed he'd found the answer. I had seen it. I would've seen it. I was the only other person working with Dr. Thomas during that time.

The answer was not only in the missing pages of his journal, the answer was in *my* memory. Could I remember it? I didn't see the paper long enough to recognize anything in my dream. The screaming had yanked me from my memory too soon.

I tried so very hard to remember the words on the pages, but my mind was a complete blank. I let out a frustrated sigh. Right about the time I was going to lose what sanity I had left, the screaming stopped. It seemed like ten minutes had passed. Ten minutes of screaming. I ran through that significant detail in my brain.

Ten minutes of screaming was the amount of time it took for the cold-blood serum to stop hurting the patients who eventually died during Dr. Thomas' studies. I began to feel hopeful that my plan may have worked—*if* and only *if* Andy had administered it on himself.

Chapter 20
DYING

The silence above was unsettling. I couldn't tell if he was dead or if he'd left. All I could do was wait and hope. Some time later, the door screeched open again and Andy entered. He was breathing hard, and his skin was sweaty. I instantly felt my entire body start to shake with fear. He walked over to the front of my chair and knelt down.

"I thought you had me there for a second."

I shook my head, not understanding. "Turns out, you were telling the truth after all. I have to tell you, that was the worst ten minutes of my life. But now I'm invigorated. I could actually feel the blood creeping through my veins. My muscles are so tight. But I feel good. It's a shame you can't try it."

I tried to redirect his attention to something else. "Can I please go to the bathroom?" I asked.

He started laughing violently. "That won't be necessary, Lenny."

"Please, Andy, I swear, I'm about to go on myself. If I don't go, I'll have to go right here. I swear."

He made a sniffing notion, as if deciding on whether he was willing to endure the mishap. "All right. I guess that's the least I can do for you." He took off my harnesses one at a time, and once he got to my last ankle harness, he issued a warning. "You don't want to try anything stupid. I assure you, I can crush every bone in your body now, and I will not hesitate for one second to do so." As I stared at his eyes in the darkness, I noticed the new gloss they possessed. Instead of fear, I felt disgust. They were blue and not nearly as pretty as Wes'.

He led me down a narrow corridor with exposed pipes overhead. I could tell we were in a basement of some sort, but it didn't feel like a house basement. The floor was made out of cement, and the walls were cinderblock. The hallway also took several narrow turns before I reached a bathroom with a metal door handle. It was definitely not homey, and there were still no windows for me to tell what time of day it was or if there was anything nearby. My chances of escape were looking slim.

The inside of the bathroom was worse. The water in the commode was the color of tea, and dirt was climbing up the walls. I thought about turning right around, but I really did have to go. I elected to go without touching a single thing, which was extremely difficult with a mangled right hand. The slightest motion sent sharp pains all the way through my arm and down my spine. It was excruciating. Even the simple task of pulling my pants up and down was extremely daunting. I concentrated very hard to do it while ignoring the pain, because I was terrified that the few minutes of privacy I had been granted would be taken away at any moment.

Once I finished, I habitually went to wash my hands, which was a mistake. The sight of my hand as I rinsed made me want to throw up. I leaned over the sink and started panting heavily while trying to push the thought of my pain out of my mind.

"Hurry up!" Andy shouted.

"I'm coming," I answered bitterly.

I took a quick look in the mirror before I turned to leave, and that's when I saw two swollen cheeks and a busted lip. I'd never in my life wished anyone else harm before that moment, but standing there looking at myself made me wish that man something awful.

On my way back from the bathroom, I thought about trying to escape. I even turned in the opposite direction from which I'd come, but I had no idea where I was or what he would do to me if my attempt didn't work, so I turned toward the hallway where he waited. I had to bank on the hope that the cold-blood would reach his heart within a few hours and then I'd be okay. And maybe, just maybe, Wes would find me.

My feet got heavier and heavier with each step I took toward that room. It was the last place I wanted to be, but I felt powerless. I felt alone and afraid. I felt the tears start to rise in my eyes as I returned to the chair. "Very good, Lenny." His praise repulsed me.

Once he bolted me back down to my chair, I saw the smug look in his eyes. He was confident and resolved. He yanked the last restraint tightly around my ankle. "All right, there you go. Now, go ahead and make yourself comfortable, and I'll be back shortly."

He left the room, and all I could do was wait. The longer I waited, the more I got worried that my plan hadn't worked. I was sure injecting straight cold-blood would kill him. That's what it had done on every patient before Wes, but my time was running out, and I could feel it.

I soon learned that Andy had a plan of his own, and it didn't include hurling over. Even if my original plan worked in the end, his trumped mine. When Andy came back into the room, he was carrying a large duffle bag and a glass of water. He dropped the duffle bag beside my chair and set the glass of water on the floor. "Okay Lenny, I'm going to make this easy for you." He pulled two pills out of his bag and picked up the glass of water.

He put the pills up to my mouth, and I turned away. His look was reprimanding. "Now, Lenny, we are done with the stubborn part. Now, take the pills." He shoved them in my mouth. "It will help take your mind off of things." I took the pills and placed them under my tongue. "Good. Now drink up."

After he put the glass back on the ground, he pulled out several IV bags and a syringe. "What is that for?" I asked.

"Oh this?" he answered, nonchalantly, without breaking his focus. "This is how I'm going to package your blood."

"Package my blood, for what?"

"Well, you see, I figure that I need some for my grandson, and I'm also thinking, that one day I could make quite a bit of money off of my discovery here. Imagine how many people will want to buy this when they find out they can have everlasting life."

Did this guy actually believe that my blood was the key to that type of medical breakthrough? He was obviously not the sharpest tool in the shed, but I was stuck between a rock and a hard place. If I told him I'd made the whole thing up, then I was sure he would kill me right then and there. There was nothing I could do.

"You're crazy," I spat.

He calmly ignored my insult, and that's when I knew he was planning to kill me.

I looked around, and there must have been a dozen empty IV bags. He was going to drain me of all of my blood. I quickly thought about swallowing the hidden pills.

"Any minute, you will be falling asleep and won't feel a thing," he said, trying to reassure me. "I'm doing you a favor. Trust me—my original plan for you was much worse."

I rolled my eyes at the lunatic and decided against swallowing the pills. Any chance I had of getting out of this situation would be diminished if I were unconscious. Instead, I began feigning drowsiness and dropped my head down, as if I were asleep.

I felt every dream of mine fade away. Every day I'd pictured with Wes was slowly disappearing right before my eyes, and yet somehow I felt hopeful I could some day see him again. It was the only thought that kept me from completely panicking. I only wished my death didn't have to be at the hands of this bitter reject. I would rather it have been on my own terms, in my own time.

After he situated his equipment, I began to hear him talking to himself. "Perfect. Now you won't even feel it as your life gets sucked out of you, my pretty little Lenny." He rolled my sleeve up and inserted the needle. I felt a stinging pinch and then my blood pull as it began to leave my vein.

I tried to remember everything I'd learned about the human body. I couldn't concentrate very well, but I remembered enough to know that more than one of those bags filled with my blood was not going to be a good ending for me. I started feeling my lip quiver, and I knew I was giving up hope.

Instinctively, I began trying to wriggle free, but it was a pointless effort. He pinned my arm down with his elbow and pressed me up against the chair with his shoulder. The stench of cigarette smoke raced up my nostrils. I turned my head as best I could and let out a cry. Nausea kicked in, followed by weakness and fatigue, as he began to fill the second bag.

I cried out as my eyes rolled toward the back of my head. The corner of the room began turning in odd directions, and I watched as the angles shifted back and forth until they began to blur. I felt weaker and weaker to the point that I couldn't think or feel anymore, and I knew it was over.

All I wanted to do was stop screaming, but I couldn't. The hollering only got louder and louder and then I realized what I heard wasn't my fearful cry. It was more like a painful, excruciating shout. I tried to open my eyes, but I was too weak. In listening to the horrible sounds, I could tell who it was. I recognized the pain—Andy's pain. He was the one shouting. It was an awful shout, a fearful one. *He* was suffering now. *I did it,* I thought—only it was too late for me.

I had no choice but to give into the sleepiness, and everything went black. I couldn't hear or see anything, and my body was weightless. I felt as though I was being lifted high over the room. I realized I was floating, and as I began my ascent away from the stench of my killer, I no longer felt afraid. I no longer felt angry. I no longer cried.

Instead, I was filled with peace. I began to wonder how long it would take to rise to heaven. Within a few moments of my journey, a new scent captivated my mind. It was refreshing, familiar, a scent I would recognize anywhere.

"No," I mumbled. "No, not yet." I wasn't ready to die. I wanted to go back.

"Shh. He can't hurt you anymore," whispered a familiar guardian. I started to panic. I didn't want to go. I started fighting the ascent, and then I heard the voice again. "Sophie, stop. I've got you." I recognized it. It was Wes' voice. The words rang in my ears like a bell, but they sounded miles away. I tried to come down, closer to the sound, but I couldn't move. I was floating and swaying like a feather. "Stop," I mumbled.

"Sophie, it's all right. You're safe with me."

I wanted to fight to it, I wanted to come back down, but I felt my body enter into a new space of flawless air, and I felt lighter and lighter. I didn't have the strength to fight anymore, nor did I want to. Instead, I let the wind carry me. It rocked me back and forth like a baby, and soon I gave in. I curled up to the familiar scent, nestled into the arms of my guardian, and suddenly I decided that heaven wasn't so bad, as long as it stayed just like this.

Read on in...

THE BROKEN LAKE, Book Two

Visit www.thepaceseries.com, for more information.

ACKNOWLEDGEMENTS

An infinite amount of appreciation goes to my husband and children. Your patience and selflessness during this creation is unmatchable, and I love you all more than you know. To my mom and dad, thank you for teaching me to go after what I want and to remember what is truly important in life. To the students at OPHS and K12, thank you for motivating me every day to bring you stories that you would enjoy. A special thank you, apart from the others, is to my mother, Lisa, for your undying support and tireless attention to detail. I know Sophie and Weston's story is better because of your care and fearless ability to tell me when something is awful! A special thank you also goes to Kenya for plowing through the story twice even though you weren't sold on Weston's anatomy before reading! Also, to my writer friends, A. J Borst and M.A Putman, who have offered great advice. Lastly, but certainly not least, I want to thank God, who is the guiding light in my life. With Him, all things are truly possible.